D0801995

Also Available from Pocket Books

Educating Caroline
Lady of Skye

PATRICIA CABOT

Kiss the Bride

SONNET BOOKS

NEW YORK   LONDON   TORONTO   SYDNEY   SINGAPORE

This book is a work of fiction. Names, characters, places and incidents are products of the author's imagination or are used fictitiously. Any resemblance to actual events or locales or persons, living or dead, is entirely coincidental.

An *Original* Publication of POCKET BOOKS

A Sonnet Book published by
POCKET BOOKS, a division of Simon & Schuster, Inc.
1230 Avenue of the Americas, New York, NY 10020

ISBN: 0-7434-1028-9

First Sonnet Books printing May 2002

10 9 8 7 6 5 4 3 2 1

SONNET BOOKS and colophon are trademarks of Simon & Schuster, Inc.

For information regarding special discounts for bulk purchases, please contact Simon & Schuster Special Sales at 1-800-456-6798 or business@simonandschuster.com

Cover art by Magué Calanche

Printed in the U.S.A.

For Benjamin

Prologue

London
May 1832

*H*e was late.

It wasn't like him. The earl of Denham was never late. His gold-and-emerald pocket watch, purchased in Zurich last year for what Emma guessed was an exorbitant amount of money, kept meticulous time. He set it to the hands of the great clock at Westminster, and goodness knew, those hands were never wrong.

Besides, the earl of Denham *always* stopped by his library after tea, to check through any messages that might have arrived while he was dining.

So where was he?

If James was late, it was only because someone was holding up his appointed schedule. And Emma hadn't any doubt who that someone might be.

Which was all very well for Penelope. She could throw herself at the earl as often as she jolly well pleased. Penelope had as much as confessed to Emma that morning at breakfast that she intended to stake her claim that very day.

"And if he isn't thinking of marriage just yet, I shall soon put it into his head," Penelope had informed her conspiratorially, while her parents, Emma's aunt and uncle, were bent over their ham and eggs, both suffering from megrims, having imbibed too much champagne at Dame Ashforth's cotillion the night before. "See if I don't."

Emma didn't doubt that her cousin Penelope was capable of putting the idea of marriage into anyone's head. Penelope had, between the two of them, been the one blessed with all the beauty, after all. Not that Emma was plain. No, she knew that she was pretty . . . passably so, anyway.

But Penelope had the raven tresses—Indian-straight, the lucky girl—and flashing dark eyes of a Spaniard, while Emma had been cursed with common, everyday blue eyes and blond hair that refused stubbornly to straighten, and instead curled riotously, making it appear inches shorter than it actually was. Besides which, Penelope stood over five feet eight inches tall, making her the most statuesque of women, while Emma's height hovered merely at the sixty-inch mark. It was no wonder, really, that she was still treated as the baby of the family, with her blue eyes and curly hair and diminutive proportions. She looked—and so was treated—like a doll.

But not anymore. Not after today. Not after she imparted what she had to impart to James.

She did not blame Penelope at all for her plan to throw herself at the earl. Far from it. Emma quite understood the impulse. James Marbury was one of the most sought-after bachelors in all of London, being darkly handsome as well as fantastically wealthy. It was a matter of some consternation to the ladies of the beau monde that he'd managed to avoid for so long the marriage noose.

But he wouldn't, Emma knew, stay unattached for much longer. Not now that Penelope had got it into her head that she'd like to be Lady Denham. No man, not even as confirmed a bachelor as the earl of Denham, could resist Penelope Van Court's charms.

Only Emma did wish her cousin would hurry up and exercise them already. It was going to look quite odd, the both of them having excused themselves from the Dowager Lady Denham's drawing room so shortly after the earl had done so himself. Emma wondered if Stuart and his aunt, Lady Denham, were feeling neglected. Well, Stuart would forgive her, she was certain, when he learned the results of her errand . . . which, Emma was quite certain, were going to be spectacular.

And then the door to the earl's library was opening. Emma leapt from the divan upon which she'd been seated and smoothed the shining blue silk flounces of her skirt. It was odd, but until now she had not felt nervous about her impending interview. Not a bit. What was there to feel nervous about? True, by saying anything of their plans to James, she was acting with complete disregard for Stuart's wishes.

But Emma did not feel that where James was concerned, Stuart was capable of being completely fair. Stuart felt that his cousin James—much as he loved him—was a profligate and a cynic. And it was true that the earl did spend scandalous amounts of his very sizable fortune on things like Swiss pocket watches and the occasional thoroughbred.

But it was James's money. Surely he had a right to spend it as he chose. And certainly he opened his purse readily enough when Emma appealed to him on behalf of the many charities for which she volunteered her time. Oh, certainly he complained . . . but lightheartedly. Emma had never gone away from the earl of Denham's study empty-handed.

And it could not be said that James wasn't generous to a fault when it came to his own relations. His mother he kept in the height of comfort in his own Mayfair town house. And to his poor orphaned relation, Stuart, he had shown nothing but the utmost beneficence, putting him through seminary school at Stuart's own request, and generally treating him as if the two of them were brothers and not mere cousins.

In light of this munificence, Emma could not help but think that what Stuart intended was wrong. James—not to mention his mother—would be terribly hurt. And what of Penelope and her parents? Emma owed so much to her aunt and uncle. It was better—far better—to do things the right way, in the open, so that no one would think there was anything underhanded about it.

And Emma would prove this to Stuart by telling James herself. Surely when he saw how enthusiastically his cousin took the news—and Emma had no doubt that James would, indeed, take what she was about to tell him in its proper light—Stuart would come to his senses, and do the thing the right way.

Still, when she heard the earl's tone as he addressed

someone who still stood in the hallway beyond the library door, she was not certain that this was, in fact, the best time to approach James on this particular topic.

"Yes, that's all very interesting, Miss Van Court," James said, not even attempting, so far as Emma could tell, to hide the impatience in his deep voice, "but if you don't mind, I have some important affairs to attend to just now, so you'll have to allow me to excuse myself—"

"Oh, but," Emma heard her cousin Penelope say, "it really is so dreadfully important that I speak with you, my lord. If I could only—"

"Some other time, perhaps, Miss Van Court," the earl said, and the next thing Emma knew, he was in the room with her, closing the door behind him with a look of relief on his handsome features.

Relief turned quickly to bewilderment, however, when James noticed Emma standing there in his private study, her hands clasped in front of her in a gesture of supplication.

"Oh, Lord Denham," she said, feeling more nervous than ever. "I do apologize. I wanted a quick word with you, but I see now that perhaps this is not the best moment—"

What an understatement! Emma had no doubt that poor Penelope, having had her advances so firmly rebuffed, had flung herself into the nearby linen closet, where they'd often hid as children, and where Penelope would know she could sob her eyes out undisturbed. It would, Emma knew, be difficult to console her. And they had the ball at Lord and Lady Chittenhouse's to attend that evening. Penelope would never recover in time.

But Lord Denham, far from appearing put out at Emma's unexpected presence in his library, merely stepped away from the closed door with a hitch of his broad shoulders—as if he'd been throwing off something unpleasant—and said with a smile, "It's never a bad time for a visit from you, Emma. To what do I owe the pleasure this time? The Ladies' Circle to Promote the Welfare of Female Inmates at Newgate? Or is it the Missionary League again?"

"Oh," Emma said, as James took a seat behind his massive mahogany desk and reached for pen and paper to jot a note to his secretary, asking for a cheque to be drawn. "Neither, actually."

James looked up in some surprise. "Neither? Don't tell me you've joined yet another society, Emma. You oughtn't allow these people to play so with your heartstrings. They take advantage of warmhearted creatures like yourself and will eventually run you ragged, I guarantee."

"It isn't a charity I'm here to see you about this time, my lord," Emma said, feeling rather as if something had caught in her throat. She coughed to clear it. Really, but this was not going to be as easy as she'd thought. She'd forgotten, in her plans, about the earl's eyes—which were hazel and highly changeable, ranging in color from the brightest gold to the darkest green, depending on the light. But whatever color they happened to be, their gaze was always the same, penetrating . . . at times even searing. Emma quite suddenly lost whatever nerve she'd earlier possessed and stood before the great desk with her hands hanging limply at her sides.

The earl, observing this, laid aside his pen and said, leaning back in his chair, "All right, Emma. Out with it. What have you done now?"

"Me?" Emma squeaked. Really, it was maddening that she should react this way, like a guilty child. He wasn't, after all, her guardian. The fact that Regina Van Court, by whom Emma had been raised, and James's mother, the Dowager Lady Denham, were the best of friends did not make them family. They weren't related—not yet, anyway. Though Emma was quite sure it was the fondest wish of both ladies that their families might one day be joined in marriage.

What they didn't know was that that day was actually right around the corner. Unfortunately, however, it was the wrong offspring who were headed to the altar.

"I haven't done anything at all," she hastened to explain. "Really. It's . . . it's about Stuart, actually."

"Stuart?" James raised a single dark brow. The earl had proved in dozens of ways, from financing Stuart's education to donating a good deal of money to Stuart's own pet charities, that he cared about his cousin . . . but that did not mean that he always approved of him, any more than Stuart approved of the earl. Quite the opposite, in fact. Stuart tended to exasperate James, who did not understand, much less agree with, his younger cousin's philosophy of life. It was all well and good, James had often pointed out, to help the poor. But wouldn't it be better to help the poor help themselves?

Stuart maintained that by educating the poor about the ways of the Lord, they'd be doing just that. But James tended to feel—and was only too happy to declare—that educating the poor about proper hygiene, the family arts, and sound financial investing might be a better answer. A soul, after all, is difficult to nourish on an empty stomach.

"If it's about this ridiculous plan of his," James went on sternly, "of taking a curacy in the wilds of the Shetlands, allow me to assure you, Emma, that no amount of pretty pleading on your part is going to change my opinion on that. It's pure and utter lunacy. I didn't pay all that money for an Oxford education for him to throw it away on a lot of toothless Scots. He'll take up a curacy here in London, or perhaps even the ministry at Denham Abbey, if he knows what's good for him. And if he doesn't, well, I can't stop him, of course, any more than I could stop him from leaving the Church of England for the Church of Scotland. But I can jolly well make things difficult for him by refusing to finance his little scheme. See how he likes living on a curate's stipend. He'll be back within the month, I assure you."

Emma, though nettled by this bombastic pronouncement, nevertheless choked back the sharp words that sprang to her lips upon hearing her beloved so maligned. It would not do, she knew, to get into an argument with her future husband's benefactor at this juncture.

"It's not about that," Emma said. "It's about . . . well . . ."

She broke off, wondering if perhaps Stuart hadn't been right in warning her not to discuss it with James. His cousin did not, after all, seem very open to the Shetland scheme. It was hardly likely he'd be receptive of the part of it she was about to describe to him, either.

On the other hand, James had always been very kind to her—not only when she'd first come to live with the

Van Courts, when the deaths of her parents left her orphaned at the tender age of four. James had seemed so very wise to her then, when at the advanced age of fourteen, he'd offered some brotherly advice on the benefits of avoiding the bees she'd been all too wont to try to pet. James had seemed every bit as wise as Stuart, only six years her senior and broodingly unapproachable, had seemed romantic.

No, even more recently than that, James had been uncommonly obliging. Since she had made her debut and enjoyed her first season out, James had not treated her at all as if she were a simpleton just stepped from the schoolroom—well, not very often, anyway—something that could not be said of many of her own family members. Whenever partners were in short supply—as they were, occasionally—she'd always been sure of being asked to dance at least once by the earl of Denham.

And when, as happened eventually, her adoration of James's cousin Stuart became too much for her to bear—particularly when Stuart seemed barely to know she was alive—James had not teased her at all about it. True, he had not been overly pleased when she'd confessed it. Still, he hadn't absolutely forbidden the two of them to see one another. He seemed to find something amusing in what he called Emma's "worship" of his cousin.

She doubted he was aware of what his tolerance of their relationship had wrought, however.

Still, she hoped he would be pleased. Of course he would be pleased. Stuart was wrong to misjudge his cousin so. James had a very generous heart. It was just that it wasn't always in ready evidence, that heart . . . like just now in the hallway, for instance, with poor Penelope. But that didn't mean it wasn't there. . . .

"Stuart and I—" Emma swallowed hard. There. She had almost got it out. Strange how much more difficult this was than she'd thought it would be. She had always considered James quite easy to talk to, not at all the ogre Stuart often made him out to be. How much of an ogre could he be if, feeling the way he did about the church—that it was all such a lot of poppycock—he had nevertheless paid for Stuart to go to seminary school? He might easily have insisted his cousin study the law instead. But he had not.

No, Stuart was wrong. James's bark was worse than his bite. He would welcome the news Emma was about to impart. Welcome it because it would mean that their two families would be united at last. Which would make his mother happy. And there wasn't anything James wouldn't do to make his mother happy.

Except marry, of course, before he was good and ready. Which, at the rate he was going, might not be until he was well into his thirties, a bitter pill for many a society matron, anxious to marry off a daughter, to swallow.

"Stuart and you what?" James asked—a little warily, Emma couldn't help noticing.

"Stuart and I," Emma said, blurting the words out all in a rush, to get it over with once and for all, "are going to get married. And, oh, my lord, you've got to talk to him, because he has this absurd notion that you aren't going to allow it, and that he and I are going to have to elope. I told him you weren't going to mind a bit, but you know how stubborn he can be. And I was hoping . . . well, I was hoping you could talk to him. Because I do so want a real wedding, you know, with you and Penny and Aunt Regina and your mother and everyone in attendance. Could you say something to Stuart, do you think, my lord? I would be most grateful."

There. It was out. It was all out. Everything would be well now. James would take care of it all, as he did everything, with such skill and proficiency. Emma had never had a problem that James Marbury had not been able to solve. Trouble with her schoolwork? James was there to untangle it. Difficulty with the owner of a hall she was trying to rent for a fund-raising pageant? James dealt with it in a single force-fully worded letter.

James always made everything right. Oh, he'd grouse about it, certainly. But in the end, he would solve the problem. He always did. Emma felt much better.

Until, that is, she got a good look at the earl's face.

"Marry?" James cried, in a tone that, she was sorry to say, did not sound very supportive. "What nonsense is this? Marry? Emma, you can't be serious."

Emma blinked at him. "I am sorry to disappoint you, my lord," she said with some indignation. "But I most certainly am."

"But . . . but you're too young to marry," the earl de-clared. "You're just a child!"

"I'm hardly that, my lord! Why, I just turned eighteen. You were at my birthday supper last month, remember?"

"Eighteen?" James appeared, for the first time since she'd met him, at a loss for words. "Eighteen is still far,

far too young to marry. Marry Stuart? Now? Do your aunt and uncle know about this?"

Emma rolled her eyes. "No, of course they don't. I just got done explaining to you, no one knows. Stuart wants to keep it a secret. He wants us to elope. He wants me to come with him to Scot—"

Emma broke off as James climbed suddenly to his feet. He was so much taller than she was that she was always forced to crane her neck to see his face when he stood as close as he did now, even though there was a desktop between them. As she looked up into his face, Emma felt a sudden, but quite definite, spurt of anxiety. James looked positively dangerous. She had seen him angry before, of course. He had a short temper when it came to things like shoddy table service at eateries and anything to do with the mistreatment of horses, having a tender spot for the creatures.

But Emma had never seen him look like this. Why, he looked . . . well, there was no other word for it.

Murderous.

"Do you mean to tell me," James said, in a voice that was a good deal more controlled than the muscles in his jaw, which were leaping about spasmodically, "that my cousin intends for you to accompany him to Shetland?"

Emma realized now that she had made a very bad error in judgment. Stuart had been absolutely right when he'd insisted they'd have to marry in secret, if they were going to do it at all . . . at least, if this were an example of the reaction the news of their union was going to inspire.

"It isn't as bad as it sounds," Emma hastened to assure him. "I'm certain Stuart will find a minister's post of his own very soon. The curacy won't last long—"

"I told him," James thundered, loudly enough to cause Emma to jump nearly from her own skin, "that he needn't waste time as a curate at all. He can have the bloody vicar's post at Denham Abbey. If I told him that once, I told him a thousand times."

"W-well," Emma stammered, "I'm certain he's grateful for it, really. But you see, he does want to go to a place—and I do agree with him—where he'll be able to do some good, where the people will really need spiritual succor, and Denham Abbey does not, I'm afraid, fit that—"

"So he intends to accept instead a post hundreds of miles away, on an isolated island in the middle of the North Sea? A post that pays close to nothing and in fact will almost certainly kill him, either through famine or disease—and *he intends to take you with him?*"

The hazel eyes had turned a deep, fiery amber. Emma almost feared to look at them, their color was so unnerving. Oh, dear, was all she could think. She had much better have kept her mouth shut. She could see that now. Too late, of course.

Fear—over what the earl might do, and to whom—made Emma brave. She had seen the two cousins in a physical fight once before—over a horse James had accused Stuart of having ridden too hard—and it had not been a pretty sight. Another such altercation must be avoided at all costs.

So with what she told herself was anger, but which was actually closer to desperation, she cried, "Really, my lord, you needn't bellow like that. Stuart and I are both adults, and capable of making our own decisions. I merely came to you in hopes that you, out of everyone, would understand and be sympathetic to our plight. But I see now that I sadly overestimated your sensibilities—"

"That's not all you overestimated, my girl," James said, with a laugh that was completely lacking in humor. "If you think for one minute that I am going to allow either of you to carry out this foolish and ill-conceived plan—"

Emma ought, again, to have kept her mouth shut. But she was too angry.

"I should very much like to see you stop us," Emma said, with a haughty toss of her head that sent her thick curls bouncing. "Stuart and I, unlike you, my lord, aren't content to sit and watch while others suffer needlessly. We both of us want to make this earth a better place for those less fortunate than ourselves. In Shetland, we will be helping people who are truly in need—"

"The only one I see who is truly in need," the earl said darkly, "is my cousin Stuart, who is in need of a sound thrashing."

Emma sucked in her breath. "Don't you dare to lay a finger on him," she warned. "If you do . . . if you do, I shall never speak to you again."

"That, Emma," the earl said, "would not be a hardship."

Without another word, the earl crossed from behind his desk, then stalked across the room to the door, which he flung open.

It wasn't until he reached the hallway that Emma heard him bellow his cousin's name. That was when she took off after him.

"No, my lord," she called. "Please, don't—"

But it was too late. She heard a crash, and then the Dowager Lady Denham's anguished cry.

"Good heavens!" Penelope, her eyes red, emerged from a nearby closet, the flow of her tears momentarily stanched by surprise. "Was that Lord Denham? Whatever did you say to him, Emma?"

"Too much," Emma informed her cousin with a groan. And then she raced off to stop, if she could, her fiancé from being murdered.

Chapter One

*E*mma Van Court Chesterton was having a bad day.

Not, of course, that today was particularly worse than any other. She'd been having bad days for nearly a year now. Oh, there'd been a few fair-to-middling days thrown in during that twelve-month period, but for the most part, they'd been bad.

She wasn't exactly sure what she'd done to bring on this spell of foul luck. She had picked up every single halfpenny she'd found and avoided walking under ladders.

Not that she believed in luck, of course. It was very old-fashioned and superstitious to do so.

But to be on the safe side, she'd visited the Wishing Tree again just last week and nailed Stuart's bedroom slippers to the trunk. She didn't have any of her own shoes to spare, and Stuart wouldn't be needing his any more, of course.

But when she woke up the next morning, she realized the shoes hadn't done the least bit of good. Her bad luck continued unabated.

The rooster had run away again.

Bad luck. That was the only explanation for it. A glance at her bedroom window revealed that the day was well advanced. The leaden sky was just light enough to indicate that dawn had come at least an hour earlier, but no rooster's crow had wakened her.

So she was late. Again.

The thought of throwing back the bedclothes to face the day was a daunting one. Emma lay still for a full minute after waking, debating whether even to bother setting foot out of bed. It was only the impatient whimpering of her bed partner—a laughing-faced dog of indeterminable breed but inestimable charm, whom Emma had rescued the week before from the docks—that finally propelled her out of bed.

Better to face a day lacking in promise, she decided, than to allow her new guest to have an accident indoors.

Hastily, Emma stuffed her feet into slippers and her arms into a dressing gown, while the dog—a female who, to Emma's admittedly inexperienced eye, appeared to be due to give birth at any moment—waddled in happy circles around her ankles, occasionally colliding with her new mistress's shins in her excitement over being let outdoors.

But when Emma opened the cottage door to let the dog out, she saw that things were worse—far worse—than she had imagined. Not only had her rooster run away, but rain—heavy, impenetrable spring rain—poured down in a thick curtain before her, turning the yard around her cottage to soggy bogs of mud. A squall had blown in from the sea during the night and was now pounding the tiny Hebridean island with its full force.

After having suffered through a half dozen blizzards since October, the sight of a good solid rainfall was not exactly unwelcome. Emma's enthusiasm for this spring shower was somewhat dampened, however, by the thought that she was going to have to wade out into that storm in order to get to the village, where a dozen children would be waiting in the schoolroom for her to conduct the day's lessons.

Emma wasn't the only one who looked upon the heavy rain with dismay. Her small guest placed a paw hesitantly in the mud, then turned to look back up at Emma, as if to say, "Must I? Must I, really?"

But it was only when that trusting, slightly perplexed expression turned suspicious and a low growl sounded in the dog's throat that Emma sensed there was something wrong with the animal other than a simple distaste for rain. Following the direction of the dog's gaze, Emma caught sight of the shadowy, hulking figure standing perfectly still just beneath the overhang of the cottage's thatch roof.

"Good Lord," Emma murmured, placing a hand to her chest. Beneath her fingers, her heart had begun to drum much too loudly. Really, she thought to herself, this is simply too much. To be accosted in front of her own cottage, while she was still in her dressing gown, for goodness sake. . . . And it wasn't the first time it had happened, either. This will not do. It simply will not do, she thought.

Opening her eyes, which she'd closed to utter a quick and silent prayer of thanks that at least she knew this particular interloper, Emma regarded the still figure.

"Really, Mr. MacEwan," she said in her sleep-roughened voice. "What *are* you doing, standing out here in the rain like this? You frightened me nearly to death, you know."

The giant—for that's what he was, really, a six-foot-seven giant of a man, who lived with his aging mother on the farm neighboring Emma's—inclined his head, causing rainwater that had collected along the brim of his hat to flow down in a stream to the toes of his thick boots.

" 'Mornin', Miz Chesterton," he said, shamefacedly. "I didna mean to afright ye. I . . . I brung back yer rooster."

For the first time, Emma noticed that there was a skinny, somewhat bedraggled bird tucked under Cletus MacEwan's arm.

"Oh, dear," she said. "Was he at your hens again, Mr. MacEwan? I'm so sorry—"

"I reckon he forgot that he don't live there no more." Cletus set the rooster on the ground. "But I don't s'pose he'll run off again. Our Charlie gave 'im quite a fight. I'm surprised ye didn't 'ear the two of 'em squawkin' all the way up 'ere."

Emma glared at the rooster, who hurried into the meager shelter provided by the overhang of the cottage's roof, then scratched aloofly at the hard ground, pretending he didn't know they were talking about him.

"I didn't hear them, no," Emma replied, "which is

why I'm running so late this morning. I can't thank you enough, Mr. MacEwan, for bringing him back."

Cletus nodded. "Well, I reckon he'll stay put this time, after the peckin' Charlie gave 'im." Then, shyly, he held out his other hand, from which a basket, its contents covered with a blue-and-white cloth, dangled. "Almost forgot," he said. "Me mam just made 'em. Scones. Fresh out o' the bakin' oven, are they."

Emma took the basket from his raw and work-reddened hands—he'd left his gloves behind again, she saw. The first warm day of the season, and Cletus MacEwan had abandoned his gloves, not remembering, as Emma did, that the weather in the Shetlands did not always abide by the calendar. It could be warm as summer in the middle of winter, and cold as February, as it was today, in the middle of May.

"Oh, Mr. MacEwan," she said, raising her voice so that he could hear her over the steady pounding of the rain. "Thank you so very much. But really, I wish you hadn't. . . ."

Emma wasn't just being polite. She really *did* wish he hadn't. Though she infinitely preferred Mrs. MacEwan's scones over last week's offering—a butchered hog—this was still far too much. Cletus MacEwan was Emma's most dedicated—and physically prepossessing—suitor, but he was also the most lacking in common sense.

"You're going to fall behind on your work, bringing me breakfast like this every morning," she scolded him gently.

Cletus only smiled at her, the trusting, friendly smile of a very young child. And indeed, he was young, at eighteen a year Emma's junior.

"Me mam says we've got to see you eat right," Cletus replied. "She says you've gotten too thin, and that you're goin' to waste away up 'ere—"

"Yes, well," Emma interrupted. She had heard Mrs. MacEwan's dire predictions before. There wasn't anything the least bit wrong with Emma's health, but Cletus's mother quite liked bragging to her friends in town about her efforts at fattening up "Poor Widow Chesterton." There wasn't any doubt that neighborly kindness was not the only reason behind Mrs. MacEwan's concern. She had an ulterior motive, and that motive was standing in front of Emma right then, shivering like a lamb before the slaughter beneath his wet clothes.

Under ordinary circumstances, Emma exercised no tolerance whatsoever for her many suitors. On this day, however, she decided to make an exception. Maybe it was the sight of Cletus MacEwan's chapped hands. Or maybe it was the heavenly smell of his mother's scones. In any case, Emma made up her mind to admit him, and so said kindly, "Do come in, won't you, Mr. MacEwan?" She moved aside to give him room to enter the cottage.

Cletus MacEwan needed no further urging. In a flash, he was ducking beneath the low-hanging door frame and filling her sitting room with his bulk.

"Much obliged to ye, mum," he said, nodding his head and this time managing to spill a good deal of water onto her clean wooden floor. "Mebbe I'll just stay fer a cuppa, if ye can spare it."

Emma smiled as she watched her neighbor move toward the hearth. Cletus MacEwan, though not terribly bright, was quite useful to have about, she'd found, especially when it came time to slaughter a chicken for her evening's supper, a task for which Emma had neither talent nor inclination.

But this skill did not engender an inclination to marry him. Emma lacked an inclination toward marriage to anyone at all.

And that was the root of nearly all her most recent trouble, the rooster not withstanding.

The ginger-colored mutt—whom Emma had decided the night before to call Una, after a character of that name in a book she'd been reading—having completed her business, turned about and scurried back into the warmth of the cottage. Emma stepped aside to avoid getting sprayed by the water droplets that flew everywhere when Una shook out her coat.

It was while Emma was in her bedroom struggling with her hair—a battle waged daily between the thick blond curls that rose from her head like a corona and the stiff horsehair bristles that seemed ultimately useless at taming them—that she happened to look up and notice something unusual:

There was a hearse in her vegetable patch.

Emma had been holding several hairpins between her teeth as she attempted to maintain the twist at the top of her head, but she nearly swallowed them when she spotted the long black carriage. The dilapidated brougham—the only vehicle in the remote island village that possessed a roof of any sort—was led by a team of twin nags, both of whom were nosing about Emma's cabbages, which had only just sprouted.

Emma stared at the brougham, her hands frozen on top of her head in her astonishment. What on earth was the village hearse doing in her vegetable patch? There had been no deaths in the area—not that she knew of. Emma's cottage was located on an isolated cliff overlooking the sea. Her closest neighbors, Cletus MacEwan and his mother, lived nearly a mile down the sharp incline that led to the Chesterton property. Surely Mr. Murphy, the brougham's owner, couldn't think either of the Mac-Ewans were dead. And obviously *she* wasn't dead.

True, Emma's husband Stuart had passed away, but that had been six months ago. And while Mr. Murphy was a bit of a drunkard, even he couldn't have forgotten that he'd already made *that* fateful pickup.

Unless—Emma lowered her arms, a cold dread growing inside her—unless Samuel Murphy was here for another reason altogether. Not to pick up a corpse, but to throw his hat into the circle of suitors—like Cletus MacEwan—who'd been so assiduously courting her since word of her highly unusual inheritance had spread up and down the shore.

"Oh, *no*," Emma said out loud. At her feet, Una wagged her tail happily, thinking Emma was speaking to her. "Not Mr. *Murphy*. Oh, please, not Mr. Murphy *too*."

It was bad enough she had Cletus MacEwan waiting on her doorstep every morning. Even worse, every time she entered the village she was besieged by eligible bachelors of all ages and descriptions, many of whom, being fishermen, attempted to woo her by waving the catch of the day at her.

But all that would be nothing, nothing at all, compared to being followed, day in, day out, by a big black *hearse*. With *fringe* hanging from its top, no less.

Determined that she would not allow this to happen,

Emma went to her bed, where she'd abandoned her shawl the night before. Throwing the heavy wool garment about her shoulders, she stalked from the bedroom, going straight to the front door without so much as a glance at the giant huddled in front of the cheerful fire upon her hearth.

The front door to her cottage was split, Dutch style, so that Emma could open the top half to enjoy the fresh ocean breeze in spring and summertime, without letting in any of the livestock that happened to be roaming in her yard. She opened the top half then, peering out through the rain at the black brougham and the lonely driver perched atop it, seemingly oblivious to the wet.

Drawing in a deep breath, Emma shouted over the steady pounding of the rain, "Samuel Murphy! What do you think you're doing? You had better have a good reason for making wheel ruts in my vegetable patch!"

Behind her, she heard Cletus MacEwan stir.

"Murphy," he burst out incredulously. "What's 'e doin' 'ere?"

Though he could not have heard the question, Mr. Murphy, atop the driver's seat of the hearse, tipped his sodden top hat politely and called across the yard, "Brung someone ta see ye, Miz Chesterton!"

It was only then that Emma noticed that there was someone inside the brougham. Since no one in Faires would ride in that wretched contraption unless he were stretched out in a pine box, no longer in a position to have any say in the matter, it was understandable that Emma would not have considered this before. But of course, in a veritable deluge like the one they were experiencing at that moment, anyone wishing to visit her without getting completely soaked would have to do so in the only enclosed vehicle in the area.

And that vehicle was, of course, Samuel Murphy's hearse.

"It's MacCreigh." Behind Emma, Cletus rose to his feet. He had to duck his head to avoid striking it on the roof beams stretched above him. Fearing for the china plates that rested on the upper shelves of the sideboard in the corner, which had a tendency to rattle alarmingly whenever Cletus MacEwan strode across the floor, Emma thrust out both her hands toward him.

"Now, Mr. MacEwan," she soothed. "Kindly seat yourself. There's no reason to think that—"

Seeing her guest's perturbed expression, and knowing how he happened to feel about Lord MacCreigh, who had called upon her at the cottage once or twice in the past—though never quite this early in the morning— Emma was not very surprised when he interrupted her.

"It's MacCreigh, I tell you!" Cletus insisted. He obliged her, however, by remaining where he was. "Sure as I'm standin' here. Too dandified to ride in the rain on his horse like regular folk, so he had to hire Murphy's hearse—"

Emma saw that if she was going to have any hope at all of keeping her china intact, she had better act, posthaste. After all, with bad luck like hers, she couldn't be taking any chances. Accordingly, she turned her face back toward the rain and shouted at the occupant of the brougham, "Lord MacCreigh, really, I am quite surprised at you. I thought I'd made it perfectly clear that my answer was—"

But as she was speaking, the brougham door swung

slowly open, admitting from the confines of the vehicle a tall man swathed in a rich, fur-lined cloak. He stepped to the ground with considerable stiffness—hardly a surprise, since the interior of Murphy's carriage had been designed not for the comfort of the living but for the security of the dead.

It was only then that Emma saw that her visitor was not Lord MacCreigh at all.

Besides the fact that, despite what Cletus had said, Lord MacCreigh was not so dandified as to hire Murphy's brougham simply because of a little downpour— he was a fine horseman who never seemed the least perturbed by inclement weather—this man was nothing like her most relentless suitor. This man was dark, while Geoffrey Bain—the baron of MacCreigh—was red-haired; clean-shaven, whereas Geoffrey Bain wore a mustache. And beneath the cloak, this man was dressed in a pair of fawn breeches and a green satin waistcoat; Geoffrey Bain had taken, since he'd been abandoned by his young fiancée earlier in the year, to wearing only black. Although the age—thirty—and the size—a little over six feet—looked about right, in every other respect the two men were complete opposites.

This man was a stranger to Emma. That in itself was odd, since strangers never came to Faires.

And they certainly never came to see *her*.

There must have been some mistake. Yes, there had to have been some kind of mistake. Because unless news of her inheritance had spread abroad—and oh, how Emma prayed that it hadn't!—there was no reason, no reason at all, why any stranger should seek her out.

And then the man started to approach the cottage, and Emma, getting a good look at his face for the first time, realized with a sinking heart that, as far as bad days went, this one really might end up being the worst.

Because this was no stranger. No stranger at all.

Chapter Two

"Oh, God," Emma murmured, her hand on the lower half of the Dutch door tightening convulsively.

She recognized him at once. The resemblance between this man and her now deceased husband had always been uncanny: the uncomfortably bright hazel eyes; the dark hair, worn just a shade longer than was stylish—than had been considered stylish, anyway, the last time Emma had been in London—and what was commonly considered to be striking looks, for a man . . . broad, un-lined forehead, clefted chin, strong, lean jaw.

Though James had always been the larger of the two—taller than Stuart by nearly a head, and so much broader about the shoulders—it had been Stuart whose slighter physical frame had housed the more spiritually vigorous soul. Or so she had always thought.

"Oh, my God," she said again, her mouth suddenly very dry.

Behind her, Cletus started forward. The china in the

sideboard trembled noisily. "That's it," the yeoman declared. "He's a dead man, baron or no."

Emma realized belatedly that she'd spoken out loud. And while she might have liked nothing better than to see the earl of Denham thrashed to within an inch of his life by her strapping young neighbor, the murder of a peer in her sitting room might be rather hard to explain to the local law officials, and she certainly didn't need *another* corpse on her conscience.

Whirling around, Emma put out both her hands, intending to stop Cletus as he rushed for the door. Her fingers met up with a wall of flesh. Trying to keep Cletus MacEwan from doing exactly as he wanted was like trying to keep a bull from charging. Still, Emma planted her booted feet firmly on the floorboards and refused to budge.

"No, no, Mr. MacEwan," she said quickly. "It isn't Lord MacCreigh. It isn't Lord MacCreigh at all."

Cletus's dark eyebrows met in a rush over his nose. "Oh, it ain't?" he demanded, obviously thinking she was trying to dupe him. "If it ain't MacCreigh, who is it then?"

"It isn't anyone," she said. "No one to concern you, anyway."

Good Lord, but he was strong! Like a steam engine, he nearly bowled her over. Cletus MacEwan was far too much of a gentleman ever to lay a hand on her without permission, but in his eagerness to best the man he perceived his rival, he'd gripped her shoulders and was attempting—as well as he could without actually hurting her—to move her bodily from his path. But Emma only took a firmer stance, determined to keep him in his place.

"Really, Mr. MacEwan," she said. She was speaking through gritted teeth now, her arms trembling in her effort to keep him from killing the earl as soon as he walked in. "Hadn't you ought to be running home now? I'm sure your mother must be missing you—"

The deep voice came far sooner than she'd expected. And it *was* a deep voice, deeper even than she remembered, a rumbling bass that brooked no disobedience. It seemed to shake the floorboards with every bit as much strength as Cletus MacEwan's enormous feet.

"What," James Marbury boomed, "is this?"

Emma raised her head. Through a tangle of curls, she saw the earl of Denham standing on the other side of the Dutch door, his expression incredulous. Giving a little groan, Emma ducked her head again, straining with all her might to keep Cletus in place.

And then, before she knew what was happening, she was lifted from Cletus MacEwan's grasp and placed, unceremoniously, upon the cushions of her own settle.

Really. That was precisely how it happened . . . or as near as she could make out. One minute she was struggling to keep Cletus from killing her husband's kin, and the next, she was on the settle, Una barking furiously at the two men before her.

And Cletus MacEwan, who had been Faires's caber-tossing champion for four years running, the largest, strongest man on the island, was staggering backward from a blow to the face that had sent him reeling—

Right into Emma's sideboard.

"No!" Scrambling to her feet, Emma darted forward just as the earl of Denham was drawing his arm back to deliver another blow. He paused to smile at her, a charming smile, made all the more convincing by the warm glow in his hazel eyes.

"Never fear, Emma," James Marbury said, courteously. "I'll see to it this young cuss learns to keep his hands to himself."

"But—"

It was too late. Cletus, still dazed from the first blow, didn't even see the second one coming. Emma stood watching in horror as her sideboard disintegrated beneath his enormous weight. The piles of porcelain teetered, then tottered, and then slowly—or so it seemed to Emma—rained down upon the hapless yeoman.

The first to fall were the soup bowls. Next came the cruet stand. That was followed by the dinner plates, then the dessert plates, and finally, in a stunning shower, the matching teacups and their saucers.

Emma was quite certain the entire demolition took place over the course of several long hours, but it could only have been seconds, really, or the earl would probably have caught more than a single teacup, which he leaned down and seized just before it joined the others in its set, in pieces on the floor all around Cletus Mac-Ewan's prone body.

When the last piece of china had slid to its explosive demise, Cletus moaned and rose to his elbows, looking confused. "What 'appened?" he asked, brushing shards of porcelain from his shirtfront.

Emma stared at the wreckage that had once been place settings for eight, fine white china trimmed around the edges with a border of hand-painted pink rose garlands. Except for the teacup held by the earl, there remained not a single salvageable piece. At her feet, Una made a snuffling sound and sat down, glaring with disapproval at the two men.

James broke the silence. Flipping the cup over, he read the mark on the bottom with raised eyebrows.

"Limoges," he read aloud. "Finely made, that."

That was all it took. Just that casual remark. And then Emma snapped. Because it was just so like him. It was just so like James Marbury, ninth earl of Denham, to destroy the only thing she had that was of any value to her whatsoever, just as he'd done once before, a year ago.

Striding forward, she snatched the teacup from his fingers.

"Yes," she shouted. Really shouted, at the top of her lungs. "It *was* finely made, wasn't it? At least until you had to come bursting in here, and smash it all to pieces!"

The earl blinked down at her. She had the impression that he was rather taken aback, but she was too angry to pay much heed to how he might be feeling.

"Bursting in here?" he echoed, as if she'd wounded him to the quick. "I beg your pardon, Emma, but when I came to your door, it appeared to me that you were being assaulted. Forgive me if I did the gentlemanly thing and attempted to protect you!"

Emma glared up at him. "*I* was trying to protect *you*, you ignorant sod. It was *you* he was trying to assault, not me."

"*Me?*" James raised his eyebrows and looked down at Cletus, who'd sat up and was carefully removing splinters of porcelain from his coat sleeve, wincing each time one of the slivers pierced his callused skin. "Why on earth would you want to attack *me?*" the earl thundered. "I don't even know you!"

Cletus looked up, startled. "W-what?" he stammered. He had not yet recovered fully from the blows he'd received, and he had to shake his head several times, as if clearing water from his ears, before he continued. "I—I did no' know it was you, sir. I thought you was Lord MacCreigh."

"Lord MacCreigh?" James turned toward his cousin's widow. "Who is this MacCreigh person?"

But Emma only shook her own head, staring dismally down at the mess on her floor.

"That porcelain was a wedding present," she said sadly. "The *only* wedding present Stuart and I received, I might add. And now it's gone, ruined, thanks to your blockheadedness—"

"Blockheadedness!" the earl interrupted. "Now see here—"

"It's gone. It's all gone. Look at it."

Emma was not exactly the type of woman who'd weep over lost china, but it had to be admitted that, for a moment, tears did prick the corners of her eyes as she gazed down at the teacup in her hands. She remembered all too vividly the day the porcelain had arrived in its wooden crate stamped "Limoges, France," and how excited and happy she'd been as she unwound the straw packing from each delicate, beautiful piece.

Stuart had chided her for it, of course. He had never valued material things. That was one of the reasons that Emma had first fallen in love with him, one of the many qualities that had set him so far above every other man she had met in her life. Stuart had always had a truly spiritual, truly giving nature. Never had Emma met anyone as devoted to helping the less fortunate and obeying the word of the Lord as Stuart. She had tried very hard to be like Stuart, to turn her mind to spiritual, not material matters—

But in this—as in so many other things, when it came to Stuart—she had failed.

The Limoges was a fitting example. How she had loved to hold her new plates to the sky, so that the sun could shine straight through them. It was, she'd insisted, like a magic trick. And when Stuart had gone on to explain the chemical process by which porcelain was made, she'd stopped her ears—though not within Stuart's sight, of course—preferring to believe in the magic instead.

Except that now, thanks to James Marbury, the magic was gone.

The earl of Denham cleared his throat. "Tell me the name of the pattern, Emma," he said, "and I'll see to it that the set is replaced—"

Angry at herself for caring so much about a silly heap of plates—but even more for showing weakness in front of James, a man to whom she now remembered having sworn she'd never speak again—she reached up to rub the corners of her eyes with some of the lace at the end of her sleeve.

"Never mind," she said. "It doesn't matter."

James said, stubbornly, "It *does* matter. If you'd just—"

"It doesn't. I told you it doesn't. Just—" Emma

looked up at him, the tears gone. "What are you doing here? I thought—"

She was interrupted by a groan from Cletus. He had managed to dust most of the broken porcelain from his clothing and was now trying, somewhat unsteadily, to rise. She placed the remaining teacup on the mantel, then went to help him to his feet.

"Are you all right, Mr. MacEwan?" she asked. "Did he hurt you?"

"No, no." Cletus, his pride wounded more than anything else, turned round to survey the wreckage that had once been Emma's sideboard. "Miz Chesterton," he cried in astonishment. "Did *I* do all that?"

Emma said, "Not at all. This one here did." And she sent a withering look in James's direction that the yeoman, still staring fixedly at the mess, missed entirely.

"Gor," Cletus breathed. "I'll build you a new one, Miz Chesterton. I promise. A brand-new sideboard. Better than the old one, I swear."

"Thank you, Mr. MacEwan." Emma stooped to pick up his hat, dusted it off, and handed it to him. "And now I think you had better go."

Cletus took his hat, but he didn't thank her for it. Instead, he leveled a hostile glare at the earl. "What about '*im?*" he demanded, rudely.

Emma folded her arms across her chest and said, "What about him, Mr. MacEwan?"

"Well." Cletus shuffled his enormous feet. "Who *is* 'e, then?"

"He's the late Mr. Chesterton's cousin," Emma replied. "The earl of Denham."

"Gor!" The ham-fisted yeoman appeared awed. He

began to knead his hat brim nervously between his thick fingers. "An earl," he murmured reverently. "I nearly pounded an *earl*."

"Yes." Emma, tight-lipped, took Cletus by the arm and attempted to steer him toward the door. "Go on home, now, Mr. MacEwan, and be sure to tell your mother all about it." *So that she can run down to the village and tell every living soul she sees,* Emma added mentally. There was no use, she knew, trying to keep anything secret in a village the size of Faires. It was better to get everything out in the open as quickly as possible, and Cletus MacEwan's mother, Emma had learned over the past few months, was quite efficacious at achieving this.

"An earl," Cletus murmured one last time, as Emma pushed him back into the rain. He'd never once taken his gaze from James, the whole time they'd been speaking. Nor did he remember to put on his hat. It wasn't until Emma shut the door firmly behind him that he seemed to recover himself, and then, she saw through the window, he shuffled slowly toward the hearse. Mr. Murphy, she noticed, had crawled inside the wretched contraption, where he was undoubtedly curled, enjoying nips at his whiskey flask while he waited for the return of his wealthy fare. The two islanders, Mr. Murphy and Mr. MacEwan, would most likely exchange stories about this illustrious personage for months to come.

Emma, however, would have given her last unbroken piece of Limoges to get him to quit her household immediately. But a peek in James's direction showed that he didn't look anxious to go anywhere. He was pulling off his gloves now—kid leather, she supposed—and looking about the cottage appraisingly. She didn't doubt he was noticing how small it was. Well, Stuart had not, on a curate's salary, been able to afford anything much bigger. And while the cottage was small, certainly, she prided herself on its neatness and charm. For it *was* neat, and quite charming, with its thatched roof—a trifle cold in the wintertime, true, but very picturesque just the same—and green door and shutters. If his lordship didn't think as much of it as she did, well, that wasn't Emma's problem.

A glance at the dining table—really just a thick plank of wood with legs attached to it—apparently showed a tabletop that passed the earl's exacting standards, since James placed his top hat there, tossing his gloves inside it.

In a minute more, Emma thought, he'll take off his boots and prop his feet up by the fire! Well, she wouldn't have it. She would not play hostess to this man, not after the way he'd treated Stuart. She would *not*.

Accordingly she said, as coldly as she could, "If you've come for Stuart's things, you've put yourself to a lot of bother for nothing." She went to the corner, where she kept her broom and dustpan. Lifting them both, she crossed the room and began to sweep up the broken shards that had once been her dining service. "I gave all of his clothes and things away to the church."

It seemed to take a second or two for her words to register. And then James had to ask for clarification, as if he wasn't certain he had heard her correctly, "The church? Did you say you gave Stuart's things to the *church?*"

"Yes," Emma replied. The porcelain made a woeful

tinkling noise as she swept it into the dustpan. "That's right."

"Do you mean to tell me," James asked, slowly, "that some tribal chieftain in darkest Africa is dashing about in my cousin's trousers?"

Emma managed to smile tightly at him. "Oh, no. There is enough of a demand for men's clothing amongst the poor right here in Faires."

James's gaze darted toward the window. So, she thought with some triumph. He'd recognized the tartan waistcoat Samuel Murphy was wearing after all.

"I see," James said. He sounded slightly mortified. Maybe, Emma thought, her heart lifting a little, maybe he'll get angry enough with me to leave now!

But James seemed to have no intention of leaving. Whatever he was here for—and why, oh, why, had he had to come?—it didn't look as if he'd leave before he got it. Not if the way he reached for one of the spindly wooden chairs—there were four of them pushed up to the table—and spun it around until it faced her was any indication.

"Put that lot down, Emma," he said, "and come sit with me. We've a lot of catching up to do, you and I. It's been a year, after all, since we last saw one another."

Emma could only stare at him.

Now that she was looking at him up close, she saw that the resemblance between her husband and his cousin was actually a trifling one. The earl was, in fact, much handsomer than Stuart had ever been. His hair was darker than his cousin's, his eyes brighter, his jaw more squared. In fact, it almost seemed to Emma as if Stuart, though the younger of the two, had been a rough draft of his cousin . . . almost as if her husband had been God's practice sketch for the earl of Denham.

But James seemed still to be laboring under the impression that he actually *was* God. Who else would arrive unannounced on her doorstep and expect her to drop everything to visit with him?

"I'm afraid I haven't time for catching up right now, Lord Denham," she said shortly. It was only with an effort that she kept her tone light. She sincerely hoped that he could not hear the *thump-thump-thump* of her heart, which seemed to have been drumming much too loudly in her ears ever since she'd first laid eyes upon him, there in her vegetable patch.

"I'm already running quite late as it is," she said. "Now, if you're not here for Stuart's things, why did you come?"

He looked surprised. Well, and why not? It couldn't be every day a woman turned down an invitation to sit and chat with the earl of Denham.

But most women, Emma thought, did not know him as well as she did.

"I beg your pardon, Emma," James said, his deep voice deceptively casual. "I hadn't any idea you were on your way out. In fact, when I came in, you seemed to be entertaining."

Emma felt herself flush. She knew what he was intimating. It was in his tone, in his expression. Emptying the dustpan containing the remnants of her porcelain collection into one of the few drawers that had not come apart when Cletus careened into the sideboard, she said, pointedly, "That was my neighbor, Mr. MacEwan. He stopped by to return my rooster."

"Your rooster," the earl repeated, without inflection.

"Yes," Emma said. "He ran away."

"Your rooster ran away?"

"Yes." Why did he sound as if he did not believe her? "He runs away quite a bit. He was a gift, you see, and he seems to miss his old roost, and is always trying to return to it."

"A gift from Mr. MacEwan?" the earl inquired, curiously.

"Certainly not. The rooster was given to me by Mr. MacEwan's mother." Seeing his raised eyebrows, she pointed defensively toward the basket on the table. "She baked those scones for me this morning. You may help yourself to one, if you like. I'm certain they're still warm."

Lord Denham ignored the basket. In fact, he did not take his gaze off her, which was strangely unsettling. His eyes had always been, she remembered, such an odd color, not really green, but not brown, either. They were almost gold, Emma thought to herself. Gold as the wedding band she'd removed so many months ago and given to someone—she could no longer remember who. Someone who had needed it more than she did. That much she knew.

"You have some very . . . attentive neighbors," was all James said, and there was that hint again, that hint of . . . something in his tone. Emma couldn't put her finger on what, exactly, that tone meant. Surely it couldn't be anything very complimentary. Not if it was coming from the lips of the earl of Denham.

"Yes," she said. "Well, Mr. MacEwan and his mother have been doing their best to look after me since Stuart passed away."

The criticism—that the earl and *his* mother had done nothing for her since the death of her husband—hit home . . . though Emma had not in fact meant it that way. It would have been accurate, of course, but not fair, given the circumstances. Still, James reacted quickly.

"Well, but then your Mr. MacEwan and his mother have known about Stuart's death a good deal longer than my mother and I. I have only had the benefit of the knowledge for a week. Really, Emma, could you not have told us sooner?"

"I couldn't," she explained, more reasonably than she felt. "You know the entire district was under quarantine. It was only lifted just last month."

"Still, you could have sent word—"

"You know you would have come," she said. "Quarantine or no. And I couldn't have your death on my conscience." *As well as Stuart's,* she just managed to stop herself from adding. She turned away and went to pluck her bonnet from the wall. "Well, you've seen me now, and you can report back to everyone that I'm quite well. And now, if you don't mind, my lord, I really must go."

"Go?" he asked. As well he might. He had, after all, just arrived. And the arrival of the earl of Denham anywhere was generally something of an occasion. He was that kind of man. "Go *where?*"

"To the schoolhouse," she replied, with more temerity than she actually felt. She knew what he was going to say when he learned the full truth. He was going to laugh . . . or worse.

"The schoolhouse?" he echoed. "Whatever for?

Not a meeting of the mission society this early in the day?"

In spite of her nervousness, Emma had trouble restraining a smile. "No. The local mission society is dedicated, I assure you, but not *that* dedicated. I must get to the schoolhouse because I am, in fact, the teacher."

"Teacher?" James stared at her. "*You* teach, Emma? Teach *what*? To *whom*?"

Well. At least he hadn't laughed.

"I teach school," she said. "To children. My lord, if you'll excuse me, I am very late. You're welcome to stay here, of course, if you wish—though I can't imagine why you'd want to—but I must go. You do understand, don't you?"

The earl of Denham did not, in fact, appear to understand. He seemed every bit as bewildered as he'd been from the moment he'd stepped across her threshold.

Still, he seemed to rally and, lifting his hat, said somberly, "I will take you into town, then, Emma."

Emma's eyes widened. "Oh," she said. "That isn't . . . I mean, it isn't in the least necessary."

James raised a single dark eyebrow as he pulled on his gloves. "You would rather walk, then, I take it? Two miles? In this rain?"

Emma gazed out at the downpour beyond her door. At her feet, Una, whom she dared not leave alone at her advanced stage of pregnancy, whined softly, not relishing the idea of stepping out into that rain any more than Emma did.

A ride. That was all the earl was offering. A ride into town. After which, with any luck, he might be induced to board the noonday ferry and go away, without ever finding out the full truth about Emma's unfortunate circumstances.

Why not? She couldn't go on having this bad luck forever, could she? Things were going to have to start looking up sometime. Why not now?

Chapter Three

At first James had thought it was only a trick of the rain.

And a hard, stinging rain it was, too, completely unlike the gentle showers back in London, or his native Devonshire. There had been such a deluge of it that morning that it had turned what apparently served as a road in this part of the country into a six-inch-deep river of mud. They'd have covered the distance in half the time, James had felt quite certain, had they been driving on macadam. But paved roads seemed to be unheard of in the Shetland Isles—much like decent coffee and indoor plumbing.

When a slight break in the downpour afforded James a better view of the woman who was standing in the doorway of the cottage they'd pulled up alongside, however, he could no longer blame what he was seeing on the rain. Instead, he simply stared.

This was not, of course, how any of this was supposed to have transpired. Emma was not supposed to have been there. Thinking back on it now, James had to admit he'd been a fool to think she'd returned to England.

But what else was he to have supposed? Stuart was nearly six months dead, after all . . . at least, according to the brief letter that had been hand-delivered last week to James's town house in London. In it, Emma explained her reasons for waiting until so many months after Stuart's untimely demise to inform them of it: since the typhus wave that had surfaced in Faires around the time of Stuart's death had resulted in quarantine of the afflicted areas, she had not wanted others to risk their own lives in an effort to pay their respects. . . .

And while it was true that Lady Denham had been quite upset by Emma's delinquency in conveying the bad news, it was fortunate for James that she'd delayed so; for if Emma had dispatched her letter last autumn, rather than last month, then to Faires James would have gone, health warnings against doing so or no—particularly had he realized that Stuart's wife was still there. It would have been unconscionable for him to leave any woman to fend for herself amidst all that filth and disease. James would not have been able to call himself a man of honor had he allowed such a thing to occur.

But it hadn't been any woman. It had been Emma. *Emma.* Impossible to have left Emma there. He would have gone to Faires at once, and insisted upon her returning to England with him. . . .

Something that he was only just now realizing her own family had apparently failed quite miserably to do.

He should not, he knew, have found this so surprising. The Van Courts, much like his own family, had not taken particularly kindly to Stuart and Emma's decision to wed. Emma's aunt and uncle had, in fact, taken steps to separate the young lovers, keeping their niece a virtual prisoner in her room for several days following her breaking the news of their planned elopement to James, who of course shared it, as was his duty, with her guardians . . . as soon as he'd finished impressing upon Stuart the foolishness of his plan.

Unfortunately, the Van Courts did not keep as close an eye on their ward as they ought, for she escaped less than a week later, disappearing into the night and across the border with his cousin, whom she married not twenty-four hours later.

And that, then, was the end of the Van Courts's interest in the girl whom they'd once adored, but whom they now considered ungrateful. The relationship between Regina Van Court and James's mother had also suffered permanent strain because of it all. James sensed that his mother found something a little romantic in Stuart and Emma's elopement, while Mrs. Van Court— quite rightly, in James's opinion—was deeply offended by the behavior of the two lovers.

Still, nowhere in Emma's letter had there been any indication that she was still living in Faires. Since the missive had been hand-delivered, James had quite naturally assumed its author was in London. James had even been tempted to call upon Emma at her aunt and uncle's home, assuming that even the Van Courts, injured as they'd been by Emma's rash behavior, would not have turned away a penniless widow . . . for penniless Stuart would have to have left Emma, as he had not possessed a cent of his own, save what he earned. And a curate's salary, James knew, was a mere pittance compared to the allowance he'd used to dole out to his headstrong cousin.

Only James's mother's gentle reminder that he had not exactly parted with Stuart and his bride on the best of terms a year earlier, and that his presence might cause the widow further pain, caused him to put off the visit. It had been decided instead that Lady Denham would pay the necessary condolence call, while James set off to Scotland to ascertain the whereabouts of Stuart's remains, and to make plans for their immediate removal, since it would not do, of course, for anyone of Marbury blood to be laid to final rest anywhere but in the mausoleum at the churchyard in Denham Abbey.

Ironically, James had actually been relieved by this turn of events. He far preferred his task, however repugnant it might seem, to his mother's. He was not at all confident he'd have been able to face Emma—and the grief she must necessarily be feeling—with the appropriate reserve. She had the sort of blue eyes, James remembered only too well, that tended to do things to a man, especially when they happened to be filled with tears. . . .

Too late, James realized that his relief had been short-lived. Lady Denham would be calling upon Emma's relatives to no avail; the widow hadn't sought comfort in the bosom of her not-so-loving family. No, not at all. Instead she had remained in Faires, having evidently sent her letter with some London-bound Scotsman, gone to the big city to seek his fortune now that the kelp beds had dried up.

And now James was going to have to face her after all. Face her and those blue eyes. Face her, those eyes, and the animosity he could tell she still felt toward him.

Surely, he'd told himself, she couldn't continue to harbor that grudge. Emma Van Court had always been an open, engaging girl, the warmest, most ingenuous person he had ever known. Surely she couldn't still be angry with him for something that had happened twelve long months ago.

Or could she? For, warm and ingenuous as she'd been, she'd also had that frustrating stubborn streak— the same streak that had caused, James was convinced, all this trouble in the first place.

It was difficult, looking at her now, seated across the carriage from him, to tell how she felt about seeing him again. Clearly she had not been particularly pleased by what had transpired back at her cottage. James couldn't really blame her. It seemed to him as if ever since he'd entered the ridiculously small house she and his cousin had shared, everything had turned topsy-turvy—not just her collection of Limoges. First he'd seen what appeared to be a beautiful woman being molested by a great hulking—well, *peasant* was really the only word—and so he had done the honorable thing, what he'd been raised the whole of his life to do, which was protect the fairer sex; only to find that Emma apparently hadn't needed protecting, and moreover, wasn't the least bit grateful to him for endeavoring to save her.

All he had was a set of sore knuckles as a thank-you.

As it was not at all unlike Emma to speak her mind—one of the many qualities Emma possessed that had always both irritated and yet, it had to be admitted, strangely attracted him, as it was a quality rare in the society misses that were continually thrust before him by their panting mammas—he ought not have been surprised.

Still, that she could be so acerbic after suffering such a loss—and he did not mean of the Limoges—was startling. He had expected tears. What he got was anything but.

But then when had Emma Van Court—Chesterton, he corrected himself, firmly. Chesterton!—ever done what was expected?

She was not even dressed in mourning clothes. The dove gray gown she wore beneath her cloak looked well worn, the lace around the cuffs a little frayed, its puffed sleeves a year out of date. But it wouldn't have mattered what Emma Chesterton put on; even a nun's habit wouldn't have been adequate to hide her beauty.

Sighing, James looked through the carriage's cracked windowpanes at the landscape they were passing through. Why anyone would want to live so close to the sea, he couldn't imagine. The cliff upon which Stuart's cottage was situated was undoubtedly shrouded in fog each morning, and bombarded with sunlight, rain, or snow the rest of the day. There was hardly a tree to be seen. A more unprotected—and less accessible—spot James couldn't imagine.

No sign, however, of a gravestone. Since James had not found it in the cemetery on the outskirts of the town of Faires, he had to assume the grave was somewhere about this desolate cliff. The Reverend Peck, Stuart's former employer, had been extremely unhelpful concerning the whereabouts of his curate's remains, claiming that so many lives had been lost in the typhus epidemic that coincided with Stuart's death that it had been impossible to keep proper records of who was buried where. When villagers had begun dying at a rate of nearly a half dozen a day, group graves had been resorted to—though James was quite certain Emma would never have consented to a group grave for her husband. That, at least, was something to be thankful for, one of the few things for which he had to give thanks since embarking on this extraordinary journey.

The real question now, of course, was, What in the name of heaven was he going to do? This was not going at all as he had planned, insofar as he'd been capable of forming a plan in the few seconds between observing Emma through the broken glass of Murphy's brougham and stepping across her threshold. He had quickly come to the realization then that his mission to retrieve Stuart's remains was likely to be a futile one.

But another mission, far more important, and entirely more pressing, had taken the place of the original. And James was determined that in this one, at least, he would not fail.

Emma, seated across the carriage from the earl, was suffering from no such internal battles. Indeed, she was beginning to feel that at last—at long last—things were looking up. Not only had the earl not asked her a thing—not a thing, thank heaven!—about Stuart's death, but he had let her have the forward-facing seat, electing to ride backward on the bench opposite hers. Emma quite hated riding backward.

But Emma soon began to feel her good fortune was not to last . . . especially when the brougham's wheels dipped into a particularly deep rut in the road, and the earl of Denham lurched toward her, very nearly thrown from his seat. For one disturbing moment, Emma thought he might actually fall forward into her lap—though why this should be so unsettling, she couldn't say. She supposed it was because he was so large, and his weight, falling on her, might prove injurious.

Fortunately, however, he caught himself just in time. Leaning back, attempting to find firmer purchase on the springless bench, he said gravely, "I beg your pardon, Emma."

She studied him from beneath her eyelashes so that he would not know she was looking in his direction. She was endeavoring to maintain an air of cool indifference where the earl was concerned—though the truth, of course, was that the tiniest glance at him set her pulse racing. Because, of course, he was so infuriating. Or so she told herself, anyway.

"It's quite all right," she said, with all the airiness she could muster. "You'll only have to put up with me as far as the schoolyard, and then Mr. Murphy will drop you at the ferry dock."

And then she awarded him a smile, a smile as sweet as nectar from a Devonshire clover.

That she was trying to be rid of him—without being implicitly rude—was evident. And James was not unaware that she had reason to be less than happy to see him. Their last meeting had not by any means been propitious for either of them. After all, the last time she'd seen him, he'd been driving his fist into the face of her fiancé.

Still, he would not be driven off so easily as that. And it was better she learned it now.

"I must say I was extremely surprised, Emma, to find you still residing in Faires," he said. "When my mother and I received your letter, we assumed that you were in London."

It was on the tip of Emma's tongue to ask just where in London he'd expected her to be residing, since her family had cut her off without a cent—as if *he*, of all people, didn't know that. But she managed to restrain herself and instead said, with what she thought was admirable calm, "Oh?"

"I would have thought," he said, "that you'd have gone home to your aunt and uncle."

Emma narrowed her eyes, but unfortunately his gaze was fastened on the landscape going by through the cracked window glass, and so he did not see her ire. Perhaps he heard it in her voice when she said, evenly, "You, sir, of all people should be aware that I no longer have a home with my aunt and uncle."

He did look at her then, and she saw his dark eyebrows constrict. "Emma," he said severely, "you cannot still blame me for telling them. You must realize now that you were far too young—"

Emma widened her eyes. "I *wasn't* too young, and I cannot believe you still insist—"

He held up a single hand, gloved palm out, effectively stanching the flow of her words. "What I cannot believe," he chided gently, "is that you haven't forgiven

your family for disapproving of Stuart. You must see by
now that it was the height of lunacy, his marrying you
when he was yet so unestablished in a career. He hadn't
a cent to his name. Of course your family disapproved.
But do you not think they would welcome you back,
Emma? I am sure they must be wild with worry for
you."

Emma blinked. Wild with worry for her? Not very
likely. The affection of her relations had come, Emma
now realized, at a price, and that price had been the ex-
pectation that she would marry a wealthy, or at least a
titled, man, and bring more prestige to the illustrious
Van Court family. Having failed to do so, she was cast
aside as thoughtlessly as a well-used dust rag.

"Still," James went on, "if you do not feel comfortable living with your family, perhaps. . . ." He cleared
his throat. "Perhaps . . . you might . . . would . . . accept
an invitation to come and live with my mother in London."

Emma thought she could not have heard him aright.
The words were spoken in so low a tone, quite without
preamble, that she was certain she could not have heard
him correctly. But the look on his face, of patient ex-
pectancy, told her she was wrong, that she had perfect
hearing.

Still, she had to ask, stupidly, "What?"

"I do hope you'll say yes," James managed to say,
though it was with an effort he kept up anything like a
politely detached tone. He was inexplicably hurt by
her stunned expression. It had obviously never occurred to her that Stuart's family might offer her anything in the way of support, financial or otherwise.

Had James really seemed that much of an ogre to her in the past?

But he supposed that, to an eighteen-year-old in love, he had committed the most heinous crime imaginable: he had attempted to keep her from the man she loved.

And his subsequent behavior—refusing to forward Stuart so much as a cent, hoping that a taste of living on a curate's miserable salary might instill some sense into the newlyweds—had probably not endeared him very much to either of them.

"Mother is quite anxious for you to come," he continued, which, while not strictly true, was not completely false. The Dowager Lady Denham had always been extremely fond of Emma, and would doubtlessly welcome her to the town house she and James still shared—James being unwilling to leave his mother, who was not perfectly well, alone for extended periods of time—with great enthusiasm.

Thinking a little admonishment on his part might be appropriate at this point, he added, "You ought to have written much sooner, Emma. It is quite intolerable, this situation. Surely you must see that."

Emma genuinely had no idea what he was talking about. "What situation?" she asked, thinking with some panic that he'd learned somehow about Mr. O'Malley and his dreadful will.

Astonishedly, James raised an arm. "Well, this, of course. All of this. That cottage you live in, quite alone, and so far from town, Emma!" He shook his head. "And this teaching business. You can't really intend to spend the rest of your life here, can you?"

Emma opened her lips to reply. But what came out of

her mouth was not a response to his question. What she said, instead, was, "Look sharp!"

And then James found himself being hurled skyward. And before he could steady himself, he found himself in possibly the most ignominious—and yet to a good many men, James included, enviable—position he'd ever been in his life: facedown between Emma Van Court Chesterton's legs.

Chapter Four

Oh, there was plenty of material—wool skirt and cotton and lace petticoats—between his face and the inside of her thighs to keep the situation from becoming . . . well, tawdry. And if embarrassment counted, well, there was enough of *that* to shield her like a coat of armor.

Still, James could not remember ever having been quite so mortified. The more so when it became clear that, far from experiencing any embarrassment herself, Emma seemed to find the situation uproariously funny.

"Oh!" She laughed in a very unwidowlike manner, her gloved hands going to his shoulders—he'd flung his arms, for want of anything better to hold onto, around her waist, and was now on his knees on the floor of the brougham, his chest between the V of her legs, his face . . . well, his face was now level with her waist, since he'd raised his head as soon as he could. "Oh, dear!"

The carriage had jerked to a halt. The only other sound, besides the rich throaty laughter spilling from

Emma, was the steady pattering of the rain on the brougham's roof. James was having a difficult time, between his embarrassment and the very distracting smell of lavender that was wafting from Emma's skirt, getting up. Despite his beaverskin cloak, James was cold. He did not realize how cold, however, until he was holding in his arms something so vibrant with warmth, he was reluctant to let go of it . . . even though that something was, in fact, his cousin's widow.

Looking up, he saw that Emma's smiling face was very close to his. Her curling lips, which were very pink and quite moist-looking, were just inches away, really. It would be a very easy thing, he thought, to reach up and capture that laughing face between his hands, then press his lips against hers. . . .

Then James heard the small door through which the brougham's driver communicated with his passengers slide back. A second later, Mr. Murphy's rough voice called down, "Sorry aboot that. Forgot ta warn ye. We're at the Wishing Tree, of course."

And that took care of that. The spell was quite broken. James tore his gaze from the intoxicating sight of Emma Chesterton's mouth.

"Emma," he said as he tried to pull himself up out of the tangle of skirts and petticoats and boots and stockings. "Are you hurt?"

She was clearly unhurt, if her peals of laughter were any indication, but he'd felt it only right to ask.

"Oh," she cried, wiping tears of mirth from the corners of her eyes. "Oh, I *am* sorry for laughing. But you looked so very surprised—"

"Well," he said, sinking onto the padded seat beside

her—he was taking no more chances riding across from her—"perhaps that's because I hadn't any sort of warning at all—"

"*Ev'rybody* knows aboot the rut in the road by the Wishing Tree," Murphy called down with some indignation.

"Well, not I," James replied. He was pleased that the rage he felt boiling in his veins was drowning out other, distinctly less comfortable feelings . . . the aching attraction, for one thing, he was beginning to realize he still felt toward his cousin's fetching widow. "*I* did not know of the rut in the road by the Wishing Tree." Then, seeing with annoyance that Emma was still struggling to control her laughter, he inquired, "Pardon my ignorance, but might I ask just what precisely *is* a Wishing Tree?"

"Ye never saw a Wishing Tree afore?" Murphy shook his hoary head. "Well, take a gander out the winder then. If'n t'were a shark, it'ud bit ye by now."

This seemed to inspire even more laughter from Emma, who now collapsed, her shoulders shaking beneath her rather well-used cloak, her face hidden in her hands. Not at all amused, James looked past her ducked head and saw, through the cracked and distorted glass in the brougham's door, an extremely curious sight. A sycamore, its gnarled branches, lightly coated in newly sprung leaves the color of absinthe, reaching toward the gray sky, stood by itself at the side of what appeared to be a split in the road. James had seen any number of similar trees since landing on this barren shore, but none sporting along their trunk what this one bore: dozens, maybe even scores, of shoes.

He squinted, but the image remained the same. People had hammered their *shoes* to a tree. James saw boots, sturdy yeomen's work boots as well as ladies' lace-up boots, wooden sabots, babies' booties, and children's sandals, even the occasional dainty lady's slipper, all secured firmly to the trunk of a tree. Most of the shoes had a bedraggled, weather-beaten appearance, as if they'd been hanging there for some time. But some of them were quite new, in particular a pair of gentleman's bedroom slippers, which looked oddly familiar to James. He recalled having given a similar pair to his cousin one Christmas.

"Well," he said, sitting back again. He dare not say what he was really thinking, which was that the Scots were a peculiar lot. "Isn't that interesting?"

Emma took her hands from her face, but she was still laughing uncontrollably. "Oh," she cried. "Oh, I *am* sorry. Only . . . only your face, when he said if it were a shark, it would have bitten you—I'm sorry."

James could certainly see the humor in the situation, but he didn't find it quite as hilarious as Emma evidently did. How could he, given the way his heart had raced when he'd found his cousin's widow in his arms? He did, however, manage a shadow of a grin, to show that he was just as willing to be made sport of as the next man.

"Yes," he said. "Well. Quite."

"It's good luck, ye know." The one-eyed drunk in the driver's box was still peering down at them. "Ta 'ammer a shoe to the Wishing Tree. Brings good luck. Specially ta newlyweds."

"Oh, yes," Emma said. She had gotten her mirth

under control. "Stuart and I nailed our shoes up when we first arrived. I think it's a lovely custom."

Lovely custom, maybe, but it certainly hadn't brought Emma Van Court any luck, James mused. After all, her husband was now dead, and she herself cut off from her family. It might not have been a bad idea, as a matter of fact, for Emma to have taken her shoes *down* from the Wishing Tree. It gave every appearance of having brought her quite the opposite of good luck.

Then the brougham gave another lurch—this one was nowhere near as violent—and they were on their way again. Shortly after clearing the deplorable road between Emma's cottage and the Wishing Tree, the brougham rolled onto smoother turf, and soon, through the cracked glass in the doors, James saw that they had reached the so-called town of Faires: so-called because in James's opinion, the existence of a pub, an inn, a mercantile, a smithy, and a church all on a single street did not exactly connote a town.

In the Shetland Isles, however, this was enough for a booming metropolis, especially since it was fronted by a pier, at which dozens of fishermen deposited their daily catch. These fishermen had wives and children who lived in shacks or cottages not far from this pier, and it was these children, apparently, who attended the school at which Emma Van Court Chesterton taught. He had not noticed the schoolhouse before, and no wonder. For as Murphy steered his horses through the narrow street and finally pulled up alongside a long, rocky outcropping that jutted out toward the sea, James saw that what served for a schoolhouse in this part of the country also doubled as the lighthouse.

That's right. Emma apparently taught school in the base of Faires's single antiquated lighthouse.

James would not have believed this had not he seen it for himself. A dozen or so raggedly garbed children dashed about on the rocks that made up the outcropping on which the lighthouse sat. In spite of the foul weather, they were intent upon a curious game of their own invention, which involved a ball apparently made of rags. The goal, from what James could tell, was to keep the ball from slipping over either side of the narrow strip of land on which the lighthouse sat and into the sea—no small feat, since the strip was hardly twenty feet wide. Surely during particularly stormy weather, the natural jetty was completely swallowed underwater. . . .

"Well," Emma said, when Murphy finally brought the carriage to a jerky halt. "Here we are."

James dragged his gaze away from the very curious athletic field. Emma, he saw, was peering past him. She appeared to be counting the children. Well, and no wonder. There was a very real possibility one or more might fall into the surf and never be seen again.

"Yes," he said. "Indeed." What followed, he knew, was going to take careful maneuvering on his part. For though Emma was obviously anxious to be rid of him, he could not leave—*would not* leave. Not without her.

And not without Stuart, he reminded himself. That was what he'd come for. Stuart, not Emma.

But now that he knew she was here as well, he could not in good conscience leave either of them on this isolated isle.

Unfortunately, he realized now that convincing Emma of this was going to be extremely difficult.

"It was very sweet of you to come all this way just to see me," Emma said. She'd been mulling over just what ought properly be said at this moment—the moment of good-bye—ever since their journey to town had begun. She flattered herself that she managed just the right note of polite distance when she extended her gloved right hand toward him and said, "Farewell, Lord Denham. Despite our past differences, I hope we can part friends, you and I."

James grasped her fingers in his before he fully realized that she was saying good-bye. Since he hadn't the slightest intention of departing, he hesitated, uncertain what to say next. He was perhaps as surprised as she was that what tumbled from his lips was an apology. "Emma," he heard himself saying, "I'm sorry. About Stuart. And about what I did to him that day you . . . well, that day you told me what the two of you were planning. I'm not saying I believe Stuart acted rightly, because I still don't. But I do want you to know that I am sincerely sorry. For everything."

Emma widened her eyes in surprise. Whatever she'd been expecting by way of response to her little speech, it had not been an apology. An *apology?* From the earl of Denham? Was such a thing even possible? She had never known James Marbury to apologize for anything before in his life.

He couldn't mean it. And yet he appeared sincere.

But then she'd been fooled by the earl of Denham's appearance before. He'd *appeared* sincere that afternoon in his library when she'd first told him about her and Stuart's plans. And yet he'd ploughed a fist straight into Stuart's face directly afterward, had he not?

No, Lord Denham's appearance was not to be trusted. Even if it was, she had to admit, a most trustworthy one. He really was a handsome man. The very least she could do was try not to be so disagreeable. . . .

"Well," Emma heard herself saying, "I forgive you, I suppose."

Then she could have bitten her tongue. Forgive him? *Forgive* the earl of Denham? Never! *Never!*

But since saying so would undoubtedly only make him hang about longer, she said instead, "Give my regards to your mother, and thank her for her kind invitation. But I'm afraid I could never leave Faires. I'm needed here, you know." She reached for the handle to the brougham door. "Good-bye."

James tightened his grip on her fingers, only to find that she'd slipped out of his grasp. She opened the brougham door and stepped out into the cold and damp. He heard the thunder of the surf as it beat against the rocks, but not loudly enough to drown out the voices of the children as they cried out eagerly upon seeing their teacher. Their voices were nearly indistinguishable from the high-pitched shrieking of the seagulls that swooped overhead.

Then she'd closed the door, cutting off the sounds of the gulls and the children, but not the rumble of the sea. James, finding himself suddenly alone, moved so that he could watch her through the cracked glass of the window. The smaller children abandoned their games and came streaming toward her, each clamoring to seize her hand, those too late to reach a hand grasping hold of her skirt. The older ones stood aloof, but much like James, they nevertheless followed the teacher with their gazes as she made her way across the jetty toward the lighthouse door, above which was suspended a brass bell. Emma seized a bit of rope that dangled down from the bell and gave it an energetic tug. The resulting ringing was the signal that released the older children from their self-induced immobility. One of them seized the cloth ball, while the rest hurried after their smaller peers, until all of them were pouring into the lighthouse through the door Emma held open for them—a door painted the same cheerful green as the one to her cottage.

It was when that door had closed firmly, shutting Emma in with all of those squirming little bodies, that James realized he'd been holding his breath. He released it in a rush, then inhaled, tasting the sharp tang of brine that hung perpetually in the air. He had no idea why he should have forgotten to breathe for so long. He supposed it was shock, really. It had only just gone nine o'clock in the morning, and already he felt as tired as if it were nine in the evening, as if he'd been all day at his desk and correspondence. Stumbling across a long-lost in-law could do that, he supposed. Particularly if that in-law happened to be Emma Van Court.

The sliding door in the roof of the brougham opened, and Murphy peered down at him curiously. "Well, milord," he said amiably, "shall I take ye back to the inn, then, ta fetch yer things afore ye ketch the noonday ferry?"

James regarded the face above him with resignation. "You may take me back to the inn, certainly," was his reply. "I shall not, however, be 'ketching' any ferry today."

The driver's eyes widened incredulously. "Wha'? But Miz Chesterton said—"

"I'm quite aware of what Mrs. Chesterton said, my good man. I am, however, better suited to making my own decisions than following the instructions of your Mrs. Chesterton." He leaned back against the uncomfortable bench.

Coffee. That was what he needed. A cup of properly brewed coffee, followed by a luncheon of thickly cut meats and mustard. Surely by the time school let out again for the day, he'd have an idea how best to proceed with this very awkward situation.

"I dunno," Murphy was muttering, up in the driver's seat. "Miz Chesterton, she won't lak it. She won't lak it one bit."

James could not help a smile upon hearing that. "Yes," he said. "I'm quite certain she won't."

Chapter Five

Emma watched carefully through the thick glass in one of the lighthouse windows. The brougham was going away. She could hardly believe it, but somehow, her little scheme had worked. The brougham was definitely going away.

Which meant that James was going away.

She could hardly credit her good fortune. She, who'd had nothing but misfortune this past year, was finally experiencing a little bit of luck. James was going away, and he would leave knowing nothing about Mr. O'Malley's will. It seemed almost too good to be true. It *was* too good to be true. . . .

No, no it wasn't! It was time, it was *high* time, for her luck to turn around. And if it wasn't going to start turning around today, well, then, it never would. He was going away, and that was all that mattered. If this luck kept up, she'd never see him again.

Which was just fine by Emma.

Except . . .

Except that that wasn't true. She didn't hate James Marbury. Lord knew she'd tried to after that day in his library. But it was simply impossible to hate anyone who'd been as kind to her, growing up, as he had. James had been the one, after all, who'd untangled her kites from tree branches they were caught in, or smuggled her dessert when she was banished to bed by her aunt without it. James, not Stuart, had been the one she'd run to with stings or scraped knees. James had always had time for her. Stuart had always had his head buried in a book.

Which, of course, had been his appeal. Still waters, it was said, run deep, and Emma had been at great pains from the age of fourteen to discover just what it would take to get Stuart Chesterton to notice her. As it happened, all it took was her expressing an interest in what interested Stuart—helping the poor. After that, she found to her delight that Stuart was always willing to lift his nose from whatever book it was tucked into whenever she happened to walk into the room.

Penelope, of course, had never understood Emma's fascination with Stuart. James, she'd insisted, had always been the better looking of the two cousins. He'd cut the more impressive figure on the dance floor, and had caused no end of sighs not only from Penelope, but from most of the women who happened to spy him.

But James Marbury's looks—not to mention his purse—weren't all that Penelope admired. He was extremely well educated, and kept himself very informed on world events. He even read popular novels, something not many men Emma knew back in London had done.

James could converse wittily on most subjects. He had always been much quicker with a joke than Stuart, who had rarely, if ever, tried to be humorous. There was too much suffering in the world, Stuart had once told Emma, for him to joke quite as casually as his cousin tended to. It was a grave thing, Stuart said, to have all the money and power in the world, and yet use it all for one's personal amusement and gain.

Emma had never, in truth noticed this character flaw before; but once Stuart had pointed it out, she grew to agree that James's priorities were in serious need of readjustment. For all his wealth—and he was one of the wealthiest men in England—James Marbury would not donate a coin to even the worthiest of causes without a certain amount of wheedling on Emma's part. He declared that he had worked hard for his money, so why should he give it away? If the poor wanted money so badly, why didn't they find employment and earn their pay, like he did? And he did not even *have* to work. There was already a substantial amount of coin in the Marbury coffers. But a man who did not work, James had informed her, was no sort of man at all.

Emma's insistence that there was not enough work for all the poor in London—for so Stuart had informed her—and that what work there was often paid so inadequately that it could not feed and clothe them never failed to engender a remark from the earl that if the poor could not afford to feed their families, they oughtn't have such large ones in the first place.

And so Emma went from thinking well of James to thinking him quite reprehensible. It became a personal mission of hers to show the earl how wrongheaded he was. If he would only have listened, instead of laughing at her, the way he had! James's stubborn immunity to her efforts to reform him became a source of continual frustration. Stuart told her she was wasting her time, and she supposed she ought to have listened. Stuart, after all, knew his cousin best. Oddly—in Emma's opinion, anyway—Stuart's own affection for James never wavered. Even after James tried to murder him—well, not murder him, maybe; but he'd still hit him terribly hard that awful day—Stuart refused to say anything the slightest bit negative about his cousin, save that he was not, by nature, very philanthropic.

Stuart, Emma reflected, not for the first time, had sometimes taken his religious training a little too literally.

Not that any of that mattered now. James was leaving, and for that, Emma could not help but rejoice, because she'd gotten rid of him without much trouble at all. And James could, when he wanted to, become quite troublesome . . . as she knew only too well. She'd been quite sure, when she'd uttered that hasty good-bye, that he wouldn't allow her to exit the brougham, that somehow he'd force her to return to London with him, since that seemed to be what he wanted.

And Lord Denham always got what he wanted.

But James had let her go, in the end. Emma supposed that Lady Denham had only issued the invitation for Emma to come and live with her because she'd thought it the polite thing to do. Surely James could not have wanted Emma to come. What man would want to share his home with the impoverished widow of his religious-minded cousin? Especially if Penelope had gotten her wish and managed to wear him down on the subject of marriage. Emma had quite forgotten to ask whether James was married yet. Not that she cared, particularly. Only that a wife—especially Penelope—might not have taken kindly to sharing her home with a poor female relation.

No, James—married or still single—had undoubtedly been vastly relieved when she had turned down his mother's invitation.

That was the only explanation, really, for why he hadn't fought her on the subject. James was the most forceful person she had ever met. If he had been determined to bring her to London, Emma would have had to have fought a good deal harder to remain where she was—standing in her schoolhouse listening to the squeak of chalk on slate. Otherwise, she might well have found herself on her way to London just now.

No, James obviously hadn't really wanted her to leave with him, which was another stroke of luck for her—though she had been quite determined to fight him, no matter how very lordly or right he seemed, or how unladylike he deemed her struggles. She would not leave her children. She was, for many of them, all they had . . . and Lord knew they were all she had now. Leave them? She'd as soon leave Una unattended in her cottage while she was away, instead of leaving her, as she had that morning, forcing Mr. Murphy to stop on their way to town, with Mrs. MacEwan.

No, Emma was staying, and James was leaving. Joy of joys, he was leaving, and she was unscathed by his visit!

Well, virtually unscathed, anyway. She couldn't help remembering, with a prickle of embarrassment, that moment when he'd fallen forward in the carriage, and landed with his arms around her. The sudden rush of emotion she'd experienced just then had been so unexpected that all she'd been able to do was laugh. James had looked annoyed by her laughter, and that had only made her laugh harder.

But what else could she do? It had been so long—months and months—since she'd last felt a man's arms around her, a man's warmth between her legs. Granted, it was *James,* but that had been the most surprising thing of all! She had *known* it was James, the man she detested above all others, and yet she'd *still* felt that rush of longing. . . .

Why this was so, she couldn't for the life of her imagine. James's arms had felt nothing like Stuart's. She had thought he might crush the breath from her for one panicky moment there, just after he'd been jarred from his seat. He had realized the same thing, she supposed, since he relaxed his grip . . . and yet he'd seemed strangely reluctant to remove his arms altogether. Had he been as surprised as she was by the sensations his embrace engendered?

And he had smelled so unlike Stuart. Stuart had always smelled of cedar—probably because of the chest in which Emma kept all of his waistcoats. James, however, did not smell like cedar at all. He smelled quite differently, of shaving soap and . . . well, home.

She could not say what had made her think of this, but there it was. James Marbury smelled of London, of clear soap and fresh oranges and rich pipe tobacco, things Emma but rarely came across in Faires, and which seemed now so very, very far away.

It was a good thing, she'd decided, as soon as that embrace had ended, that James was returning to England. A very good thing. No man—especially a man such as James Marbury, who would betray someone the way he'd betrayed her—had a right to smell that good. That sort of thing, those sort of smells, well, could *do* things to a girl. Even a widow.

"Miz Chesterton?" A small voice, accompanied by a decisive tug on her skirt, jerked Emma back to reality. She looked down and saw little Flora Mackay standing there, clutching her piece of slate.

"What are you doing out of your seat, Flora?" Emma asked. "I thought you were working on your arithmetic."

"I was, Miz Chesterton," Flora said, her voice dropping to a whisper. "But I thought you should know, the answer you wrote down for nine hundred and sixty-seven divided by twenty-four is wrong."

Emma winced and lifted her gaze guiltily to the large piece of slate she'd had Samuel Murphy, the community's jack-of-all-trades, hang up along one gently curving, whitewashed wall. The sums she'd been correcting glared at her. In her distraction today over the earl of Denham, she had been a bit careless, she now saw, with her long division.

"Oh, dear," Emma said. "Could you fix it for me, please, Flora?"

The little girl nodded, took the chalk from Emma's hand, and went to the board to correct the problem. Emma, watching her, felt a familiar flash of guilt. She was not, she knew, a very good teacher. In fact, she was probably a downright bad one.

But what, Emma asked herself, not for the first time, was the alternative? It was Emma's school for the children of Faires, or no school. No one else had volunteered to run it after the schoolmaster had fallen prey, along with so many others, to typhus last fall.

Still, Emma had to admit the children—especially the brighter ones—deserved better. A *real* teacher, not just the town curate's poor widow, ought to be conducting their lessons, teaching them French and science and history and geography. And they ought to have desks, not just long wooden benches, upon which they jostled one another for elbow space as they bent over their pieces of slate, working their sums. And a *real* schoolhouse, not the wretchedly cold, invariably leaky bottom floor of the lighthouse, with a wood stove that would never stay lit. She could see now that it had gone out again.

Damn that wood stove, anyway. It rarely worked, and on the few occasions when it did, it didn't keep the room anywhere near warm enough, and it smoked besides. If only she'd kept her head about her, and remembered to ask the earl if he'd be at all inclined to donate funds for a new stove. . . .

But she doubted that, given all that had passed between them, James would still be as willing as he'd once been to support her favorite charities. And for that, she supposed she couldn't blame him.

And it had to be admitted that he *had* done something rather kind. He had, after all, come all the way from London, just to invite her to come live with his mother. He may have had ulterior motives—Emma was convinced he'd only done it to assuage his guilt over that last awful argument with Stuart—but it had been a sweet thing to do, just the same.

Still, even if Emma hadn't had the schoolhouse, how could she have accepted Lady Denham's offer? She couldn't. Not with O'Malley's will. Imagine, if she'd moved to London, and that got out! She'd be the laughingstock of Mayfair.

"John," Emma said, after giving a final glance out the window to convince herself that James was well and truly gone, "give me a hand with the wood stove, will you? I think it's gone out again."

Obediently, the boy sprang up, still ungainly after a sudden summer growth spurt had sent him shooting up five inches. "Yes, Mrs. Chesterton," he said, and he put aside his slate and hurried to the front of the room to tackle the temperamental stove.

It was a shame, Emma thought, watching him, that there wasn't any money to send him away to school. John had a brilliant mind, and in six months there'd truly be nothing left for her to teach him.

She ought, she thought regretfully, to have asked the earl if he wouldn't consider sponsoring some sort of scholarship in Stuart's name, to pay for the more deserving boys to go to college. Not that the earl would easily have agreed to such a thing. "Let them work their way through school," she could almost hear him say. "If they're hungry enough for an education, they'll find their own way to pay for it."

Still, there was always a chance he'd changed. He'd come all the way from London merely to inquire personally how she fared, and she knew very well how much he despised Scotland. Perhaps he'd have been more open to suggestion than he'd once been. Stuart's death might have softened him, just as it had, to a certain extent, hardened Emma. Certainly it had taught her a few painful truths about herself.

Perhaps she could write to him. Yes, that was it! A nice, safe letter . . .

But then, she'd thought the letter she'd sent his mother a safe one, and look what *it* had wrought!

"Oh, dear," Emma said to herself, and then one of the children raised a hand to ask her why she'd written that five went into thirty seven times, when the answer was clearly six, and she quite forgot the earl of Denham altogether.

Chapter Six

The earl of Denham, however, had not forgotten Emma. Not at all.

How could he? He had a nicely aching hand to remind him of their meeting earlier that morning. Now that he'd had his valet bind his knuckles, James felt at least a little better.

And soon he found himself seated at the local pub's finest table—or at least that's what the barmaid, a buxom young woman named Mary, assured him, as she hurriedly wiped down the seat of his chair with a cloth before urging him to sit. James wasn't in a mood to dispute her. Though the table was in full view of the swinging door to the kitchen, he was at least seated with his feet to the fire.

James was offered no menu. Instead, Mary informed him that the ploughman's lunch was superb and asked him if he wanted beer or cider to wash it down. James decided he was willing to take the risk, and asked for whiskey. Mary beamed—an expression that did not become her because it revealed her startling lack of incisors—and rattled off a long list of peat whiskeys that could be had at a nominal fee. James picked one at random, mostly to make Mary and her toothless gums go away, and a few moments later was sitting with his hand curved around a small glass, the contents of which, whenever he brought it toward his lips, caused his eyes to water mercilessly.

James sat at his table, the only customer in the Sea Cow at noon on a working day, and stared into the fire. He was in a quandary, there was no doubt about that. He hadn't the slightest idea how next to proceed. He could not, it seemed, extract his cousin's widow from this place, any more than it seemed he could ascertain of the location of his cousin's final resting place.

Which reminded him of his other problem. Stuart! What was he going to do about Stuart? Where could Emma have buried him, if not his parish's graveyard? And why was it, when he asked people if they knew where the late curate was buried, they looked so strangely at him? He ought, he supposed, to have come straight out and asked Emma about it, but dammit, it wasn't something a man liked to bring up to a grieving widow. Particularly since he wasn't asking because he wanted to lay flowers on the grave. No, he wanted to dig it up. He didn't doubt Emma was going to have a few words to say about *that*.

James had not been cheered by the minister's words upon his asking if he had any idea where Stuart's final resting place might lie. " 'Twas a hard thing," the Reverend Peck had assured James, "to deny Mrs. Chesterton, the wife of my own curate, grave rights for her husband, but what could I do? There wasn't any room." The minister had then confided to James, "My fear is that, wherever Mr. Chesterton is buried, it isn't on consecrated ground. Mrs. Chesterton has some odd ideas about things, I've found. One of them is that *all* soil is God's soil. But we can't allow that, now, can we? Otherwise, people would be burying their loved ones right in their own front yards. . . ."

The only real option left, of course, was to inquire of the deceased's spouse, but he'd managed to bungle that, hadn't he? From start to finish, he'd looked a fool, first because of that bumbling yeoman, and then because of Emma herself. Who would have thought she'd turn out so . . . well, differently? Really, a year earlier, when he'd last seen her, he'd never have predicted she'd grow into such a . . . well, he didn't know what, precisely, Emma had turned into. What had happened to the sweet, idealistic girl who'd badgered him so mercilessly for donations to her various charities, and with whom he'd danced at so many balls and cotillions, that winter of 'thirty-two? The girl who'd enchanted everyone with her doll-like grace and her laughing indigo eyes? Though, truth be told, he'd seen far more of fire than laughter in those eyes. She'd been forever chastising him about his selfish and errant ways, a habit he'd have found obnoxious in anyone else.

But he'd rather enjoyed being catechized by Emma. It had always been far more entertaining than the fawning praise that came from most of the other women in his acquaintance.

Maybe, James thought as he stared grimly into the

fire, nothing had happened to Emma at all. Maybe she had simply . . . grown up. Maybe *that* was what she'd become.

A woman.

That thought was the one that finally caused him to lift his glass and bring it, unswervingly, to his lips. He downed the contents in a single swallow, lowered the glass—

And heaved a powerful, shoulder-shaking shudder.

Good God. What were they trying to do? Kill him?

Eyes watering, throat burning, James looked around frantically, convinced he was dying. Someone had poisoned him, someone who knew why he'd come to Faires, and despised him for it. But when he swung his head around toward the bar, he saw, through his tears, a tall man standing behind the counter, wiping down a tankard and chuckling. Chuckling at him.

"May I ask," James croaked, "what is so amusing to you, sir?"

"You," the barkeep laughed. "Here." The large man filled the tankard he'd been cleaning with something from a tap, then stepped round the bar and placed a foam-topped beverage in front of James. "Drink that. It'll help, a little."

James, only because his gut was burning, did as the barkeep bid. The yeasty brew immediately quelled the flames in his belly. When James could speak again, he asked, in an unsteady voice, "What *was* that?"

"What you ordered." The barkeep lifted the innocent-looking glass that had held the toxic liquid and held it up to the gray light that crept through the mullioned window. "One of our local distillers. Got a bite to it, eh?"

"A bite?" James shook his head. He had to admit, however, that the ache in his hand had ebbed a bit.

"Right. Another?"

"I think not," James said, and turned his attention back to the fire. What had he been thinking, anyway? Oh, yes. Emma. What to do about Emma.

It should not, he knew, have been so complicated. And with any other woman, it would not have been. James knew he could be quite charming when he wanted to. True, his romantic affairs tended to be just that—affairs. Similar to business affairs, he'd found, but much more straightforward and far less complicated. A sensible arrangement, overall. Much more sensible than this feverish thing people called love.

It had occurred to him, of course, that it would be far less expensive in the long run to marry. And if he chose a bride prudently, he could actually profit from the deal. There were quite a few unmarried ladies in England who might be induced to join allegiances with the Denham estate and bring to it a sizable dowry. Certainly James's mother had been at great pains these past few years to introduce him to these young ladies— Penelope Van Court primary among them.

The drawback to such a plan was that when one tired of one's wife, one could not give her a diamond bracelet and bid her a polite adieu. And James had not met a single woman—save one—of whom he could not imagine tiring at some point. Penelope Van Court might be radiantly beautiful and have ten thousand pounds a year, but she was also, in his opinion, completely insipid. And the eldest daughter of the earl of Derby might possess fifty thousand pounds and an estate in

Shropshire, but her incessant talk of hounds had caused James hastily to drop her. To be saddled for the rest of his life with *that*? No amount of money was worth it.

" 'Ere you are now. Ploughman's lunch, fit for a king."

James looked down at the plate Mary had slid before him. A large wedge of cheese, a lump of bread, some pickles, something unidentifiable, and an onion. That, evidently, was what ploughmen subsisted upon.

Noticing James's expression, Mary said defensively, "That's haggis, that is," pointing at the unidentifiable, steaming heap of brown at one side of James's plate.

He looked up at her and managed a smile. "Thank you so much."

It had been a mistake to smile. It caused Mary to smile back, and he had another glimpse of her gums. "Think nofink of it, I'm sure," Mary said, and she hurried away to wait upon another customer, a middle-aged man who'd only just entered the pub.

MacTavish, over by the bar, grinned as he watched James pick at his food. "Here on business, are ye, then?" he asked, pleasantly.

James lifted a limp cabbage leaf with his fork and said, shortly, "Of a sort."

"Right. I didn't take you fer one of Lord Mac-Creigh's friends, fer all your fancy duds. They don't usually come into town. Stay at the castle, mostly. Too good fer the likes of us, I s'pose."

James, who'd been chewing a bit of the cheese—it wasn't bad, actually—looked up. Well, he thought. At least he might find out something that had been bothering him all morning.

"And who," he said, after washing the cheese down with a swallow of beer, "is Lord MacCreigh?"

"You never heard of Castle MacCreigh?" When James shook his head, the barkeep said amiably, "Well, it's up the road a bit. You can see it from the King's Crag. Built in the sixteen hundreds, it was, and looks it. Belongs to the eighth baron of MacCreigh, Geoffrey Bain. Not a farthing to his name, but he's got his castle. Does quite a bit of entertaining, him an' his sister, Miss Bain. Me mam cooks for 'em every once in a while. Don't like her goin' up there by herself, though, so she don't do it on any regular basis."

"Why don't you like your mother going to Castle MacCreigh?" James asked curiously.

"Aw, it's nothin', really." The barkeep looked sheepish. "Wild stories, mostly, I suppose. You know. About banshees and all that, roamin' the 'alls. After Lord MacCreigh's betrothed disappeared—"

"Disappeared?" echoed James. The conversation was suddenly getting more interesting.

"Well, run off, MacCreigh says. Last year. With his valet. Could be true. Might not be. Don't suppose no one but MacCreigh knows for true. So o' course, people talk. That she didn't run off at all, that MacCreigh found her in a clench with another man and killed 'em both. MacCreigh himself doesn't do much to dispell the rumors, if you know what I mean. Takin' to ridin' a coal-black charger, wearin' a black cape—when he comes to town, which isn't often. Leastways it wasn't, not till he found out about O'Malley's will."

James placed a bit of cheese onto a portion of bread

and ate it. Surprisingly good. "O'Malley's will?" he echoed, after he'd chewed and swallowed.

"Oh, you haven't heard about that one yet?" Mac-Tavish reached for another tankard and began to dry it absently. "Fellow by the name of O'Malley killed a man, oh, about six months ago. Didn't mean to, of course. O'Malley was a big man, a whaler, you know. Had a temper, and didn't much know his own strength. Well, the feller he pummeled popped off. They hanged him fer it. O'Malley, I mean. Though O'Malley, he was right sorry about it. Sorry enough about it to ask the assize judge, the one what sentenced him to death, to help him make out a will, leavin' everythin' he had to the dead man's widow."

MacTavish set the beer tankard down and reached for another. " 'Course, what nobody knew was that O'Malley, he had quite a bit. Added all up, it came to a total of ten thousand pounds." MacTavish laughed. "You could say that since Lord MacCreigh found out about *that*, he's been in town quite a bit more." He winked. "Because the curate's widow—he was a curate, did I mention that? The one what died. Well, she's a looker, and rich now, besides. If you know what I mean."

Chapter Seven

*J*ames did not, in actual fact, know what the barkeep meant. All he knew was that suddenly the bread and cheese he'd been swallowing lodged in his throat and stuck there, like nettles. Reaching hastily for his tankard, he downed what remained of his beer. That dislodged the bread and cheese, but did nothing for the feeling of horror that had crept over him.

Lowering the empty tankard, he asked in strangled tones, "Are you trying to tell me that Stuart Chesterton—the curate—was *murdered?*"

MacTavish looked at him curiously. "Aye," he said.

"But that's . . . that's impossible," James said. "He died during the typhus epidemic, six months ago."

"Aye," MacTavish said. "That he did. But it wasn't typhus what killed him. It was a man called O'Malley."

James blinked at the barman. His mind flew back to the wording of Emma's note. True, she hadn't specifically described the cause of Stuart's death—only that he'd died, and that due to the quarantine, she'd been unable to get word of his death to them sooner. James and his mother had only assumed that Stuart had died from typhus.

But murder? *Stuart?* Why on earth would anyone want to kill Stuart? Besides James himself, of course, who'd felt very much like murdering his cousin . . . but only just the once.

"This O'Malley," James said. "Why did he do it? Kill Mr. Chesterton, I mean?"

The barman shrugged. "No one rightly knows. Out of his head he was. O'Malley, I mean. All I know is, curate went to give last rites to O'Malley's wife, and next thing I knew, three people was dead: the curate, O'Malley's wife, and O'Malley himself, when he was strung fer it. . . . "

So perplexed was he by what he'd heard that James did not notice that MacTavish had refilled his tankard. He took a healthy swallow, then asked, "And you say the curate's wife—Mrs. Chesterton—inherited *ten thousand pounds* from her husband's killer?"

"Well, she *will* get it," MacTavish said, companionably, "soon as she marries agin."

James stared at him. "When she *marries* again? What are you talking about? Does Emma Chesterton have ten thousand pounds, or doesn't she?"

"She doesn't," came a mildly irritated voice from behind them. James looked around and saw that the middle-aged man who'd been seated some moments before had thrown down his napkin and was regarding them from his seat at a table by the window with some disgust. "And I thank you, Sean, for bringing up this subject just as I was trying to enjoy my lunch. You know how it puts me right off your mother's haggis."

The barkeep suppressed a smile. "Sorry, Your Honor."

James stared at the stranger. "Lord MacCreigh?" he asked dubiously, though from the impression he'd received from the barkeep, MacCreigh was not the portly, haggis-loving type.

"Not MacCreigh," the gentleman—for gentleman he clearly was, the first James had come across since landing in the Shetlands—growled. "Lord chief justice. Reardon's the name. I'm the judge who ruled six months ago, during my last trip to the island, that O'Malley hang." He took a healthy draught from his own tankard, lowered it, belched, and said, "Ah," with some satisfaction.

James looked from the assize judge to the barkeep and back again. After a second more of deliberation, he pushed back his chair and hurried to the judge's table. Reardon looked up at him suspiciously.

"I beg your pardon, Your Honor," James said. "But might I join you? I have some involvement with this case, I believe—"

"Case?" Reardon glared up at him. He was a red-faced man, not yet grossly overweight, but getting there. Still, there were laugh lines etched at the corners of his eyes and mouth that whispered of a good humor James had yet to glimpse. "What case? There is no case. The case is closed. O'Malley killed Chesterton; Chesterton's widow gets O'Malley's fortune soon as she remarries. And if it's marryin' her you're thinkin' of, get in line. There's about twenty fellows ahead of you, young man."

Without waiting for the older gentleman to invite him to sit—James had a pretty good idea no such invitation was forthcoming—the earl slid into the chair opposite the judge's and leaned forward.

"Excuse me, sir. My name is Denham. James Marbury, ninth earl of Denham, to be exact. Stuart Chesterton was my first cousin."

Reardon raised his eyebrows until they almost disappeared beneath the old-fashioned powdered wig he wore. "Earl of Denham?" he echoed. "I see. I knew Chesterton was related to someone hoity-toity, but I always heard tell it was a duke."

James remained silent, refusing to take umbrage at being referred to as hoity-toity. Finally, *finally* he had met someone who might be able to shed some badly needed light on his cousin's death and subsequent burial—not to mention Emma's curious refusal to return to England. Accordingly, he said nothing, merely looked at the judge with a solemn expression that gave no indication of the mad impatience he felt inwardly.

"Well," Reardon said, slowly. "I suppose you *do* have an interest in the case, then." Pushing back his chair to make more room for his belly, which swelled out from beneath a gold-and-green-striped waistcoat, the lord chief justice called, "Sean, another beer, there's a good lad. Let me see now. First cousin to the curate, eh? You've got his look about you, now that you mention it. I can see it a little in the eyes. You're a good deal strappier, though. O'Malley wouldn't've killed *you*."

"Not very likely," James agreed. "So might I ask, sir . . . why the condition?"

Reardon had lifted his fork and was poking at his haggis again. "What condition?"

"The, er, rather curious condition you just mentioned, that Emma—er, Mrs. Chesterton—has to remarry before she can receive O'Malley's ten thousand pounds."

"Oh." The judge washed the haggis down with a mouthful of ale. "That. Well, use your head, man. You obviously know her. She married your cousin, after all."

"Yes," James said, somberly. "I know her."

"Well. Would *you* trust that woman with ten thousand pounds?" James opened his mouth to reply, but the judge continued, "No. Of course you wouldn't. She'd take that ten thousand pounds and donate it to the mission society, or use it all to buy supplies for that damned excuse for a school she's running. Who knows *what* she'd do with it? But nothing sensible, I can tell you that."

James took a sip of his beer. He had a feeling he was going to need it. "Yes," he said. "Well. So you made the condition that she couldn't have a penny of O'Malley's fortune unless she was married as a sort of guarantee that the money would be spent, er, wisely?"

"Precisely." Reardon slammed a hand onto the table, causing James to jump. "Exactly. For her own good, you understand. Nothing worse than a tenderhearted lady with a lot of coin. Or, from the point of view of a shyster, nothing better. I wager that if I'd let her have that ten thousand last December, she wouldn't have a shilling left today. But this way, the money is quite safe, and turning over a healthy bit of interest in an account I set up, just for her. When Mrs. Chesterton chooses to marry, I will turn the account over to her husband, who can administer the funds to her as he sees fit. Though I can't say as I expect that will happen anytime soon. The widow Chesterton appears to be in no sort of hurry to marry again, much less claim what's owed her."

MacTavish, chuckling as he moved forward with two fresh tankards, remarked, "I asked 'er last month. Caught 'er outside of church. She thanked me for askin', but said she had no intention to marry just yet, still bein' in mournin' for 'er husband."

Reardon raised his cup toward the young barkeep, whom, James noted for the first time, was a tall, athletic-looking chap, not at all the type of man to inspire animosity . . . though his revelation had engendered in James a sudden and very intense antipathy.

"My sympathies, young man," the judge said to the barkeep. "If anyone were good enough for our Mrs. Chesterton, it'd be you, Sean."

MacTavish shook his head. "Guess she'd seen me out walkin' with Myra McAllister one too many times. She called me a fool to marry for money rather than love, and tol' me to stick with Myra." He scowled at the judge's hearty laughter. "Weren't *that* funny," he grumbled. "Myra won't 'ave me either, till I get me own place. Says she won't live with me and me mam."

Reardon shook his head, making sympathetic noises. "See?" he said, turning back to James. "That's how things work here in Faires. Only come here twice a year, you know, for the assizes, but I know these people. Know 'em like the back of my own hand."

"This is preposterous," James declared, extremely put out, though not sure whether it was because of Reardon's bombastics or the barkeep's admitting that he'd proposed to Emma that irked him most. "We are talking about a widow, sir, a penniless widow whom you are—"

"Looking out for," Reardon said quietly.

"I beg to differ, sir." James shook his head. "I am quite certain that there isn't a single precedent for such a provision anywhere in England, and that if Mrs. Chesterton wanted to, she could appeal this ridiculous decision of yours to any court in the land and win, hands down."

Reardon eyed him, all hint of laughter gone now. "She could, but she won't. You forget, my lord, I am looking out for Mrs. Chesterton. She hasn't a father to do it, nor a brother, nor a husband, not anymore. She is all alone in this world, and so I have made it my business to see to it that she isn't taken advantage of. She is a good woman whose only failing is a tendency to open her heart—and her purse—a little too readily." Reardon set down his cup and gave James a steely-eyed look over the tabletop. "I don't know who you are to her, my lord, but I will say that this is the first I've seen of you. If you're so fond of the girl and so set on keeping her from being cheated, where have you been these past months, since her husband passed? That's what I'd like to know."

James stared at the older man incredulously. "Now see here," James began, leaning forward. "I don't know what you're implying, but I will have you know that I only received word of my cousin's death a week ago. I came here just as soon as I could. I have already offered Mrs. Chesterton a permanent place in my mother's household, which, I might add, she turned down—"

"Well, of course," the judge interrupted mildly. "She won't leave those children she teaches. Or professes to teach, anyway. There seems to be some contention as to whether or not that is what she's doing. They seem as ignorant as ever to me, just better versed in the works of Walter Scott. But I don't suppose it is so unusual, this attachment Mrs. Chesterton has to them, considering she and her husband were not blessed with children of their own."

James, upon hearing this last bit, looked up sharply. Children of their own! Oddly, it had never before occurred to him that his cousin and Emma might have wished for, much less attempted to produce, offspring.

But of course children are a natural consequence of marriage. Why he should find the idea so very unsettling, he could not imagine. Only he had—stupidly, he now realized—never considered that Stuart, whose nature leaned so strongly toward the spiritual, might actually . . . And with Emma, of all the women in the world!

Good Lord. The thought completely unmanned him. He could feel the blood draining from his face. He was, he knew, being ridiculous. After all, the two of them had been man and wife. What had he supposed they'd married for, if not—

He didn't want to think about it. He didn't want to think about it *at all*.

Judge Reardon regarded James, his good humor

seemingly suddenly restored. Apparently he found something amusing about James's discomfort with the topic of his cousin's marriage bed. This, of course, only served to embitter James even more against him.

"Who did you say you were, sir?" Reardon demanded cheerfully. "Her husband's cousin?"

"Yes," James said. "There was a bit of a falling out, you see, between Stuart and me shortly before he and Emma married. We didn't speak as a result of it. I came as soon as I heard of his death—"

"To pay your respects to his widow?" Reardon asked, with deceptive nonchalance.

"Um, yes," James replied. There was no need, James felt, to admit the real reason he'd come all the way to Faires. Somehow, he did not think Justice Reardon cared much about family mausoleums. "Yes, of course. And to invite her to come live with me. I mean, with my mother."

Reardon smiled. It was a strange smile. James wasn't sure he liked the look of it. "I see," was all he said, though. "And she turned you down."

"Yes."

"So now you're returning to the mainland?" He glanced at the clock behind the bar. "You've missed the only ferry today, you know."

"No, I'm not returning. I thought I'd . . ."

And all at once, James knew. James, who only moments before had been sitting in abject misery, not having the slightest idea how next to proceed, knew precisely what he was going to do.

"I'm going to stay," he said, firmly. "Stay and ask her again, when she's had a little more time to think about it."

"How gallant of you," Reardon observed. "And you didn't even know about the ten thousand pounds."

"No, of course not," James said, casting the judge a sharp look. "I have no need of ten thousand pounds that once belonged to my cousin's murderer." Seeing that the lord chief justice looked skeptical, James went on indignantly, "I felt it my duty to come, you see, to offer Mrs. Chesterton my protection—"

"Which she turned down."

James pressed his lips together. He wished Reardon would refrain from pointing that out. "Well. Yes. For now."

"Interesting." The judge's gaze was bright with interest now as he studied James. "Very interesting. You and your cousin had a falling-out, you said? What was it about? Not Mrs. Chesterton, I hope?"

James felt it was high time to put an end to the conversation. "Well, sir," he said, pushing back his chair, "I see that I've troubled you long enough. I'll return to my own table now."

Reardon folded his hands over his considerable belly and looked up at James with an enigmatic expression on his round face. "Denham," he said, thoughtfully. "I suppose you're in the baronetage."

So the old cuss was going to try to look him up! Well, let him. He'd find nothing in the baronetage except the information that the Marburys were one of the oldest and most respectable families in England.

James tugged on the points of his waistcoat. "Most certainly, sir."

"Thank you." Reardon inclined his head, like a cat who'd had her fill of cream. "It's been a pleasure."

James returned to his seat and, without thinking about it, lifted a fork and began devouring the haggis on his plate. Of all the ridiculous, backward things he'd ever heard, Emma's situation with this man O'Malley's will was the most outlandish. It was barbaric, that's what it was. Who was this man to withhold a woman's fortune from her because she happened to have a generous nature? Why, it was ludicrous. It was insulting. It was . . . it was . . .

It was ingenious, really. Because of course Reardon was perfectly correct. Emma could not manage money. What could she possibly know about finances? She had never had any money of her own. She'd been raised around wealth, certainly, but at the age of eighteen she'd married someone who hadn't a penny to his name. She'd been church-mouse poor ever since.

James had to hand it to the judge. He'd come up with a perfect solution to the problem. Perfect in every way except one.

Emma was not rising to the bait. Evidently, she had no more intention of marrying than James did.

The only difference, of course, was that not so very long ago there *had* been someone of whom James had entertained thoughts of marrying.

And his cousin had beaten him to it.

Chapter Eight

*E*mma lifted the first piece of slate from the pile beside her and read, "When I'm growed up, I want to be a fishman, like my da, and sale the ocean seas. I will sea new worlds, and ketch many fish. Then I will come home and marry you, Miz Chestertown."

Emma laid down the slate, after making a few spelling corrections and scribbling, "Thank you, Robbie" in the margin. Good Lord, things were at a sorry pass when nine-year-olds were proposing to her. Though Emma had to admit that of all the proposals she'd received thus far, Robbie's was certainly the most sincere.

When Emma lifted the next slate, Bridget Donahue's boldly printed words, "When I grow up, I want to have curly hair like you, Missus Chesterton," caused her to reach a hand up to her hair. As usual, the thick curls had slipped from the pins with which she'd tried to restrain them, and were cascading in snaky tendrils all around her face. *Why* had she been cursed so? She'd have given anything in the world to have controllable hair, like Bridget's, which was stick-straight and well-behaved.

Emma was writing as much in the margins of the little girl's piece of slate when she heard the lighthouse door blow open. Giving the pocket watch at her waist a perfunctory glance, she said without looking up, "You're late again, Fergus. If you've got to run home after school every day to feed your cat, you could at least not dawdle about it. I've got to get home to feed my own animals, you know, after our tutoring session."

"My sincerest apologies, Mrs. Chesterton," said a much deeper voice than what she was expecting. "I shall cease my dawdling at once."

Startled, Emma looked up and nearly upset the pile of slates beside her. "Oh!" she cried. "Lord MacCreigh. It's you."

Lord MacCreigh grinned at her as he strolled casually down the aisle between the two rows of benches upon which the children sat, when school was in session. Emma stood up hastily. When she saw that the pile of slates beside her was wobbling, she reached out a hand to steady it.

"I didn't mean to startle you, Emma," the baron said as he approached. His long black cloak was so full that it brushed against the ends of the benches as he walked. "I only stopped by to see whether or not you'd heard the news."

Emma had backed up as far as the bench would allow, and now stood so close to the stove that she could feel its heat straight through her wool skirt and plentiful petticoats, hot enough upon her thighs to singe them.

"News, my lord?" she echoed weakly. She hoped to high heaven he was not referring to the earl of Denham's early-morning visit. Added complexities to her already troublesome relationship with Lord Mac-Creigh, who seemed set on marrying her, if she'd just say the word, Emma did not need.

"Aye." Lord MacCreigh was dressed in his riding clothes, all of which were coal black, to match his horse, which, Emma assumed, was tied up outside. Lord Mac-Creigh had taken rather too much to heart his fiancée Clara McLellen's abandonment of him, and had accordingly adopted a dramatic—almost theatrical—style of dress to suit his role as jilted lover. He lifted a heavily booted foot and placed it beside the pile of slates, then leaned an elbow upon his knee. Emma had to grab at the pile with both hands to keep it from tumbling down.

"Chief Justice Reardon's back for the winter assizes," he said conversationally. "Saw him in the smithy's shop on my way into town, holding court. You know what that means, don't you, Emma?"

Emma began disassembling the pile of slates, since she was quite certain Lord MacCreigh was going to knock them over, one way or another.

"No," she said, careful not to look him in the face. The baron's attempt to pass himself off as a man who'd been through a great tragedy, dressing all in black and sulking moodily about, was somewhat hampered by the fact that from his head rose a great crown of extremely bright copper-colored hair, nearly as curly as Emma's own. This misfortune was further compounded by a visage that, rather than being rutted with deep lines arcing from his flaring nostrils to a wide, full-lipped mouth, as a romantic hero's face ought to be, was actually quite childishly plump, and was furthermore thickly frosted with freckles.

And though at least the baron's eyes were bright blue, they were, to his great regret, not at all unsettling or menacing, but rather the color of the sky on a summer's day.

"Um," Emma said. She had split the slates into three piles now, the ones she'd finished grading in one, and the others left to be read in two smaller stacks. "No, I'm afraid I don't know what that means, my lord."

Lord MacCreigh made an impatient gesture with his gloved hand. "Come, Emma! Obviously, now would be an excellent time to post the banns."

Emma looked past him, toward the door, which was, unfortunately, firmly closed. All of the children had gone home, and none of them were coming back except for Fergus, whom Emma tutored specially three days a week, his failing eyesight making reading especially difficult for him.

"Banns?" Emma asked, with purposeful stupidity. Maybe, she thought, if I drag out the conversation long enough, Fergus will come. Fergus will distract Lord MacCreigh. He wouldn't dare to try anything with a little boy in the room. . . .

"Emma," Lord MacCreigh said with a chuckle. Fortunately, his elbow still rested upon his knee, his gloved hands relaxed and not looking at all as if they were about to reach out and grab her, for all he stood just about a foot away. "You know precisely what I mean. I think we ought let the chief justice know of our plan to wed, so he can start drawing up the paperwork for your inheritance."

Emma shook her head. "That's *your* plan, Lord MacCreigh," she said. "Not mine. You know I have no intention of marrying again."

"Don't be ridiculous, Emma," MacCreigh said. "Of course you'll marry again. What else are you going to do? Teach in this sorry excuse of a school until you rot?"

"If I choose to," came Emma's calm reply.

Petulant as a child, Lord MacCreigh did not want to hear this. Emma felt more sympathy for him than she did any of her other suitors, with the possible exception of Cletus. The mysterious disappearance of Lord Mac-Creigh's young fiancée had caused no small bit of gossip about the baron. Had she really run off, as Lord MacCreigh insisted, with his valet? Or had he, stumbling across the pair of lovers, dispatched the two of them with his sword, and thrown their bodies—as the rumor went—down the castle's cistern?

Though Emma did not particularly like the baron, she, out of everyone on the island, knew he was not a murderer. Had he behaved, in fact, with a little more circumspection, she might almost have felt sorry for him, living as he did in that decrepit castle, rumored to be haunted by banshees and ghosts, with only that dreadful sister of his for company.

But that did not mean she was willing to *marry* the man. Even if she were not convinced that the only reason the baron wished to marry was so that he might use Mr. O'Malley's ten thousand pounds to refurbish his ancestral home, which was slowly but steadily crumbling, she could not see herself wed to a man who smelled so strongly, she was sorry to say, of horse.

The baron made an impulsive gesture, removing his foot from the bench and reaching up to run a hand impatiently through his wildly curling red locks.

"Why all this infernal quibbling?" he demanded. "The fact is, you and I are eminently suited for one another, Emma, and I don't want to have to wait until the winter assizes for the money, when we might as easily get him to sign it over to you tomorrow." He reached for her, circling her upper arm with fingers that, though they didn't hurt, exactly, weren't at all gentle. "So let's go. Now."

Recognizing in the baron's voice a new note of conviction, Emma realized he actually did mean business this time. Still, she tried to make a joke of it—though, truth be told, she found nothing amusing in the situation. Justice Reardon might have thought he'd been doing her a service in making his bizarre ruling concerning Mr. O'Malley's will, but the money had become nothing but a curse to Emma.

"Really, my lord," she said, laughingly, even as she pulled away. "Your eagerness quite takes my breath away."

Lord MacCreigh's grip did not loosen, despite her attempts to free her arm. Looking up into his face, seeing that his square jaw was set firmly, Emma began to feel just a little afraid. Which was ridiculous, of course, because when they reached the judge's chambers, all she had to say was no.

It was what might happen to her *after* she said no

that had Emma worried. She knew perfectly well that
Geoffrey Bain had not murdered his fiancée—

But that did not mean he was incapable of such a
thing.

"Really, Lord MacCreigh," Emma said, her voice becoming a trifle shrill. She tried to lower it. "Really, I
can't go right now. I'm . . . I'm waiting for Fergus
MacPherson."

"That half-blind brat again?" Lord MacCreigh
rolled his eyes. "Emma, I believe you take your teaching
duties too much to heart."

"He should be here any minute," Emma said, glancing anxiously toward the door. "I wouldn't want to
upset Fergus, Lord MacCreigh. He's had such a hard
life—"

Lord MacCreigh only growled, and yanked her toward
the hook on the curving wall where she'd hung her cloak
and bonnet.

"Come on," he said. "The boy can have his lesson
another day. Reardon will only be here until tomorrow
or the day after. We haven't time to dally."

Emma, glancing through the windows cut into the
thick walls of the lighthouse, strained her eyes to see if
she could spot Fergus approaching. Though what a
nearly blind eleven-year-old boy might be able to do
about the six-foot-tall baron menacing his teacher, she
hadn't the slightest idea.

As it happened, Emma's prayers were being answered, though not in the manner that she'd hoped.
Outside the lighthouse, Fergus MacPherson, whose eyesight had never been good, and was getting steadily
worse, *had* noticed Lord MacCreigh's stallion. He also

noticed a very tall man in a top hat coming up the lane from town on foot, swinging a silver-topped cane. The man, Fergus couldn't help noticing, even with his troubled eyesight, had also noticed the horse, and seemed right put out by it. He stopped swinging the cane and stared, and then, when he noticed Fergus standing there in the wind and spray from the sea, demanded, "I say, there. D'you know whose horse this is?"

Fergus cocked his head to squint at the man. The odd manner in which he cocked his head to see had a tendency to make most people feel ill at ease, but the tall gentleman did not appear to notice. He was looking quite intently at the glow in the lighthouse windows, which indicated quite clearly to Fergus that Mrs. Chesterton was still there . . . just as the horse indicated that she was not alone.

"Well," Fergus said slowly. "I reckon that there is Lord MacCreigh's horse."

"Lord MacCreigh?" The gentleman did not look at all pleased. "Of Castle MacCreigh?"

Fergus furrowed his brow. "Aye, sir. That's the only Lord MacCreigh what lives in Faires. 'E's—"

But the stranger had suddenly begun stalking forward, striding very rapidly toward the lighthouse door. Fergus, seeing him pass by as a mere blur in front of his eyes, called out, "Mister? Wait! Mister?"

But the stranger apparently couldn't hear him over the thunder of the surf. Fergus raced after him. After all, Mrs. Chesterton was always saying that it was their duty to look after those of unsound mind and frame. This stranger was clearly of unsound mind if he thought interrupting the baron while he was proposing—

again—to Mrs. Chesterton was a good idea. After all, everyone knew Lord MacCreigh had murdered his own bride-to-be.

Fergus thought it best to let the stranger know about this, and so he hurried after him, holding onto his cap as the bitter wind off the sea tugged at it.

"Mister," he called, panting. "Mister, I wouldn't go in there, if'n I were you."

The stranger, who had very long legs, didn't slow his stride. "Run along, little boy," was all he said. "Go on home to your mother."

"Really, mister," Fergus called, panting as he ran up alongside the determined newcomer. "I mean it. You don't know Lord MacCreigh. 'E's a killer. Killed 'is own betrothed, they say, when 'e found 'er with another man. 'E's right dangerous, that 'un."

"Then you'd best hang back, little man," the stranger said. He'd reached the lighthouse door now and, like someone who was preparing for a fight, paused to strip off his leather gloves. "Leave Lord Mac-Creigh to me."

Fergus frowned. It wasn't anything to him, certainly, if this lunatic wanted to get himself killed. Still, a few words of advice seemed to be in order.

"Well," Fergus said conversationally, "if you're goin' to hit 'im, hit 'im low. Below the belt's the only way to knock a man like MacCreigh off 'is feet."

"I most certainly," the stranger said, loosening his cravat, "shall not strike the baron below the belt. I'm astonished you'd even suggest such a thing. Gentlemen do not strike one another below the belt."

"They ain't supposed to kill their fiancées, neither,"

Fergus pointed out, accepting the stranger's top hat and cane as they were thrust toward him. "But that didn't stop Lord MacCreigh."

The stranger grimly tossed his gloves into the hat, threw back the ends of his cloak, and laid his hand upon the door latch. "We'll see about that. Wait here," he commanded. "If you hear gunplay, run for the local magistrate."

Fergus snorted. *"Magistrate? In Faires?"*

Chapter Nine

$\mathcal{J}$ ames was not certain who looked the most surprised when he suddenly threw open the lighthouse door: Emma, or the man who was gripping her arm, quite literally dragging her across the floor with one hand, while clutching her cloak and bonnet in the other.

"Hello," James said, mildly enough. Although of course he didn't feel mild at all. In fact he felt rather murderous, seeing Emma being manhandled in this way.

And evidently this must have showed, as the baron seemed suddenly to feel it prudent to drop Emma's arm. Emma staggered a little at being released so abruptly. Then, to James's complete astonishment—and, he had to admit, utter delight—she tripped forward until she'd seized with both hands his arm, which she clung to as if it were a lifeline.

"James," she cried, in tones—if he was not mistaken—of ecstasy. "James, what a pleasant surprise!"

That's when he knew how badly alarmed Emma had been: never in her life had she addressed him by his given name. It had always been "Lord Denham," or "my lord," but never, ever, James. Not to his face. Not in all the years he'd known her.

And *never* had she seemed ecstatic to see him.

"I thought you were going to catch the noonday ferry," Emma said. He could feel her heart hammering against his arm, she was holding onto him so tightly. Her tongue seemed to be wagging every bit as fast as her heart was beating, as if the two muscles were in a race for some unseen finish line. "Whatever happened? You didn't miss it, did you? Well, never mind. I'm sure it's not too late to take a room at the Puffin Inn. Or, if Mrs. MacTavish is full up, there's always the settle back at the cottage. It isn't luxurious, but you don't mind that, do you, James? After all, you're family!"

James, aware that she was shaking a bit, reached out and anchored her to his side by wrapping an arm securely about her waist. When she did not protest at all, but seemed to shrink even closer to him, until her right cheek was pressing against his waistcoat, he knew.

MacCreigh was going to have to die. That was all there was to it.

The baron seemed to be aware that his life was in danger. There was wariness in his features as he slowly leaned down to lay Emma's cloak upon a bench, the sort of wariness that appeared on the face of a buck just before a hunter let loose a barrage of shot in his direction.

A muscle in MacCreigh's jaw twitched, just once, in

the light that gleamed from a lantern on the windowsill. James saw it. MacCreigh knew he'd seen it. And yet neither man said anything. There was nothing to say, really.

Well, nothing for James to say. Emma, on the other hand, had a good deal to say. But then, when had she not?

"Lord MacCreigh, I don't believe you know Stuart's cousin, his first cousin, the earl of Denham. James Marbury. Lord Denham, this is Geoffrey Bain, the baron of MacCreigh. I'm sure you saw Castle MacCreigh from the boat on your way across the water, James. You can't miss it. It's just above King's Crag, it quite monopolizes the horizon. . . ."

Emma was speaking at breakneck speed, a sure sign she was distressed. As James knew only too well, Emma only prattled when she was very happy or very nervous. The rest of the time, she was far from quiet, but she was not, as she was now, incoherent.

"Castle MacCreigh was built in sixteen-eighty-four, you know, James, and is really quite thrillingly ancient. I mean, it has a dungeon and turrets and, well, just about everything, doesn't it, Lord MacCreigh?"

MacCreigh smiled. It was a confident smile, much more confident, James guessed, than MacCreigh actually felt. Or ought to have been feeling, had he known James better.

"Just about," he said, pleasantly. "You really ought to bring your cousin to see it, Mrs. Chesterton. But then, I don't imagine he'll be here in Faires for that much longer." A pair of thick red eyebrows rose questioningly, though there was enmity, not enquiry, in the baron's bright blue eyes. "Will you, sir?"

James said, coolly, "As a matter of fact, I only just decided to extend my stay indefinitely. I'd very much like to see Castle MacCreigh, sir. Especially by dawn's early light." James smiled magnanimously. "Perhaps tomorrow morning?"

MacCreigh got the message. James was quite sure MacCreigh got the message.

But instead of acquiescing as a gentleman ought when he's been challenged, MacCreigh said, "You've got to be joking. Dawn? That's much too early for me, my good man. Make it noon. You can come for lunch, and meet my sister, Fiona."

"I think not," said James, in slightly mortified tones. He did not make a habit of dining with men he intended to kill, let alone with their sisters.

"Noon it is, then," the baron said, as if James hadn't spoken. To Emma, MacCreigh said, "Well, Mrs. Chesterton. I suppose that, in light of your cousin's unexpected arrival, we shall doubtlessly have to postpone our trip to see Judge Reardon."

"Oh," Emma said, and James, when he looked down at her, saw that she was blushing fiercely. "Oh, yes, I'm afraid so. I *am* sorry, Lord MacCreigh."

"Of course." MacCreigh, with every appearance of gentlemanly gallantry, clicked his boot heels together and gave a courtly bow. "Far be it from me, madam, to deny you the pleasure of the company of your husband's family. Until the morrow, then, sir."

The baron started to sweep by them, but James's cold voice stopped him short.

"*Noon,* tomorrow," he said, affecting a tone of pleasant nonchalance for Emma's benefit.

He had the satisfaction of seeing the baron's broad shoulder twitch, just once. "Of course," Bain said with a broad smile. "I shall look forward to it, sir."

And then, with a sudden burst of wind and salt spray, the baron was gone.

James felt Emma sag against him, as if it had been only her reluctance to show weakness in front of Lord MacCreigh that had kept her on her feet at all. Now that he was gone, her knees appeared to have gone quite weak beneath her.

"All right, Emma," James said, tightening his grip on her waist to keep her from slumping to the floor. He looked down at her reprovingly, taking in her hot cheeks and unnaturally bright eyes. "Are you going to tell me what that was all about?"

Emma, though clearly upset by what had occurred, dissembled handsomely. Had he hands to spare, he'd have applauded her performance. As it was, he was far too busy supporting her to clap.

"Whatever are you talking about?" she asked innocently, her blue eyes wide. "Honestly, my lord, you do speak in riddles sometimes. The baron and I were merely talking, that's all. Sometimes he stops by the lighthouse after school is over, and we talk, oh, about literature, and things. . . ."

James nodded. "I see. And it was during the course of one of these literary discussions that he suddenly thought it might be a good idea to drag you into town to see Judge Reardon?"

The blue eyes grew troubled, the blush increased, and she dropped her gaze. "I . . . I don't know what you're talking about," she stammered.

"No," James said. "I'm sure you don't." He sighed, keeping a firm hold on her. "Emma, I think it's high time we had a discussion ourselves, you and I. And not a literary one."

Emma glanced up at him, just once, apparently to gauge the seriousness of his expression. She must have seen that it was very serious indeed, since she looked down again, at her fingers, which had been playing quite unconsciously with the gold buttons on his waistcoat. "Must we, James?" she asked, in the faintest of voices. "I'm sure I'd rather not."

"I'm quite aware that you'd rather not," James agreed, trying not to admit to himself how very much he liked hearing the sound of his name on her lips. Refusing to allow himself to be distracted, he took firmer hold of her and said, "Really, Emma. How long did you think you could keep such a thing from me?"

When she lifted her eyes again, he saw that now they were wide with feigned innocence. "Keep what from you, James?" she asked.

"Don't try using that tone on me," James said severely. "It's the same one you used to employ on your aunt when she caught you with your fingers in the pudding when you were supposed to be in bed. You know perfectly well what I'm talking about. Stuart. How long did you think you could keep me in the dark about that, eh?"

Emma's eyes widened further, but this time with guilt. "Well," she said, some of the familiar asperity with which she normally addressed him creeping back into her voice, "if you'd left on the noonday ferry, like you were supposed to, I'd have kept it from you forever, wouldn't I?"

"And if I'd left on the noonday ferry," James said, "what would have happened just now with Lord Mac-Creigh, had I not come in?"

"Nothing," Emma said, but without much conviction.

"Nothing? I don't think *nothing* is what would have happened, Emma. I think—"

But James never got to finish saying what he thought—at least, not just then—since the door blew open again. Only this time, it was not Lord MacCreigh that stood there, but the boy to whom James had entrusted his hat and cane.

"Miz Chesterton?" the boy called, as he slipped into the schoolroom. His gaze swept the premises, only stopping to rest when it settled on Emma. Cocking his head to one side, the boy said, "Oh, there you are. Everything all right then?"

Emma let out a sound that was halfway between a sob and a laugh, and then, to James's disappointment, she pushed away from him.

"Oh, Fergus," she said, sinking down onto a bench just opposite from where the boy stood. "Of course everything is all right. What do you have there, in your hands?"

Fergus held up James's hat and cane. "The gentleman's things, mum," he said, with a nod in James's direction. " 'E passed 'em to me before 'e came in 'ere to give Lord MacCreigh a piece of 'is—"

"Yes, yes," James interrupted quickly. He crossed the room to take his belongings from the boy's hands, which, he saw with some dismay, were quite grubby. "Thank you, son. Um, here's a sovereign for your trouble."

And to keep your mouth shut, James added silently. He didn't need to say it out loud, he soon saw, since the boy was so distracted by the coin in his hand that he'd been rendered nearly speechless.

"Gor," he cried breathlessly, holding the sovereign up to the light. "Is that what I think it is, Miz Chesterton?"

"Yes, Fergus," Emma said. "It's a pound. You'd best put it away, if you want to keep it. You don't want any of the bigger boys finding it on you. Now, where were we with our reading? Do you remember? Had we gotten to the part where Mr. Van Winkle wakes?"

James, watching her with some amusement, said, "Eager as I am sure you are to tutor this, er, promising young lad, Emma, I'm afraid we have some rather more pressing business just at the moment. Wouldn't you agree?"

Emma looked up at him, her expression blithe. "Oh, that can wait, I'm sure, Lord Denham. Fergus simply must have his reading lesson—"

So it was back to Lord Denham again, was it? Well, he wouldn't allow that to bother him. Why should it? It had been Lord Denham for the entire time he'd known her, up until about five minutes before. It could be Lord Denham again.

For now.

"Yes, well, we're all quite impressed by your dedication, Emma," James said drily as he tugged on his gloves. "But now I think it would be best if young Master Fergus ran along. I've had Mrs. MacTavish pack a hamper. I am going to escort you back to your cottage, where you and I shall have a nice long talk over dinner,

and see if we can't make some sense out of this little
mess you've gotten yourself into. All right?" After placing his top hat dapperly over his head, he reached down
and lifted her cloak, then shook it, beckoningly, at her.
"Come along, Mrs. Chesterton," he said. "No dillydal-
lying. I'm paying Murphy by the hour, not by the trip.
He's waiting for us just outside the inn."

All hint of cheerfulness had left Emma's face. She did
not look troubled so much as confused. "Mrs. Mac-
Tavish packed a hamper?" was all she asked, and that
came out sounding rather faint.

"Yes, a lovely hamper, full of delicious sundries." He
shook the cloak again, and this time Emma rose and,
walking as slowly as if she were in a dream, came
toward him, turning round obediently when he ges-
tured for her to do so, so that he could drape the well-
used garment over her shoulders.

"I believe there's some pickled herring in sour
cream," he said as he turned her about again and began
fastening the toggles on her cape. "And some sort of
meat pie. Lamb, I think. And a stew. Oyster, if I'm not
mistaken. There's a nice loaf of bread, fresh from the
oven, and a bottle of claret." He lifted her bonnet and
skillfully placed it over her thick, wildly curling hair. "I
hope you won't mind the liberty, but I thought that,
after a long day of teaching, you'd hardly feel like cooking for yourself." He concentrated on securing her bonnet beneath her chin with an attractive bow. "And
there's a nice meringue for dessert. Mrs. MacTavish insisted it was impossible to bake a meringue today, the
weather being so damp, but it appears that I managed
to convince her otherwise."

Passing a critical eye over Emma, who was still looking up at him with a stunned expression on her face, he
said, "There we are, now. Have you any gloves?" She
reached into the pocket of her cloak and pulled out a
wadded-up pair of red leather gloves. "Capital," James
said, extending his elbow invitingly, "Mrs. Chesterton,
if you'll allow me to escort you to Mr. Murphy's carriage. . . ."

Emma took his arm like a woman in a daze, only
seeming to remember where she was when they reached
the doorway. There she turned and called, worriedly,
over the sound of the wind and surf, "Oh, Fergus, put
out the lamp before you go, will you? You know how
angry Mr. McGillicutty gets when we leave the lamp
on—"

"I will, Miss Emma," Fergus assured her.

"And the wood stove. Don't forget to make sure the
fire in the wood stove is out—"

James saw Fergus roll his eyes heavenward. "I *will*,
Miss Emma."

"And the benches." Emma continued to hesitate in
the doorway, one hand on her head to keep her bonnet
from being swept away by the wind tugging so fiercely
at it and her skirt, the other still in the crook of James's
arm. "When he gets here, have Mr. McGillicutty help
you to move the benches away from the stove, because
sometimes when the wind is high, sparks can come flying out even after you've put out the fire, and we
wouldn't want the benches set aflame—"

"That's quite enough, Mrs. Chesterton," James interrupted mildly. He took firm hold of her arm and
began to steer her outside. "You've put this off as long

as is humanly possible. I don't think even you could possibly think of another delaying tactic."

She looked up at him, her blush belying her indignant response. "I don't know what you mean, Lord Denham. I was merely—"

"I know precisely what you were doing. Say good night to the boy."

Emma waved a little desperately at Fergus as the tall man propelled her out into the sea spray. "Good night, Fergus! We'll continue our lesson tomorrow, I promise—"

"Good night, mum," Fergus called happily. If he was at all concerned by his teacher's evident reluctance to leave with the tall stranger, that concern didn't last very long. Lord Denham, Fergus could tell, was a right enough chap. Didn't Fergus have a sovereign now, to prove it? He was richer than he'd ever been in his entire life, richer even than his own father had ever been, since any money that found its way into Mr. MacPherson's fingers had a tendency to slip right out again, over the Sea Cow's bar.

Not certain how he was going to spend this vast fortune, Fergus did know one thing for certain: there was more to be had where that had come from. He was going to keep his eye on Mrs. Chesterton's friend, Lord Denham. Oh, yes, a *sharp* eye on him.

Chapter Ten

Emma sat stiffly on her well-padded settle, unwilling to relax even a little bit. When they'd been growing up, her aunt had instructed Emma and Penelope that it wasn't proper for ladies to slump in their chair. One's spine, Aunt Regina Van Court had explained, must never touch the back of one's seat.

But Emma had realized long ago that most of what her aunt had told her growing up was either untrue or patently ridiculous. A lady, she'd discovered, could sit any way she wanted to, and still remain a lady. It wasn't how one *sat* that determined one's breeding. It was how one, in spite of all odds, persevered. In that, Emma felt, she had more than proven that she was a lady.

So that was not why she was sitting so stiffly in her seat. That was not why at all. She refused to relax because she knew that at any moment, James was going to ask her about Stuart, and how he had died, which would naturally lead to Mr. O'Malley, and his dreadful will.

She did not know which she was more loath to discuss—her husband's murder or the fortune left her by his murderer. Both topics were particularly repellent to her. Couldn't James see this? Couldn't for once he be merciful, and just let it be? No, Emma was not about to relax. She could not allow herself to be lulled into a false sense of security by the warm fire, the savory food in front of her, and most of all, her nicely padded settle. No, she was waiting for the proverbial other shoe to drop.

Still, she could not help but be a *little* grateful. After all, James *had* rescued her from Lord MacCreigh. When James had asked her, back at the lighthouse, what she thought might have happened had he not walked in, and Emma had replied, "Nothing," she had of course been lying. She was not at all convinced that *nothing* would have happened.

Oh, she knew the rumors about Lord MacCreigh having killed his fiancée weren't true—knew it better than anyone in the district, with the exception of Lord MacCreigh himself.

Still, Lord MacCreigh really did have something of a temper. Clara, his fiancée, had once described to Emma a family supper at which he had hurled a plateful of eels across the room when he found them not pickled to his liking.

And he was in dreadful need of money. The rooftops at Castle MacCreigh were made of wood and had lately started to decay. The baron needed to install all new rooftops—slate ones, or stone, at the very least—or lose his precious heirlooms, amongst which were some very fine, if slightly moth-eaten, fourteenth-century tapestries. . . .

So while she knew Lord MacCreigh was unlikely to try to kill her, she certainly would not put a little forceful coercion past the baron.

Only he hadn't had a chance, because James had been there, and had put a stop to it.

And Emma really was very grateful to him. Not just for stopping Lord MacCreigh, either. He had gone to considerable trouble and expense to arrange this supper, which, although she wouldn't allow herself to relax, she had to admit was delicious. Mrs. MacTavish was the best cook on the island, and it was rare that Emma got an opportunity to sample her excellent cuisine. Though the innkeeper had very sweetly provided Emma with many hot suppers those first few nights just after Stuart had died, she had not been able to keep doing so forever, of course.

"More claret, Emma?" James asked. Without waiting for an answer, he refilled her glass, which she'd only just touched with her lips. She did not want, on top of everything else, to become giddy, and so she was drinking sparingly.

James, however, seemed to have no such fear. He'd consumed a third of the bottle of claret by himself. He was in as good a mood as Emma had ever seen him, which surprised her, since he certainly hadn't started out his day at all propitiously, having split his knuckles open on a yeoman's jaw in the first few hours of the day. He seemed to have forgotten all about that, however, and was doing thorough justice to Mrs. Mac-

Tavish's oyster stew, which he was consuming from a bowl—an earthenware bowl, the only crockery Emma had left, now that he'd destroyed her Limoges—in his lap, having eschewed the only table for the warmer, cheerier hearth.

Despite what he now knew about his cousin's demise, James had been in a good humor from the moment they had climbed into Mr. Murphy's brougham—this time he'd followed her advice, and sat beside her on the forward-facing seat—all the way to the cottage, not complaining a bit when the carriage tipped and swayed along the road. The rain, which had stopped at last, had nevertheless left the road slick with mud, making the journey quite treacherous.

But James had not uttered a word about the condition of the road. Instead, he had asked her quite amiably about her school, and Emma, cautiously at first, and then with growing enthusiasm, had told him about John McAddams and Flora and Fergus, and her troubles with the stove, which sometimes acted up, and the very great shortage of desks and books and paper and ink. James listened carefully, she thought, and did not, as he might have done a year ago, reprove her for wasting her time trying to improve minds "not worth saving," which was how he'd used sometimes to refer to the offspring of the underclasses, she remembered.

He did look a little stern when, in answering a polite inquiry of his, she inadvertently let slip the smallness of the stipend paid to her by the town for her work. But when she explained, hurriedly, that after the typhus outbreak, there'd been little money left in the Faires treasury to pay a teacher's salary, he nodded as if he understood perfectly. She mentioned nothing of Lord MacCreigh, but to her dismay, he'd asked, quite casually, just as they were passing the Wishing Tree, if this was the first time the baron had called upon her while she was alone at the lighthouse. He had not looked at all pleased when she replied that the baron came two or three times a month, no more, and that certainly this was the only time he'd ever "gone off his head," as she'd—diplomatically, she thought—put it.

And then she'd nearly ruined everything by adding lightly, "But that only happened because Judge Reardon's come back to town," after which she could have bitten her tongue. Lord! And she had sworn to herself she wasn't going to bring up that subject—it was entirely possible that James, though he might have learned the truth about the nature of his cousin's death, had not yet heard about Mr. O'Malley's will.

To her relief, he hadn't. At least, it did not appear he had. He certainly did not bring it up during the carriage ride home. Indeed, he was all that was polite and attentive during that ride.

And when, after a stop to retrieve Una from a highly talkative Mrs. MacEwan (whose loquaciousness quickly died upon noticing Lord Denham; Emma didn't doubt it would soon be all over Faires that she had dined alone in her cottage with a man—never mind that that man happened to be a relation . . . well, by marriage, but still), Mr. Murphy had pulled up his team outside her cottage, James had alighted and handed her down from the brougham as gallantly as if they'd been arriving at St. James Palace, and not her humble little home. He had been quite patient while she'd torn about, starting a fire, lighting the lamps, and feeding the animals—the dog, the mother cat and kittens that had taken refuge in her woodshed, the chickens, and the goat—all at the same time. Really, if she hadn't known differently, she never would have guessed that the James standing in her cottage then, and the James she'd known a year previously, were one and the same person.

And now he was offering her a piece of meringue and speaking quite amusingly of mutual acquaintances they had known that winter of 'thirty-two. Really, but James could be charming when he wanted to be. Emma felt almost at ease with him, sharing the wide settle they'd pulled so close to the fire. Its high back protected them from the winds that sometimes seeped beneath the door, and surrounded them like a protective wall. She really did fear that, in her great comfort, she was going to let down her guard. Why, it would have been so easy to forget that the two of them were on an isolated cliff, with the wind from the sea howling against the windowpanes. They might almost have been back in London, sharing a midnight feast in James's town house, as they'd done several times a year ago, after a long night of dancing.

There was just one notable difference, really: Stuart wasn't there with them.

She wondered, as she listened to James describe a gown Penelope had worn to the opera not long ago— the two of them were not, she was interested to learn, married, or even engaged, a fact that must have irked Penelope no end—if he was as conscious as she was of Stuart's absence. Did James, she mused, miss Stuart? The two of them hadn't spoken for the six months before Stuart's death, but they had been, in spite of their differences, as close as brothers.

Before Emma had put her foot in it, that day in James's library.

Oh, how much she would have liked to relax! Maybe she was being silly. James didn't know anything about Mr. O'Malley. How could he? Really, it was ridiculous of her to be—

"So, Emma," James said conversationally as he leaned over and plucked a piece of meringue from the basket on the hearth. His tone was so nonchalant, his manner so easy, that Emma thought he was going to say something about the weather, or at the very most, the ill health of King William.

She was perfectly unprepared when what came out of his mouth instead was, "What really happened to Stuart?"

Oh, dear.

Chapter Eleven

*J*ames, at the very moment Emma was wondering whether or not he missed his cousin, was as far from missing Stuart as he could be. Stuart was nowhere in his thoughts.

Perhaps he ought to have been. It would have been only natural if he were. James was, after all, sitting on Stuart's settle in the cottage Stuart had lived in during the last months of his short life. On the mantel top above him rested Stuart's pipe. On the shelves behind him stood Stuart's books. Through the door leading from this room was Stuart's bedroom. The very air James breathed was permeated with the memory of Stuart Chesterton. . . .

Especially since, seated beside him, looking very fetching indeed with her light blond hair, bright blue eyes, and scarlet cheeks, was Stuart Chesterton's widow.

And yet, strangely, James had never been less aware

of Stuart than he was at the particular moment. Perhaps because at that particular moment, all he could think of was Emma, and *this* Emma, the one seated beside him, seemed as unlike the Emma he had known in relation to Stuart as she could be. *That* Emma would have been, like Stuart, trying to impress upon James the errors of his profligate ways. *That* Emma would have been at pains to convey to James her disapproval of what she considered his dissolute lifestyle, though she would have done it charmingly. *That* was the Emma that Stuart had loved, the Emma that Stuart had married.

That was not the Emma that James was sitting beside. *That* Emma would not have started her own school. *That* Emma, though she might have expressed an interest in doing so, would never have been successful, let alone have carried on with it for as long as this Emma had. *That* Emma would have been too frightened to remain in this cramped cottage on this isolated island, so far from her family and friends, where this Emma had built a life for herself, independent of everyone she had ever known and loved—and seemed quite content to continue living that life, despite the obvious hardships she encountered while doing so.

This woman sitting next to him was completely different from the woman he had known a year earlier . . .

. . . and yet oddly the same. For though she seemed stronger and more sure of herself, she was still vulnerable—how could he forget how she'd clung to him in the lighthouse?—and, when it came down to it, still as warmly feminine as she'd always been.

Still, he couldn't help wondering whether the change in Emma had come before or after Stuart's death. And if it had come before, what had Stuart thought of it? Had theirs been a happy marriage? James wondered. Did Emma miss him? Surely she must. Any woman who was willing to throw away all that Emma had in order to marry a man must have loved him a great deal.

But once she'd finally gotten Stuart, had he made her happy? James wondered if he would ever know. It was not, after all, the sort of thing he felt he could ask. Not the way he'd asked about Stuart's death.

He had been trying for some time to put her at her ease. It was quite clear she was nervous as a cat, no doubt over the realization that her secrets—the ones she'd been trying to keep from him so assiduously since his arrival—must necessarily be revealed now. He did not know why she was being so mysterious about it. It wasn't her fault, after all, that Stuart had been killed, any more than it was her fault the lord chief justice had made up the ridiculous condition that she must marry in order to receive the money due to her.

But now that he'd brought the subject up, he could tell it was going to be a hard one—harder, even, than he'd suspected. Emma had had time to grieve, certainly. And since his arrival, he had not seen very many signs that she still felt Stuart's loss very actutely. Until now, that is. Now that he'd brought up the subject of Stuart's death, Emma—her hair, having completely escaped the pins into which she'd tucked it, glowing a burnished gold in the firelight—looked miserable.

"Oh, James," she murmured. "I don't want to talk about it. Please don't make me."

James said, firmly, "Emma, I've got to know. You

know I do. I won't tell anyone back in London, if you like, but I really must know the truth. You can understand that, can't you?"

She passed a hand over her eyes, so he could not read her expression.

"I suppose so," she said.

"So," James said gently. "Tell me. How did Stuart die?"

She sighed, and then, lowering her hand, she said, her gaze on the dancing flames of the fire before them, "He was killed. A man named O'Malley . . . they had a disagreement, he and Stuart. And Mr. O'Malley hit him. He didn't mean to kill him, of course. Only Stuart . . . well, he wasn't expecting the blow, and he fell back, and hit his head on the hearthstone, and—"

"And died," James finished for her, softly.

"Yes." Emma looked up, tears sparkling on the ends of her long, dark eyelashes. "I'm so sorry, James."

"It wasn't your fault," James said. "Will you tell me . . . *can* you tell me . . . what the disagreement was about?"

Emma shook her head. Her gaze was faraway. "I . . . I'm not sure," she said. Then she added, "It was over in an instant. I do know that, James. I'm certain he didn't suffer. Not as . . . not as Mr. O'Malley did, later."

"Emma," he said. He longed to put an arm around her slender shoulders, to comfort her the way he'd used to, back when she'd been a child and had suffered some hurt or slight.

But he dared not do so now. Not because she was his cousin's widow, either. No, he dared not because it was just the two of them, alone in this isolated cottage, and there was no one, nothing to stop him if putting an arm around her proved not to be enough . . . if from there he was drawn, as he knew he would be, to press his lips to that smooth forehead, or, God forbid, lower, to that sweet, rosebud mouth. . . .

No. He shook himself. These kinds of thoughts wouldn't do. He had a task to perform, and perform it he would. He would not be distracted by the magnetic pull she seemed to have on his heart. . . .

"And the money, Emma?" he asked her, clearing his throat. "The will?"

She turned her head to stare at him owlishly. It was clear that of all the questions he could have put to her, this one was the least welcome.

"How did you find out about that?" she asked him, stunned.

James gave her a stern look. "Emma, really. Faires is a small village. My only surprise was that it took as long as it did for someone to bring it to my attention." He smiled at her reassuringly. "Now the question is, just what are we going to do about it?"

Emma shook her head just the slightest bit, so that her long curls swept her shoulders. "Do?" she echoed, faintly.

"Yes. It's perfectly ridiculous, Emma, this stipulation that you must be married in order to receive this . . . inheritance. If you'll allow me, I'd like to consult a friend of mine who often tries cases like this in London before the Court of the Exchequer Chamber. I believe we have a very good chance of winning an appeal of this ludicrous decision by Justice Reardon."

"I don't want to," Emma said in a low, but quite emphatic, voice.

James smiled tolerantly. "It won't be any trouble, Emma," he told her. "Well, hardly any. I'll simply have my attorney submit an appeal, and you'll be asked to appear before——" She was shaking her head so hard that now he could feel a lavender-scented breeze coming from her side of the settle. He broke off, surprised. "Emma, really! Why are you so resistant to the idea? Don't you want the money?"

"Of *course* I want the money!" Emma stopped shaking her head and stared at him as if he were simpleminded. "But I can't leave Faires to appear before any court."

James, taken aback, said, "Can't leave. . . . But, Emma——"

Suddenly Emma could stand it no longer. She had sat on that settle for over two hours, waiting for exactly this to occur. Now that it had, she couldn't sit still a minute more. Scrambling to her feet, Emma left the glowing warmth of the hearth to pace in the darkness of her cottage's front room.

Oh, Lord, what was she going to do now? Exactly what she'd prayed wouldn't happen *had* happened. James had found out about the money. James had found out the truth about Stuart—well, most of it, anyway—and now he knew about the money, too. Oh, Lord, would her bad luck *never* abate?

"Emma." James had risen from the settle as well, and now stood with one elbow resting along its back, watching her as she strode furiously from one side of the cottage to the next. "Emma, really, you must be rational about this. I know it must upset you to discuss it, but it's *ten thousand pounds*. You could live comfortably, and for the rest of your life, on ten thousand pounds—"

"I know that," Emma said shortly, to her washbasin, directly before she turned her back on it to pace in the opposite direction. "Do you think I don't know that?"

James shook his head. "Then why won't you appeal Reardon's decision? Surely you can't think it *fair* of him to insist you must be married before you can collect the money—"

"No," Emma said. "I don't." She kept pacing, her arms folded across her chest as if to ward off a sudden chill.

James shook his head. "Emma, be reasonable. This is far more money than you are likely to see in a lifetime. I can't imagine Stuart left you anything—"

"He did," she said, stopping short to stare at him with indignantly glowing eyes. "You're standing in it."

"Very well. So he left you this cottage. But that's all. Emma, Stuart died as penniless as he was the day he married you, and God knows your family won't help—"

"Oh, yes." She tossed her head and started pacing again, her long skirt whirling out around her ankles as she spun on one heel. "*You* would know all about that, wouldn't you, my lord?"

James chose to ignore that remark. Instead, he spoke as calmly and as kindly as he could. "You haven't any money, Emma," he said. "You won't accept my invitation to live with my mother in London. The salary you earn teaching in that school isn't enough to—"

"I'll manage," Emma said, not looking at him.

"Oh? You will manage? And how do you intend to do that?"

Irritated by her pacing, he stepped forward just before she stalked past him, effectively blocking her circuit back toward the washbasin.

"Is there something you're not telling me, Emma?" He peered down into her face and saw confusion written there. Still, he had to ask. "Is it possible that there is someone . . ."

The blue eyes were wide, and as without guile as they'd been a year earlier, when she'd looked up at him and confided her intention to marry his cousin. "Someone?" she echoed.

"Yes." James cleared his throat. "Someone who, perhaps, you intend to wed, in order to get the money? That Cletus fellow? Is it him?"

Emma, rolling her eyes in disgust, tried to step past him, but he reached out and took hold of her arm.

"Well?" he demanded. "If not him, then someone else? Is there someone, Emma? Is there?"

"Of course not!" Emma wrenched free from his grasp. Then, like a cat, she stood a few feet away, smoothing her gown where his fingers had crushed the puffed sleeve and attempting, not very successfully, to tuck her hair back into the drooping knot on top of her head. "Honestly, Lord Denham. My husband's hardly been dead six months. What do you take me for?"

James exhaled slowly. He felt as if an immense weight had been lifted from him. He had not realized how very much he'd been dreading her answer. He managed, however, not to let a hint of his relief show.

"Forgive me, Emma," he said. "But you must admit

that the question was a natural one. Why else would you be so resistant to the idea of appealing Judge Reardon's decision?"

"I already told you," Emma said. "Appeals like the one you're talking about can take years. And I cannot leave Faires for that long."

James frowned. "In God's name, Emma, whyever not?"

She looked at him as if he were quite dense. "The *children,*" she said.

"Children?" he echoed. Then, remembering the conversation he'd had with Justice Reardon, comprehension dawned. "Oh. . . . Your schoolchildren."

"My schoolchildren." Emma stalked past him and reached for a woolen shawl that hung from a peg near the hearth. She flung the garment about her shoulders and faced him with her chin lifted. "I can't leave them."

"Whyever not?" James demanded. "Is it an orphanage you're running, or a school? Don't they have parents?"

"Not all of them. Quite a few of them lost loved ones in the typhus epidemic. The school—my school—is the only place on the island where many of them feel valued . . . feel safe. I can't go traipsing off to London to waste my time before the courts, demanding they hand over money I don't want or deserve, when I'm needed—badly—elsewhere."

"Yes, but Emma—" James heard the change in her voice, but didn't understand it. "Emma, it isn't your *duty* to see to it that the children of the village of Faires learn to read."

"Oh, isn't it?" Emma tugged on her shawl, bringing the wool closer about the lace collar of her dress. "Then whose is it?"

"I don't know," James admitted. "The minister, I suppose. Let him do it." James had met the minister, of course, and very much doubted that he bothered himself with the spiritual well-being of his less than well-off brethren. That would have been his curate's duty . . . if he still had a curate, of course. The Reverend Peck had apparently failed to lure a new one from the mainland, news of the fate of the last one having undoubtedly already spread through seminaries across the land.

"It isn't your affair, Emma," James said, firmly. "You oughtn't involve yourself."

"Oh, that is just so like you." Her voice was filled with bitterness. "It's never any of *your* affair, is it, Lord Denham? You've never liked to bother yourself with people who had the bad misjudgment to be born poor. Even though, having all the money in the world, more than you could ever possibly need, I don't know who could do more for them."

James heaved an exhausted sigh. This was not precisely how he'd pictured the evening progressing. Oh, he'd known that Emma was going to be resistant to the idea of discussing her strange predicament.

But he'd rather hoped their interview would not descend, as it evidently now had, into their usual old argument.

Glaring at her now, in the half-light cast by the fire, James found it hard to believe that such an angelic-looking young woman could be capable of such vexing behavior, for despite the physical hardships she'd endured over the past year, Emma Van Court Chesterton was still beautiful. Really, there wasn't a woman in James's acquaintance back in London who wouldn't have envied Emma's glorious hair and eyes, but it was her overall presence that would have aroused the most admiration. Was it, he wondered, slightly appalled at his own sentimentality, but nevertheless unable to keep from considering this new thought, a glow that came from some kind of spiritual satisfaction?

Good God, he had to get away from Scotland. He was becoming pukingly romantic.

"Very well, Emma," he said finally, folding his arms across his chest. He chose his words with care, conscious that she was watching him warily as that cat he'd seen slinking in and out of the shadows of the cottage. "I can see that this is a subject upon which you will not be swayed."

Was it his imagination, or did she look relieved? In any case, the chin lowered, just a little bit.

"It is, my lord," Emma replied with gravity.

So that was that. They were at a standstill. On this subject, anyway. But there was another . . . one that James was loath to bring up, but which he felt obligated to mention. Really, he had no other choice.

"Emma," he said. "About Stuart."

She looked at him curiously. "Yes? What about him?" Then her expression grew defensive. "Honestly, my lord, I've told you as much as I—"

"No," he said, raising a hand to stop her. "Not about his death. I want to ask . . . about his burial."

Her eyes went round as saucers. "His burial?"

"Yes. His grave. I went to the Reverend Peck, and he was unable to tell me where Stuart had been buried. And I was wondering—"

"Because Reverend Peck doesn't know," Emma said,

quickly. Too quickly. "There were too many other people dying at the same time Stuart did. Reverend Peck couldn't officiate at his funeral. I couldn't even—"

"Bury him in the churchyard," James finished for her. "Yes, Emma, I know. And I am grateful, frankly, that you didn't. A group grave would have been inexcusable. I'm not at all angry that you put him in unconsecrated ground—which I am assuming you did. It doesn't matter in the least, you see, because I do think that—and I'm sure you'll agree with me—he'd be happier back at Denham Abbey."

She frowned. "Back at Denham Abbey? I don't know what you mean."

"I mean," he said, slowly, "that I would like to retrieve Stuart."

Her eyebrows came down in a rush over her nose. "Retrieve Stuart? Whatever do you mean?"

"To disinter him," James explained. "For transferal to the family mausoleum at Denham Abbey. That really is, Emma, the only appropriate place for him. He really ought to be laid to rest with his parents. They would have wanted—"

"*No!*"

It was more of a gasp than a word. But James heard her easily enough. Heard her, and saw the sudden pallor in her face.

"Emma," he said, truly shocked by her appearance. "Are you unwell? Can I get you something? Here, have some wine—"

But Emma, who had reached out and grasped with white-knuckled fingers the back of a nearby chair, seemed hardly to hear him.

"You can't," she said, shaking her head until her curls swayed. "You can't possibly. No. No."

"Emma—"

"I won't allow it," Emma said, meaning, James was certain, to sound far more authoritative than she actually did. It was probably quite difficult, he thought, to sound authoritative when one was as close to collapse as he feared she was. "Do you hear me? I won't."

"Emma," he said. "You are overwrought. Sit down, please. Let me get you some wine—"

"I don't want to sit down," Emma said, some of the color, he was relieved to see, starting to come back into her cheeks. "I don't want wine. You're not to dig him up, James. Do you understand? He's to stay where he is."

"Emma—"

"He's my husband," Emma said, in a voice that shook.

"Emma, I'm not disputing that. I'm only saying that there's a space reserved for him, where he'll be with the rest of his family, where his grave will be tended to—"

"He's staying here," Emma said. "With me, right here in Faires. You're not to touch him. Do you understand? *You're not to touch him.*"

Chapter Twelve

Emma rolled over, giving her pillow a hearty punch to fluff it up again. She couldn't sleep, and no wonder.

She ought to have expected it, of course. She couldn't believe she'd been so naive as not to have thought of it before. Of course the earl would want to see his cousin properly interred in the family mausoleum. Stuart had, of course, been a sad disappointment to his family, but that did not mean he wasn't still just that . . . family. They would want him buried alongside his parents—and probably, Emma thought morosely, when her time came, they'd want to put her in alongside Stuart.

Well, that wasn't going to happen. Not if she could help it.

And she could help it, simply by refusing to tell James where his cousin was buried.

She hadn't any doubt that James thought her horribly sentimental, perhaps even superstitious, in her refusal to reveal the whereabouts of Stuart's final resting place. She didn't care. She didn't care what James thought. He certainly didn't care what she thought. If he had any sensitivity to her feelings at all, would he currently be sleeping, not back at the Puffin Inn, where he'd taken rooms, but out on the settle, in her very own cottage? Of course, she had offered back at the lighthouse, but she hadn't seriously thought he'd take her up on it. It had been mostly for Lord MacCreigh's benefit, after all.

No. Because she had let him know, in no uncertain terms, how she felt about *that* plan. She had, after all, only just been recovering from her shock at finding him standing in her vegetable patch, and then the discovery that he knew, actually *knew* about Mr. O'Malley's will, when he'd turned around and fired another shot from the hip, this one about Stuart . . . and then about staying the night. How was a woman supposed to combat these sneak offensives? It was more than could be reasonably borne.

"I think it best that we retire for the evening," he'd said. "You are, I am sure, done for, as am I. If you'll just point me where you keep the spare sheets, I shan't trouble you again till morning."

Emma had been appalled. Sleep here, in her cottage? Was he mad?

"Perhaps you hadn't noticed," James had replied, "but Mr. Murphy is gone. I have no way of getting back to the village."

"Oh!" Emma had interrupted. "Oh, but you could certainly walk there. I'll go with you, to show you the way. It *is* quite steep—"

He'd cocked a dark eyebrow at her. "Emma, really. You're being a bit missish, aren't you? I am done for— the sea air, I suppose. I shall merely spend the night on this settle."

"But Mrs. MacTavish, down at the inn," Emma cried, with mounting urgency. "She'll know that you didn't spend the night there. She'll wonder where you *did* spend it—"

He'd waved his hand dismissively. "Mrs. MacTavish will think nothing of it, Emma."

But when Emma assured him that he was wrong, that it would be the talk of the town upon the morrow, James had merely looked at her and said, in a chiding voice, "Really, Emma. It isn't as if we're strangers, you and I. We *are* family, are we not?"

Family! The very idea! Emma could not lie still at the thought of it. Indeed, Una, beside her in the bed, looked up sleepily at her mistress several times, seeming to wonder when, if ever, Emma was going to calm down and go to sleep.

But *family!* The nerve! After what he'd done . . .

Granted, it had been a year earlier, that horrible day in his library. But still. Family! What kind of family physically attacked one another simply because some-one announced he was marrying?

Still, what could she do? It wasn't as if she could order him out of the house. Well, she supposed she could have—she could have demanded he go and sleep in the barn, with Tressida, the goat.

But she didn't. Instead, she'd gone wordlessly to the chest where she kept her spare bedclothes and taken out a quilt. She'd been surprised when he'd seized hold of the corner of the comforter and helped her to shake it out, then lay it over the settle's padded seat. He'd insisted upon helping to wash the dishes and, to Emma's great surprise, even volunteered for the odious washing part, allowing her the easier task of drying. She had *almost*, watching him plunge his hands into the freezing water, felt a companionable warmth toward him at that point. After all, she could not imagine that the earl of Denham had ever offered to wash anyone else's dishes.

But she had quickly squelched the gentle emotion. She could not let herself be lulled into a false sense of security around the man. Look at what had happened the last time she'd allowed herself to trust him. . . . He'd very nearly killed Stuart himself!

And now here he was, asking permission to do a thing that would, Emma knew, only result in heartbreak, not to mention further scandal. . . .

No. She would not allow herself to feel warmly toward him. To do so would only make it that much harder for her to say no the next time he asked her— and she knew there'd be a next time—for permission to dig up Stuart. And that she could never allow.

But Emma had never been very good at hating. She was quite out of practice at it. The only person whom she'd ever actively hated was the earl of Denham, and though she'd hated him in fits and starts this past year, it had never been for more than a few minutes at a time, and sometimes with weeks and months stretching between bursts. Really, it was quite taxing, keeping up a good solid hatred of someone. She was going to have to concentrate on it very hard, if she was going to go on hating him until he finally left the island . . . whenever that might be.

What if, she wondered, he kept on doing kind things for her, like defending her from Lord MacCreigh, and bringing her hampers from Mrs. MacTavish, and helping her with the dishes? How was she going to keep hating him then?

Still, she could not allow herself to be swayed from her enmity for him.

She lay in her bed, listening hard to determine whether or not he was sleeping yet. Was he, as she was, lying awake, blinking at the ceiling? She could hear not the slightest sound from the outer room. All she could hear was the rhythmic breathing of Una, in bed beside her, and the wind outdoors . . . much of which was seeping in through the bedroom window, casting a chill across the room.

It had been a serious design flaw of the cottage, having only one fireplace, and that in the cottage's center, instead of in the bedroom, where it might have done some good at night. It had not been so much of a problem when Stuart was alive. But now that Stuart was gone, and the door to the bedroom was shut—as it necessarily had to be, lest James see her in her nightclothes—it could get cold as a tomb inside.

Emma was ruminating on the coldness of her bedroom, and just what exactly she was going to say to Mrs. MacEwan in the morning, when the woman asked—as she surely would; there were no secrets in Faires—about James having spent the night, when she heard a sound other than the wind and Una. It wasn't snoring, either. It was the sound, Emma was quite certain, of someone trying the front door.

Emma did not know what time it was. She had lain

awake for hours, it seemed, ruminating on James and his unexpected visit. It could have been midnight, or it could have been dawn, since the sky—what she could see of it through the diamond-shaped panes of her window—was hidden by dark clouds. Lord knew her rooster was not particularly reliable. Dawn could have come and gone with her never being the wiser.

On the whole, however, Emma thought it closer to midnight. Who on earth, she wondered, could be skulking around outside her cottage at midnight? She had become quite used to having her sleep disrupted back when Stuart had been alive. During the typhus epidemic, Emma had sometimes been roused two or three times a night by parishioners frantic for last rites to be read for loved ones who'd taken a turn for the worst.

But Stuart was gone now. Whoever it was surely had good reason for seeking her out at such a late hour.

A good reason, or a very nefarious one . . .

Without thinking twice about it, Emma was out of bed and running for the bedroom door. She tore it open, then ran to the fireplace. The embers had died almost completely on the hearth, casting the room in a strange red glow. She didn't pause to admire it. Instead, she lifted the trailing hem of her nightdress, climbed up onto the stone hearth, and heaved the hunting rifle from the hooks upon which it had hung. Emma was not particularly proficient with the weapon, and had not the heart to aim the barrel at any living animal. In fact, were it not for Mr. MacEwan's generous contributions to her table, she would live only on bread and vegetables.

But, though Stuart would have been horrified to

know it, Emma was not particularly opposed to shooting humans, should the need arise.

Tucking the rifle under her arm, she went to the front
door. She'd latched it securely, not because she feared
robbers but because the force of the wind from the sea
had often flung it open in the past. The only way that
anyone could enter her cottage, once the door was
barred, was through one of the many windows, which
could be opened quite simply from the outside by pop-
ping out a pane, reaching inside, and lifting a lever.
They all opened out to let in the fresh sea breeze, and
could be propped ajar with a metal hook.

Emma saw no hand reaching up to tap out one of the
small diamond panes, seeing as how whoever her midnight caller was, he'd failed to pry open the door. She
did, however, hear a noise behind her, and she whirled,
bringing the heavy gun to her shoulder, her heart in her
throat, her eyes wild—

Only to have the weapon yanked clean out of her
possession by an irate earl of Denham, who cried,
"Emma! For the love of God!"

Emma responded by letting out a startled shriek.
She had quite forgotten in her panic over the noise
outside that James was in the house. The sight of him,
looming so close and so large, in only his linen shirt
and breeches, completely undid her. She screamed
until he seized hold of her and clapped a hand over her
mouth. Then, conscious of the fact that he was holding her against his body—which was still warm from
the settle—and equally conscious of how well that
body was defined against the very thin material of her
nightdress—beneath which she wore exactly nothing—

she came back to her senses and, not knowing what else to do, bit him.

"Ow!" James wrenched his fingers from between her teeth and flapped them in front of her face. "Stop that," he hissed.

"Let go of me, then," Emma suggested, but James only shushed her. It appeared that he, too, had heard the door rattling. Now he stood still, waiting to see if he'd hear it again.

Emma knew, of course, that was what he was doing. He was certainly not holding onto her so tightly because he *enjoyed* the feeling of her all-but-naked body against him. No, no, far from it! And the fact that his right thigh was sort of, well, *between* her legs wasn't of the slightest consequence to him. Of course not! He had hold of the rifle, didn't he, as well as her waist? A man holding onto a rifle could not *possibly* be thinking of anything but what he was about to shoot.

But *Emma* wasn't holding onto any rifle. *Emma* didn't have anything to keep her mind off the feel of his body against hers. She was excruciatingly aware of the thick muscularity of the thigh pressed up against her, fully sensitized to the strong fingers sunk into the flesh just above her hip bone. Not only that, but she could smell him. The masculine scent of him filled her nostrils, that same distracting odor that had emanated from him that morning in the brougham, those mingled scents of soap and London. And he was so warm! Hot as Una, with whom she'd been sharing her bed, but significantly less furry, and with much better smelling breath.

That breath now tickled her ear. "I don't hear anything anymore," he whispered. "Do you?"

Emma was far too busy concentrating on not smelling him, not feeling that hard thigh pressed between her legs, to answer. But when she cocked her head and listened, she didn't hear anything anymore, either . . . for a second or two. Then she did hear it again. Whoever it was out there, he was trying the door once more.

James heard it, too. Abruptly he released Emma's waist and, placing a heavy hand on her shoulder, pushed her firmly down onto the settle he'd just abandoned.

"Stay here," he commanded, not looking at her, even when he seized hold of the bedclothes and flung them up, over her. "I'll go and see who it is."

Emma, cocooned in the residual warmth left from his body, protested, "I should go. It might be one of the children."

He gave her an incredulous look. "The *children?*"

"Or one of their parents," Emma said. "Sometimes they do come to me, if there's something they need to be read, or—"

"At one o'clock in the morning?" James demanded.

Emma said, "Just promise me you won't shoot them."

"Why should I?" James sat down briefly beside her, but only to pull his boots on. "You were going to."

"But I was going to ask who's there first, and only shoot if it were . . ."

"If it were who, Emma?" he asked, curiously.

Emma's gaze fell. "No one," she said.

"Hmmph. Just as I suspected." He stood again, cracked open the rifle, and squinted down the barrel.

"Emma," he ground out in a highly irritated voice. "This isn't even loaded."

Emma pulled the comforter high until she could tuck it beneath her chin. The sheets, she noticed, already smelled like James, clean and manly.

"Well," she replied, in a whisper, "it would be silly to leave a loaded gun hanging over a hot fireplace, now, wouldn't it?"

James lifted his eyes toward heaven. "Where," he hissed, "did Stuart keep the shot?"

Emma hissed right back at him, "In the sideboard by the washbasin. What's left of the sideboard, anyway." She started to fling back the comforter. "I had better show you—"

"At your peril," he said ominously from the doorway, "do you move from that settle. I'll find it myself."

"But—"

"For God's sake, Emma," James snapped. "Stay where you are, or I . . ." Apparently unable to think of a threat that sounded dire enough, James finished with, "Or I shall be very displeased indeed."

Then he moved into the shadows.

Emma, in the warm spot he had abandoned, watched tensely, wondering who on earth could be trying to pay her a midnight call. It wasn't entirely out of the realm of the possible that it was someone perfectly harmless. Emma had had midnight callers before . . . just not in a great while. But it was possible that behind that door stood someone with a perfectly logical reason for being there. . . .

On the other hand, supposing that it was Lord Mac-Creigh out there, and James happened to shoot him? Oh, dear!

The same thought had, of course, occurred to James, almost the very second he'd heard the latch catch on the door. Hadn't he insisted upon spending the night here at the cottage for this very reason? Not that Emma, of course, knew it. Lord only knew what she suspected, so far as his motivations for remaining under her roof.

But while he'd suspected the baron might make a rash move like this, he hadn't, in his heart, really believed MacCreigh would be so stupid—or so evil. It was incomprehensible to James that a man would choose to terrorize a woman in this manner. What sort of black-hearted bounder would stalk an innocent widow in her own home, in the dead of night?

Well, it was no use, James had learned long ago, wondering at the twisted workings of the minds of men. He knew, even if Emma didn't, that there was far more evil in the world than good. This was a prime example. Still, he had thought MacCreigh cold, but not mad.

For this, surely, was the act of a madman.

He found the shot with little trouble, despite not having dared to light a candle. If MacCreigh hadn't heard Emma's screaming—and there was the slightest chance that he might not have, due to the shrieking of the wind outside—then surely he'd see a light, and become aware that they were alerted to his presence. Surprise was crucial. MacCreigh mustn't suspect either that Emma was not alone, or that anyone knew he was about. James wanted one thing, and one thing only, and that was a good clean shot. . . .

His eyes had adjusted almost at once to the darkness that permeated the little cottage . . . the darkness, and the cold. Christ in heaven, he hadn't noticed it before then, but the place was like a tomb, it was so cold! Still, he managed to locate the ammunition and load it into the rifle, all the while never taking his eyes off the two windows, one on either side of the front door.

For a few seconds, all he saw was rain. It had started up again, and was falling thick and fast. Then a dark figure—just the briefest of shadows—passed by the first window. The sound of a stick breaking beneath a heavy weight was clearly audible above the pounding of the rain. In a second more, James knew, MacCreigh would try the door again.

It was now, James knew, or never.

In four long strides, he was at the door himself. In a neat, single motion, he simultaneously lifted the wooden bar that kept the door locked, and raised the rifle butt to his shoulder. The wind did the rest. It hurled the door open with an explosive force, sending rain flying indoors.

And outside, looking miserably into the mouth of the rifle James had leveled at its head, stood a very wet, very confused cow.

Chapter Thirteen

"Oh!" Emma cried, from behind James. "It's Louise!"

James lowered the rifle barrel. He could not quite believe what he was seeing. It was not Geoffrey Bain at all. It was a cow. A black-and-white cow. As he stared at it, it lifted its head and let out a pathetic *moo*.

Emma, jostling James aside, reached out to lay her hands on the cow's velvet nose. "Oh, poor Louise," she cooed. She dropped her head until her cheek rested between the cow's eyes, and all of her long blond curls tumbled about the cow's face. "Did you run off again? I'm sure Mr. MacEwan must be very worried about you. Well, you did the right thing, coming to me."

And then, to James's utter astonishment, Emma lifted her head and actually began tugging at the cow's halter, urging it inside.

Inside the *cottage*.

"Emma," he said. It was rather hard to be heard

above the pounding of the rain. Still, he made an effort. "Emma, *what are you doing?*"

"Well," Emma grunted. After some initial reluctance, the cow began a slow lumber into the cottage, its heavy hooves clattering against the wood floor. "We can't just leave her outside," Emma said. "It's pouring. We'll let her spend the night here, and then Mr. Mac-Ewan can fetch her back in the morning."

James watched in disbelief as the cow moved past him, her udder swaying beneath her enormous black-and-white girth. "Emma," he said, as a long tail swished against his leg, "have you gone mad?"

Emma appeared to be ignoring him. She had moved one corner of the settle out of the way, and was stoking the fire, murmuring soft assurances to the cow.

"Emma!" James could take it no longer. He strode forward, intending to seize his cousin's wife and shake some sense into her. Unfortunately, the cow blocked the way. Emma stood on the opposite side of the animal, blinking at him in surprise.

"Whatever is the matter, my lord?" she asked, innocently.

"Emma." James placed the rifle, carefully, on the table. Angry as he was just then, he didn't trust himself not to use it on her . . . or the cow. "Emma," he said, with forced calm. "You simply cannot keep a *cow* in the front room of your cottage."

She had climbed up onto the hearth, where she was applying a poker to the log she'd just laid. "I fail to see why not," she said, into the fireplace.

"Because what if it . . . what if it . . ." James was completely incapable of finishing that particular sentence.

"Then I'll just clean it up." Emma rolled her eyes at him. "Really, Lord Denham. You have more in common with Stuart than I ever thought. He, too, was always very unkind about poor Louise, whenever she got lost like this."

James, hearing this, completely changed his opinion of their midnight visitor. After all, they couldn't very well leave the pathetic creature outside to drown.

"Well," he said, hesitantly, since it wouldn't do to appear to have changed his mind *too* abruptly. "I suppose, if it's just for one night . . ."

It was then James noticed that, standing where she was, so near the dying fire, Emma's body was silhouetted by the light from the glowing embers against her thin nightdress. He could make out quite clearly every curve, every hollow, every . . . *everything*. Even now, he could see that her nipples had become distended from the cold. They pressed insistently against the front of her nightdress.

James knew this was not something he should be seeing. James knew that, as a gentleman and a peer, it was his duty to look away. This was his cousin's wife, a widow, entirely without power or protection in the world.

And yet, try as he might, James found he could not take his eyes off her. It wasn't until she turned around, presenting him with a very fetching but not quite as revealing view of her backside, that he drew breath again.

Really, James thought to himself. This was more than a man could be expected to endure. Wakened from a dead sleep, thinking his home was being invaded, only to find out he was going to have to spend the rest of the night in the same room as a cow.

Then, as if that wasn't bad enough, catching a glimpse of his hostess's nipples.

Really, he hadn't *asked* to see Emma's nipples. That had not, when he'd insisted upon spending the night here, been his intention at all.

And it wasn't as if, after all, he hadn't seen them before, and a good deal more clearly than just now. Emma had been wont to wear extremely low-cut ball gowns a year ago, and thanks to the rigors of the quadrille and his height, which afforded him a perfect view into her decolletage, James had been awarded frequent glimpses down Emma's bustiers.

"Here," James said, with ill grace. "Give me that." He strode forward and wrenched the iron poker from her hand. She looked at him in surprise. James, ignoring her with an effort—her gown was even more transparent, up close—went to work building up the fire. "Go back to bed. You'll catch your death, otherwise."

"Oh," Emma said, cheerfully. "No, I won't. I've never been sick a day in my life. I'm quite hearty, really."

"Emma." He glared up at her now. "Do as I say."

Something in his tone must have persuaded her that he meant business, since she said, in a meek voice, "Yes, my lord," then turned tail, jumped off the hearth, and disappeared into her bedroom.

James, alone at last, turned his head to look at the animal beside him. He was not particularly well acquainted with the bovine species, but he supposed that as cows went, Louise was a pleasant enough one. She had been shivering piteously when he'd first caught sight of her, but she seemed to have warmed up a little. Now she regarded him passively through limpid brown eyes, her pink lips moving rhythmically as she chewed her cud.

James said to her softly, "Let's not make a habit of this, shall we, Louise?"

"Excuse me?" Emma, coming out of the bedroom, struggled to get her arm through the wide sleeve of a maroon satin robe while holding onto the lace cuff of her nightdress, to keep its sleeve from riding up as she donned the outer garment. "Were you speaking to me, my lord?"

"I was not," he said, looking closely at the robe. "I say, Emma, isn't that Stuart's?"

She glanced down as she tied the fringed sash in a bow at her waist. "Yes, of course it is," she said.

He narrowed his eyes at her. "I thought you said you gave away all of Stuart's things."

She looked up quickly. A blush, faint as the dawn, crept over her satin cheeks. "Oh," she said. "Well. Not *all* of them."

"No," James said, more hurt than he supposed he had a right to be. "Apparently not." And then, before he could stop them, the words slipped out. "You know this can't go on, Emma."

She blinked at him. "What can't?"

"You. Living here. All alone like this. Supposing it hadn't been Louise at the door. Supposing it had been MacCreigh."

Emma laughed . . . but not very convincingly. "Oh, but he'd never . . . "

"Wouldn't he?" James shook his head. "I've heard

the talk in the village, Emma. I know they say he killed his fiancée—"

"Oh, but he didn't," Emma said . . . then, too quickly, she snapped her mouth shut. James looked at her curiously.

"You sound awfully certain," he said. "I thought the woman disappeared without a trace. How can you be so sure MacCreigh didn't have something to do with it?"

"Oh," Emma said, suddenly nervous again. "Because I just . . . well, I know Lord MacCreigh. And he'd never—"

"Never what?" James demanded. "Try to take a woman by force? Isn't that what he was doing today when I came across the two of you at the lighthouse?"

"Oh, that," Emma said. "Well, he was just trying to take me to see Judge Reardon, you know. That's a far cry from killing me."

"Still," James said. "There's a woman missing, and MacCreigh's the one said to have killed her—"

"Honestly, Lord Denham," Emma said, "the baron hadn't a thing to do with Clara's disappearance. She ran off with a man—Lord MacCreigh's valet."

"How do you know?" James asked, curiously. "Everyone else says he killed her."

"Yes," Emma said, looking at her bare feet. "I know they do. But I can't help that. I can only say what I know, and that's that Clara ran away to marry the man she loved. Her father would never have approved, you see, and so she felt she hadn't any other choice—"

"Rather like someone else I know," James said drily as he leaned the poker back where it belonged.

"Yes," Emma said, blushing a little. "But at least I wasn't engaged to another man at the time, like Clara was."

"No," James said, thoughtfully. "You weren't." Then, as if it were a confession that had been wrenched from him, he said, "I only did what I thought was best for the two of you, you know. Stuart was in no position to marry. He hadn't established himself in his profession. He hadn't any money."

Emma regarded him with almost as much passivity as the cow. Only the cow wasn't blushing. "He said we didn't need money," she said, in a voice that had gone a bit throaty with emotion. "He said all we needed was love."

"Well," James said, "he would have, wouldn't he? I suppose it seemed romantic enough . . . his first post, and all of that. Who cares if it happened to be in the wilds of northern Scotland, and would necessitate living conditions not quite on a par with what you were used to? The two of you had one another."

Emma's chin slid, just the littlest bit, out in protest of his sarcastic tone. "We came here," she said, "to help others less fortunate than ourselves. Something *you* wouldn't know anything about."

"Perhaps," James said. "On the other hand, it appears that one of those poor unfortunates wasn't very grateful for that help, was he? Considering how he thanked Stuart for his kindness—"

"It wasn't Mr. O'Malley's fault," Emma said. "Anymore than it was Lord MacCreigh's fault that Clara—"

But then, as if an unseen hand had been placed across her lips, Emma snapped her mouth shut and only looked guilty. The silence, broken only by the howling wind outside and the sound of Louise chewing her cud, was palpable.

"Wasn't Lord MacCreigh's fault that Clara . . . what?" James asked, gently. It seemed to him that whatever Emma had been about to say was important—mightily important, if the stricken look on her face was any indication.

"Emma," James said slowly. "Just what happened to Lord MacCreigh's fiancée? You said she ran off with his valet. Is that all there is to the story? Or is there something more?"

There was. He saw it in the way the color drained suddenly from her face. She knew perfectly well there was more to it than a simple elopement. Only she wasn't willing, apparently, to share that information. At least not at the present time. No longer blushing—in fact, pale almost as death—Emma lifted that outthrust chin and said, "I don't care to discuss it right now, Lord Denham. I'm tired, as I imagine you are. I think it might be best if we both went back to bed."

She saw his eyebrows go up, way up, as if he were very surprised indeed by this response. The earl of Denham was not used, of course, to being put off.

This time, however, he seemed to take it rather well.

"Well," he said, "I suppose you're right, Emma. The midnight hour is never a good one for sharing confidences, I've found. It can lead to all sorts of"—she saw his gaze dip toward the V where Stuart's robe gapped a little away from her chest—"complications."

Gasping a little, Emma moved instinctively to tighten the robe, then said sharply, "You needn't worry about any such *complications* ensuing here, Lord Denham. Good night to you."

So saying, Emma turned on her heel, stalked toward her bedroom door, and closed it emphatically behind her.

"Emma?" James stared at the closed door in bemusement. What had he done? What had he done to rile her *now*? Good God, this woman's temper was almost as short as his own. "Emma?"

There was no response. In the bedroom, Emma heard his soft call but chose to ignore it. *Complications,* she fumed to herself, as she threw back the comforter and climbed into her cold bed, not bothering to remove Stuart's robe. Complications, indeed! If he actually thought she'd—he could not possibly think she—

Why, she very much doubted James Marbury had ever been in a *complication* with a woman in his life. What woman would be good enough for him? The man expected perfection in every single person he met.

She could only hope that come the morrow, James Marbury would be long gone from Faires. She had had such wretched luck this past year. Couldn't she ask just this *one* thing? Just this one?

For it wasn't only that James Marbury was infuriatingly superior that she wanted him gone. It was also the memory of the way his body, when it was close to hers, made her feel—as hot as if she had a fever, and breathless as if she'd just run a mile. It was not to be borne that a man could be so exasperating on the one hand, and so very attractive on the other!

Sadly for Emma, James had no intention whatsoever

of leaving Faires. Not before he'd seen that his cousin's widow had been adequately provided for, anyway.

But really, he thought. Really, it was hard work indeed, trying to look after someone who was so very insistent that she needed no such looking after.

Sighing, James turned to make sure the fire didn't need any more stoking. It wouldn't do at all for Louise to start complaining in a few hours because she was cold. He'd had his rest disturbed quite enough by this stray bovine. He had a long day ahead of him.

He still had a baron to kill, after all.

Chapter Fourteen

~

Castle MacCreigh was plainly visible from the village of Faires on a clear day. And the morning having dawned every bit as clear and as warm as the day before had been cold and wet, Castle MacCreigh made a vivid sight indeed, towering above the small village, its turrets seeming to skim the robin's-egg blue sky. Faires was a very different place in fair weather than in foul. James, observing it through the diamond-paned windows of Emma's cottage, could only marvel at the sudden lushness the rains had brought to the new spring grass, so richly dotted with wildflowers and flocks of white-fleeced sheep.

And yet, fairy-tale kingdom though it looked, there was nothing very picturesque about the steep climb to the top of the cliff upon which Castle MacCreigh was situated . . . as James found out for himself, all too soon.

Still, the day had begun promisingly enough. He'd

wakened to bright sunshine streaming through the windows of Emma's cottage, and the sound of Emma herself, humming as she pottered around her room. It was, James felt, one of the most pleasant wakings he'd ever experienced in his life.

At least until he felt a strange sensation on his toes, and glanced down the length of his body to see Louise gently nosing the soles of his feet.

Not a propitious way to start the day. And when, a short time later, James threw open the door to steer Louise back into the yard, he found Cletus MacEwan standing there with a rooster for some reason tucked beneath his arm, he knew that his day would only get worse. Although it was not, perhaps, as bad for him as it was for Cletus. The expression on the young man's face when he saw James there had been something to behold.

The fact that his cow had spent the night in the cottage's front room was nothing in comparison to the fact that James had spent the night there as well, apparently, since MacEwan couldn't do anything but stare at him, and not at his cow, for a full five minutes. Even when Emma came bustling out from her room to explain to him gently that James had stayed upon the settle, and only because of the lateness of the hour, MacEwan still stared, one hand holding limply to Louise's halter, the other continuing to clutch the sorry-looking bird. James almost felt a little sorry for the man . . . but not much. He had not forgotten the look on Emma's face the night before, when he'd found her—quite heedless of his presence in her fear—with that heavy rifle in her arms. He had known then that, for her all protestations otherwise, she suspected as he did that MacCreigh might do something rash, and had been just as convinced that it was the baron out there in the rain, trying to find a way to break into her cottage. It irked James that MacEwan, while seeming to feel possessive toward Mrs. Chesterton, had taken no real steps whatsoever to ensure her safety.

His irritation with the man, however, did not stop James from inquiring in a low voice, when Emma had left the room to fetch her cloak and bonnet, if MacEwan would act as his second that afternoon.

"Your *what?*" had been the predictable reply.

James sighed. He had given the matter considerable thought, and had come to the conclusion that, since the village of Faires lacked a physician, his valet would have to act as surgeon during his duel with Geoffrey Bain. This was no great hardship for Roberts, who had attended a good many duels in his master's company and was well used to tying off wounds and stanching blood.

But it meant, of course, that James needed another man to act as his second. The yeoman clearly shared James's dislike of the baron, and James had always found it expedient to call his enemy's enemy his friend.

To MacEwan's confused inquiry, James said only, while Emma was out of earshot, "Nothing. Show up at the Puffin Inn at precisely half eleven, then go with me to Castle MacCreigh, and I shall give you a guinea."

That MacEwan apparently understood, since with a wide and happy smile, his first since having arrived and seen his precious Mrs. Chesterton in the presence of a man he'd been struck by the day before, he said, quite firmly, "Aye, me lord!"

Emma, for her part, had been behaving in a flustered and embarrassed manner all morning, ever since she'd seen he was awake. He knew she resented him, of course—and that after what he'd confessed to her that night, about his true reason for coming to Faires, her resentment was likely greater than ever.

And he supposed he could understand it. A young widow was bound to be sensitive about her husband's final resting place. Emma had loved Stuart, and would necessarily want to remain near him, even in death.

And yet . . .

And yet there was a part of James that couldn't quite believe that this was the reason behind her refusal to allow him to bring Stuart home to Denham Abbey. Emma was attached to Faires, that much was obvious. But it seemed to him to be the living residents of Faires, the schoolchildren, to whom she was so devoted, not the memory of her dearly departed husband. He could not say exactly what made him feel this way. It was only a perception. . . .

But there it was.

It nagged at him all through the carriage ride back into town—he'd instructed Samuel Murphy to pick him up at eight in the morning, and the driver, with his hearse, arrived promptly. It did not help, of course, that Emma sat, silent and thoughtful, beside him during the trip, having accepted his offer of a ride to her schoolhouse. James was uncertain whether it was the admission about his true reason for being in Faires or merely his continued presence that most irked her. It wasn't until Murphy pulled up in front of the lighthouse—to which, for the second time in two days, she'd been conveyed by carriage, a fact of which her students took note, watching round-eyed as James handed her down and elbowing one another meaningfully—that she asked, without looking at him, "And will it be today, then, that you shall be returning to the mainland, Lord Denham?" and he had his answer.

James had looked down at her, admiring the way the wind from the sea—as gently warm today as it had been fiercely cold the day before—brought out the pink in her cheeks and bow-shaped mouth, and said with grave politeness, "I haven't yet decided. I shall see how the day progresses," only to see the corners of that mouth droop with disappointment.

"Oh," was all Emma said, and then, with an effort at cheerfulness, she managed a tremulous smile, and added, "Well, you know where to find me, then. Good morning."

She had gone into the lighthouse with the breeze snatching loose curls out from beneath her bonnet, sending them bouncing about her face.

James had chosen to breakfast at the inn, a wise decision, he thought, since Mrs. MacTavish's sausages could not be rivaled even by his own cook back in London. As Emma had predicted, Mrs. MacTavish commented on the fact that she had stopped by his room with a bed warmer the night before, only to find the chamber unoccupied.

The woman was too conscious of his rank, however, to come right out and ask where he'd been. James, wiping his mouth on a napkin, did not give her an explanation, saying merely that he appreciated the gesture, and that a bed warmer was a welcome thing on a rainy night. Then he went upstairs to find that Roberts had already prepared a hot bath in anticipation of his lordship's return. Informed of the pending duel, the valet's calm reaction was typical. He inquired merely, "Pistols or blades, my lord?"

James, shedding his cravat, which he'd tied too tightly in his valet's absence back at the cottage, grumbled that the baron hadn't yet chosen a weapon, and that he'd best bring them all, to be on the safe side. This Roberts understood, and he packed the pistols neatly in their leather case, and sheathed the sword after oiling it until it gleamed.

At precisely half after eleven, James emerged from the Puffin Inn to find Cletus MacEwan waiting for him. When James informed him that they were taking Murphy's brougham to Castle MacCreigh, not walking, MacEwan seemed excessively amused, but it wasn't until they were struggling up the steep hill to the castle that James understood why. The road to Castle Mac-Creigh was very nearly as impassable as the trail to Emma's cottage, with its pits and ruts. At several points, they were forced to get out and walk alongside the carriage, since Murphy's horses could not find their footing on the incline with their weight to pull. When this happened, MacEwan trudged happily alongside the conveyance, nimble as a mountain goat, while James and his valet labored some yards behind, unused to such muddy, strenuous climbing.

Eventually, however, they made it to the portcullis that guarded the dilapidated structure's entrance. Castle MacCreigh was in fact a real castle, with actual turrets, battlements, and, James supposed, even a dungeon. Made of crumbling stone by some ancient relative of the current baron, it was a dark and hideous fortress, and James imagined its occupants must be very uncomfortable indeed. It wasn't any wonder that the baron was so anxious to marry Emma; he must surely have longed to use the money left to her to renovate.

Drawing his horses beneath the deep shade of the portcullis, Murphy pulled back the sliding trapdoor and peered down at James.

"Well," he said, "I reckon someone ought to knock."

"I'll go, my lord," Roberts said, rising from his seat and attempting to climb out of the brougham. This necessitated maneuvering around MacEwan's enormous legs, an act that proved easier said than done.

"Never mind." James exhaled gustily. *"I'll* do it."

He let himself out of the carriage and approached the door to Castle MacCreigh, a massive affair of thick dark wood and metal rivets. James looked around for some kind of bell to pull and found none. He was lifting a gloved fist to give the portal a thump when it swung open as if of its own accord.

"Lord Denham?" asked a lilting, and definitely female, voice.

James squinted. His eyes, accustomed to the strong sunlight outdoors, were having trouble discerning the speaker. All he saw was a hallway that, except for the glow of a single candle flame, was perfectly dark. Then he noticed that the candle was held by a woman. He could not tell what sort of woman, young or old, thin or fat, servant or lady. It was simply too dim to distinguish that much.

"Won't you come in?" the lilting voice inquired, and there was a hint of honeyed laughter that suggested to James, who knew about such things, that the speaker was not only young but attractive and not unwilling to be admired. "We've been expecting you."

James cleared his throat. This was not at all what *he'd* been expecting. "Um," he said. "I'm not alone—"

"Oh?" The voice became decidedly less honeyed. "You didn't bring Mrs. Chesterton with you, did you?"

Confused, James said, "No, no, my valet, Roberts, who has some experience as a surgeon, and my second, Cletus MacEwan. Roberts? Mr. MacEwan?" he called, and the men obediently clambered down from the brougham, the sudden lifting of MacEwan's great weight causing the carriage to rise nearly a foot off its springs.

The woman with the candle laughed again, this time in relief.

"Oh, Mr. MacEwan, what a delight," she cried, as if she meant it. "Come in, come in, all of you. You, too, Mr. Murphy. Come in and warm yourself. Maura's just laid a kettle on down in the kitchens."

James, feeling dazed, followed the dancing candle flame down a maze of dark corridors, until suddenly he found himself in an unexpectedly bright great hall. Sunlight streamed through narrow arched windows, carved high into either wall, just beneath a vaulted ceiling, from the beams of which hung a few tattered banners depicting the MacCreigh family crest, a gold goat on a green background. The furniture inside the hall was sparse and almost randomly arranged, except for a long table, laid for lunch, James saw, and set as close to an eight-foot-wide fireplace as it could be without being actually *in* the fire.

Now he could see clearly the woman who was guiding him, and he was pleased to note that he'd been correct in his assumption that she was young and attractive. She was red-haired rather than blond, and built on a larger scale than Emma, but her figure was nevertheless pleasing, being full and womanly, though she was actually, James thought, still only just past girlhood, close to Emma's age in fact, maybe eighteen or nineteen.

"Ah," she said, after she'd blown out the flame on the candle she'd been clutching and set the tallow down upon an ancient sideboard. "That's much better. Now I can see you properly." Her gaze roamed up and down James appraisingly, and he saw approval in her soft eyes, eyes as blue as the sky outdoors, and as shiny as the copper-colored hair she wore in a loose curtain about her shoulders.

"You have the look of Mr. Chesterton about you, my lord," the girl said finally. "But only just. You're much bigger than he ever was. Bigger and better-looking, I must say."

James, not a bit taken in by this very obvious attempt at flattery, said in a dry voice, "Thank you. I'm very grateful, for both the compliment and the hospitality. May I ask to whom I'm obliged for both?"

The girl, who was very fetchingly garbed in a white muslin dress that was both too young for her and too light for the season, made a pretty curtsy. "The Honorable Miss Fiona Bain, my lord. And I'm very honored that you should call upon us here in our lonesome hideaway."

James gritted his teeth. Damn it! MacCreigh's sister. He should have known. This simply would not do, this fraternizing with the enemy and his family. Hadn't her brother told her that James had come for the express purpose of killing him? Or maybe he had, and that was at the root of the girl's flattery. Either way, the situation was not to James's liking.

Not so with his companions, however. Murphy and MacEwan had both stumbled in behind him, their hats in their hands, their jaws agape at their surroundings. Here, where James saw only decay, they clearly saw grandeur, a grandeur unparalleled by anything else they'd ever seen in their lives.

"Gor," breathed MacEwan, as he gazed at the ragged banners overhead, which swayed slightly in the wind that whistled through the drafty hall. "It's e'en bigger'n the *church*."

"An' this is only the room what they *eat* in," Murphy agreed worshipfully. Both men stood with their heads back, their mouths ajar, looking up.

Fearful that his second was quickly warming to the enemy, James turned away from them and asked Fiona Bain, "Where might I find your brother, madam? I've an appointment with him that I shouldn't like to break—"

"Ah, Denham, my good man! What a delight."

The voice rang out clearly in the enormous room, echoing loudly from some point just before the fire, where, James saw, Geoffrey Bain had suddenly risen from a high-backed chair. He was dressed, as usual, in black, and held a glass of amber liquid in one hand, which he raised in James's direction.

"Join me, join me, my lord," he cried, urging James toward him with his free hand. "Get out of the draft. It's terribly damp and chilly in here, I know, after last night's rains. That's why I had the table set so near the fire. Come, come, we don't stand on ceremony here at home."

Furious, James glanced at the baron's sister. She was smiling prettily at him, either oblivious to the true reason he'd come or cunningly hiding that knowledge. Knowing her brother to be filled with similar conniving tricks, James assumed she was feigning ignorance—especially when she stepped forward and, taking his arm, began guiding him toward the fire, one pert young breast pressed very forwardly against his biceps.

"Come, Lord Denham," she said excitedly. "It's so very rare that we get visitors here at Castle MacCreigh. We used to entertain your cousin and his wife quite a bit, back when . . . well, my brother's fiancée was still with us, and of course before Mr. Chesterton died so tragically. But now we hardly see anyone at all. I can't wait for you to try Maura's mushroom soup. It's her own family recipe. She started making it last night, when Geoffrey told us he'd invited you. She's so excited to try it out on someone new. I'm so sorry Mrs. Chesterton couldn't come to luncheon as well." Her regret sounded perfectly false to James. "But then, she's got her little school to keep, hasn't she?"

By the time they'd reached her brother, James's ire

was at its peak. Imagine, a grown man hiding behind the skirts of a young girl! Well, he didn't know why he was surprised. After all, a man who thought nothing of terrorizing one woman shouldn't feel any compunction at all about seeking protection from another.

MacCreigh, James saw, when he was close enough, was drinking whiskey. His own family recipe, James didn't doubt.

"Ah, Denham," the baron said, grinning broadly. "So glad you made it. Road didn't trouble you too much, I hope? Sometimes after a rainfall like yesterday's the mud's so deep, we don't see a caller for weeks, do we, Fiona? You've met my sister Fiona, haven't you, Denham? Well, what can I get you? Whiskey? Or are you more for port?"

James could overlook the baron's familiarity. He could even ignore the fact that MacCreigh was addressing him as a friend, which he most definitely was *not*. What he could not accept, however, was the fact that the baron looked in no way ready to fight. There was not a pistol box or sword in sight, and unless the baron's sister was acting as his second, no one to perform that service for him! James, mightily irritated, growled, "I believe we had an engagement for noon, sir."

"Yes, yes," MacCreigh said, waving a hand dismissively. "Luncheon will be served anon. But I always enjoy a little whiskey before a meal. Cleanses the palate, so to speak. Do have some."

"Our engagement," James said, in a voice that he hoped was low enough not to reach the hearing of the baron's sister, "was not for luncheon, and you know it,

MacCreigh. Now be a man, and fetch your sword. I intend to kill you and be off again. I have luncheon waiting for me down at the inn."

"Ah, a luncheon prepared by Mrs. MacTavish." MacCreigh nodded appreciatively. "I can certainly see where you'd prefer her cooking to anything you're likely to find here. Though our Maura does try her best, poor thing. But what's this about killing me?" The baron did not lower his voice at all. In fact, he spoke loudly, with a good deal of bravado. "I'm afraid I haven't the slightest idea what you're talking about."

James glared at the younger man. "You know perfectly well what I'm talking about," he said, icily. "I called you out yesterday evening, when I found you attempting to compromise my cousin's widow."

"Compromise her?" MacCreigh laughed outright. "Oh, come. I was merely trying to *persuade* her, not *compromise* her."

"That's not what it looked like to me," James declared. "It looked to me like you were trying to force yourself upon her. Now, you'll fetch your sword and face me like a man, or by God, I'll—"

"You'll what?" MacCreigh inquired, tiredly. "Really, this is stupid, Denham. Surely we can settle this without one or the other of us having to lose life or limb."

"The only way we could do that," James asserted, "would be if you give me your word as a gentleman that you won't go near Mrs. Chesterton again." Although of course he didn't believe for a moment that MacCreigh would keep any promise of the sort.

MacCreigh made a face. "Now, look, Denham. I

can't do that, and you know it. We're talking about ten thousand pounds, here!"

"We're talking," James shouted furiously, all patience gone, "about my cousin's wife!"

"Your cousin's widow, you mean." MacCreigh drained his whiskey glass and set it down upon the wooden mantel. "And as long as she remains unattached, she's fair game for any man, Denham. You're just going to have to get used to it. The only hope you have of putting a stop to it, you know," he said, with a shrug, "would be to marry her yourself. As if she'd have *you!*"

James did not know how much MacCreigh knew about his relationship with Emma. He did not know what Stuart might have told him—after all, it appeared that the two men had once been friends, if what the man's sister had said about their frequently entertaining Stuart and his wife was true.

Perhaps the baron meant only that Emma, known for her idealism and good works, would hardly be likely to align herself with a man of his rather more, er, practical principles.

But it didn't really matter, in the end, just what Mac-Creigh meant by the remark. What mattered was his tone, the sneer in his voice, the derisive expression on his face. Those were what provoked James into drawing back a fist and sending it, with all the force he had, into the baron's face.

The baron, who had clearly not been expecting the blow, fell backward into the table. Plates and cutlery flew, chairs tipped over, and feminine screams pierced the air. MacCreigh lay in a tangled jumble of table legs and overturned soup bowls. James, seeing that he was dazed but still conscious, had stepped toward the baron to deliver another punch when an all-too-familiar voice cried out in horror, "Stop, James, stop!"

It was only then that James realized that the baron's sister was not the only lady in the room.

Chapter Fifteen

~~~

*E*mma could not believe her eyes.

She had been skeptical when Mrs. MacTavish had interrupted her history lesson with the news that the earl of Denham was headed toward Castle MacCreigh with the intention of killing the baron. Why on earth, she'd asked out loud, would Lord Denham do something so absurd? She was quite aware that he didn't like the baron, but *kill* him? Whatever for? Really, the idea was simply too ridiculous.

But when Mrs. MacTavish pulled her aside, out of the children's earshot, and imparted the details of the matter—that the earl's valet, whom he'd taken with him, had been carrying both a sword and pistol case; that James had asked for a prepared lunch at one o'clock, a clear indication that he had not been invited to dine at the castle; and that, of all people, he'd been joined by Cletus MacEwan—well, Emma had to admit it certainly sounded suspicious.

Still, she hadn't been *completely* convinced. She wasn't

completely convinced there was any real need to worry until she'd gone—reluctantly—with Mrs. MacTavish to address her fears to the lord chief justice. Judge Reardon, who'd been enjoying a break in the property dispute trial he'd been hearing in the smithy's shop, listened to them gravely; then, with a tired sigh, he set aside his bowl of haggis and reached for his hat. That was when Emma began to feel truly afraid. Judge Reardon would *never* allow a meal to be interrupted. . . .

Not unless someone's life was in peril.

And now, standing in the doorway to Castle Mac-Creigh's great hall, Emma saw more than enough to convince her that Mrs. MacTavish's fears had been perfectly well founded. The baron's life *was* in jeopardy. James had delivered him a blow stronger even than the one he'd dealt Cletus MacEwan the day before— stronger even than the one he'd dealt Stuart, that day back in Lady Denham's drawing room!

And yet he stood there so calmly, looking at them, waving his smarting knuckles in the air.

"Oh," James said when his gaze fell upon Emma, standing between Judge Reardon and Mrs. MacTavish's son Sean, who'd driven her—along with his mother and the lord chief justice—to the castle in his delivery wagon. "Hullo there, Emma."

Emma brought her hand down from her mouth. She was completely flabbergasted. Never, in all the time she had known him, had she ever seen James Marbury be-have so bizarrely. Why, ever since he'd set foot in Faires, it seemed, he'd been completely unlike himself, extending invitations to widows to come live with him, volunteering to wash dishes, tossing sovereigns to little boys. . . .

And now here he was, defending her honor for the second time in two days! Lord Denham, who'd always seemed to consider Emma nothing more than the sweet little girl from next door. Why, he was almost behaving as if he recognized the fact that she was actually a full-grown woman now.

It was all simply too astonishing to be believed.

"Well, Mrs. MacTavish," Judge Reardon drawled laconically. "It looks as if your suspicions were correct. There *does* appear to be a duel under way here in Castle MacCreigh, though dueling is, in fact, illegal." He made a tisk-tisking sound with his tongue. "And amongst gentlemen of rank! I am astonished. *Quite* astonished. What have you got to say for yourself, Lord Denham, eh?"

James regarded the judge coldly. "Only this," he said. "That if it weren't for your ridiculous ruling that Mrs. Chesterton couldn't collect the money due her until she was married, none of this would have happened."

"Oh-ho," the judge said, seemingly quite unperturbed by the accusation. "So that's what you two are about." He had crossed the room as he spoke, and then, leaning over to right an overturned chair, sat down on it and said, with a wave of his hand, "Well, carry on, then, carry on. May the best man win, and all that."

Emma sucked in her breath. *"What?"*

Judge Reardon glanced in her direction. "I *am* sorry, Mrs. Chesterton," he said, rising hastily. "I ought to have offered this seat to you. Take it, take it, by all means."

Emma was convinced she'd walked into a room full of madmen. "No," she said, shaking her head. "Your Honor, you cannot possibly allow this. They'll kill one another!"

"They might," Judge Reardon agreed, as he sank back down onto the chair. "They might indeed."

"But you can't let them!" Emma hurried forward until she stood between the two gentlemen brawlers, who were both observing her interestedly, James from where he stood, poised above the baron, and Geoffrey Bain from where he lay collapsed against the table. "This is absurd! You cannot allow it. They must be stopped!"

The lord chief justice drew a pouch full of tobacco from his waistcoat pocket and began thoughtfully to stuff his pipe. "That may well be, my dear," he observed, kindly, "but I'm not going to try it. I have found, in my years upon the bench, that it is quite useless to keep one man from trying to kill another. If a man is really intent upon murder, nothing and no one can stop him."

Emma stared for several seconds at the portly judge, uncertain she had heard him correctly. Then, seeing the calmness with which he lit his pipe, she burst out, "Why on earth did you agree to come up here with me, if not to stop them?"

Justice Reardon raised his eyebrows at her in surprise. "Why, to watch the fight, of course. My money's on the earl. How about you, MacTavish?"

Sean MacTavish, still standing in the doorway to the great hall, rubbed his chin thoughtfully. "I'm for the baron," he said, finally. "He's smaller, but I expect he'll fight dirty to make up fer it."

Emma shook her head. This was simply too much. Whirling toward the earl, she said, "Honestly, James, you must stop this. Whatever can you think you're accomplishing?"

James blinked at her uncomprehendingly. "What do I think I'm accomplishing?" he echoed in disbelief. "Emma, this man insulted and threatened you. I have every intention of teaching him a sound lesson for it. Now be a good girl, and go back down to the village." Scissoring an aggrieved look at the judge, he muttered, "I don't know what anybody was thinking in the first place, bringing you up here. If you ask me, this place is populated entirely by madmen." Then, seeing that Emma hadn't moved, he said, more loudly, "Step aside, Emma. I haven't time for this foolishness. You're only prolonging the inevitable."

"Inevitable? Now see here." The baron rose up onto his elbows and glared at James from where he lay amidst the broken dishware. "I'm tired of these assumptions that I'm going to lose this fight. And by the by, I never insulted her. I might have threatened her, yes. But I never insulted her."

James regarded the fallen man dispassionately. "For someone of your ilk even to speak to her is an insult."

"My ilk?" the baron echoed. "Say, what do you mean by that?"

"I think you know," James said, tersely. "Considering what everyone back in the village says about your fiancée."

Geoffrey Bain's mouth opened and shut like a salmon. "Clara? Is that who you're jawing about?"

"You have another fiancée?" James inquired, mildly.

"Dammit," the baron said, launching himself from the tabletop with a kick of his long legs. "How many times do I have to say it? I didn't kill Clara!"

Grasping Emma's shoulders, James moved her aside before striding forward to meet the rushing baron head on.

Unfortunately, this time Lord MacCreigh was ready for him. Just as James's fist sunk into the baron's ribs, MacCreigh wrapped his hands round the earl's waist and, with a grunt and a well-timed pull, sent the bigger man toppling to the flagstones.

James landed with a crash that caused the Honorable Miss Fiona Bain to squeal and run toward the ruins of what had once been her dinnerware.

"My mother's chafing dish!" she cried, throwing herself into the melée. "Oh, if either of you've dented it, I'll kill you both myself!"

Emma let out a startled shriek as the men then slammed into a sideboard a few feet away. Then, to the judge, she wailed, "Oh, you're mad if you don't try to stop them!"

"Mad?" The judge puffed away at his pipe. "Hardly." Observing that the earl had apparently lost the upper hand, as the baron had wrapped his fingers round the bigger man's throat, the lord chief justice interrupted himself, leaning forward in his chair to bellow, "Denham! I say there, Denham! Use those fists of yours. That's right!" Leaning back again, Justice Reardon said, in a normal tone of voice, "So sorry, my dear. What were you saying?"

Emma flashed the judge a look of anguish. "If you won't do anything to put an end to this," she declared, "then I see I shall have to."

And then, as she'd done a half dozen times a day since taking on the role of schoolmistress, Emma strode out into the fray to separate the squabblers.

It didn't actually dawn upon her that this time, she wasn't dealing with ten-year-old boys, until a ham-sized fist came barreling in her direction just as she'd insinuated her way between the two men. By the time Emma noticed the danger into which she'd put herself, it was too late to step out of the way, or even to duck. And the baron, to whom the fist belonged, had put far too much of his weight behind the blow to stop it mid-flight.

It was fortunate, then, that the reflexes of the earl of Denham were so much faster than an ordinary man's. Because just as Emma, with a faint murmur of dismay, was closing her eyes, anticipating the collision of hard knuckles with her face, James flung out a hand. Seizing the baron's arm, he stopped the projectile just inches before it reached its target, so that instead of feeling the breaking of delicate bones, Emma felt only a breeze, a breeze in which the scents of the two men—James's expensive soap, the baron's more pungent odor of horse—were curiously mingled.

When she dared to open her eyes again, she saw that both the earl and the baron were standing completely still, frozen to the spot. Well, their limbs—raised on either side of her, as if they'd been dancing a quadrille—were frozen, in any case. Both of their chests, however, were heaving with the exertion of their battle. Emma, after uttering a brief, silent prayer of thanks—her first ever expressing gratitude for the existence of James Marbury—said, "Now stop it, both of you. Aren't you ashamed of yourselves? It's all fun and games, isn't it, until someone gets hurt. That's when laughter generally turns to tears."

This was the exact same speech she gave to the little brawlers in her schoolhouse. It was a good speech, a speech her aunt had often delivered to Emma and Penelope when they'd played together too roughly. And it seemed to have the same effect on grown men as it did on little boys and girls—well, the both of them dropped their arms, anyway.

"Now," Emma said severely, "shake hands and apologize." Seeing truculence in the set jaws of both men, she reached out and seized the right hand of either. "Didn't you hear me? *Shake hands and apologize.*"

James, recognizing that Emma meant business, and that she was unlikely to move out of the path of danger until he complied with her wishes, grasped Geoffrey Bain's hand in his and squeezed.

"Sorry," he said, without a hint of remorse in either his voice or mien. "Didn't mean to dent your mother's chafing dish."

"And I," MacCreigh said, with equal insincerity, "didn't mean to strangle you."

"There," Emma said, well satisfied by the way things were turning out. "That's better." Then, flicking a glance at the chief justice, who was still comfortably seated, giving every appearance of a man who was enjoying himself immensely, she said, not without a certain amount of smugness, "You see, Your Honor? Matters like these can be resolved without having to resort to—"

It was at that moment Lord MacCreigh changed his handshake to a head lock, securing the earl's neck against his side with both arms.

"I'm going to marry her, see?" the baron bellowed into James's ear. "And there's nothing you or anybody else can do to stop me."

Emma whirled once more toward the lord chief justice. "You must put a stop to this!" she declared. "Don't you think there's been enough violence and bloodshed in Faires? If you don't do something, they'll kill each other, just as Mr. O'Malley killed my husband!"

"If *I* don't do something?" The judge took his pipe from his lips and, tearing his gaze away from the struggling men, studied her with some perplexity. "It seems to me the only person who can stop them is you, my dear."

"*Me?*" Emma threw him an uncomprehending look. "How can *I* put a stop to it?"

"Well," the judge said, calmly enough. "By marrying one of 'em, of course."

Chapter Sixteen

*Abruptly, the fighting stopped. Two heads came up—one dark, one the color of brightly scoured copper. Both swiveled to peer in Emma's direction.

Emma, uncomfortable under the glare of two such intent gazes, took a quick step backward.

"Oh, no," she said, firmly. "*No.*"

"Right." Cletus strode forward, his chest thrust out. "Because Miz Chesterton's goin' to marry *me*, not one of *those* two."

Judge Reardon observed the younger man's protestation with interest. "You see," he said to Emma, pointing at Cletus with the mouthpiece of his pipe, "you're never going to put a stop to any of this until you make a choice."

"Choice!" Emma cried, hardly able to believe what she was hearing, much less what she was seeing in front of her, which was that both the baron and the earl had released one another, and were straightening up and trying to put their clothing back to rights. "What kind of *choice* do I have? In order to keep a murder from taking place, I have to *marry* someone? This is completely—"

"Marry Geoff," the Honorable Miss Fiona sidled up to Emma to suggest, in a low, sly voice. "He'll do right by you, Emma. I'll see to it."

"Lord MacCreigh!" Mrs. MacTavish, who was no great supporter of the baron's, snorted. "A man what murdered his own fiancée?"

"For the last time," Lord MacCreigh began tiredly, "I did not murder Clara. She ran off with that upstart valet of mine, and I never heard another word from 'er!"

Mrs. MacTavish looked unconvinced. "That's your story, my lord," she said, primly. "And I suggest you stick with it. But in the meantime, Miss Emma, if you're going to be marryin' anyone aside from my Sean here, by rights it ought to be Lord Denham. Or"—here the innkeeper's eyes narrowed meaningfully—"didn't he spend the whole of last night up at your cottage?"

This last was uttered with such dark insinuation that Geoffrey Bain cried, "Emma! That's no' true, is it?"

" 'Course it's true," Mrs. MacTavish said, with no end of satisfaction. "And when the minister finds out, he'll have something to say about it. Mark my words."

Emma blinked at the innkeeper. "You're mad," she said. Then she glanced at James and Lord MacCreigh, both of whom were staring at her with heaving chests and extremely bright gazes, one the color of amber, the other the color of a warm summer sky.

"*All* of you," she added, with sudden heat. "Mad. And if you think I'm going to stand here and let you manipulate me into marrying any one of you, you are sorely mistaken."

Then, with a hammering heart, Emma turned around and attempted to flee from the room. She hadn't the slightest idea where she was going. All she could think of was escaping from the many gazes that were trained upon her . . . one of which was particularly unsettling, though Emma could not for the life of her explain why. After all, it belonged to the earl of Denham, who, though she was beginning to think she did not quite hate him as much as she once had (how could she, remembering that moment the night before when he'd held her, and how her body—treacherous thing that it was—had reacted to his touch?), was still the man who had tried, as best he could, to keep her from the one she loved . . . or had thought she'd loved, anyway?

So it was all the more alarming when, just as she was about to find safety by ducking through a nearby door, she felt a firm hand upon her arm and heard an all-too-familiar voice say, with some urgency, "Emma. Wait."

Before she could utter a word of protest, James was pulling her not back into the room she'd been fleeing, but through the very doorway she'd been heading for.

"My lord," she said, with a futile attempt to dig her heels into the flagstones beneath them. It didn't much matter though, since he merely slipped an arm around her waist and lifted her the last few feet through the doorway. Still, she tried to hold onto what dignity she could, even as he kicked the door closed behind them and propped her up against a nearby wall with an arm on either side of her to keep her from escaping again. "I am not at all interested in discussing—"

"Shut up a minute, Emma," James said tersely, "and listen to me."

She did shut up, but not out of any desire to oblige him. She shut up because she was stunned he'd been so short with her. What had happened, she wondered, to the smoothly sardonic earl of Denham? He had never in his life spoken to her like this before. Always, always he had been the levelheaded one, ever ready to help her with her problems and wipe away her tears. Now here he was, even more agitated than she was! It was quite a shock.

"Reardon's right," he said, speaking rapidly in that deep, gravelly voice of his. Because of his proximity, Emma was given all too close a glimpse of the damage the baron had done to James's face: there was a shallow cut in one dark eyebrow, and one side of his jaw had already started to purple. Was this, she could not help wondering, the same man who, back in London all those months ago, she'd once witnessed send his soup back because it wasn't hot enough to suit his taste?

"This is an intolerable situation, Emma," he said. "But there is a perfectly obvious solution to it—I ought to have seen it at once—that will, if you'll agree to it, satisfy everyone."

Emma opened her mouth to declare that it certainly wouldn't satisfy her. Though she wasn't about to admit as much to James—the last thing she ever wanted to let him know was that he'd been right to try to stop her from marrying Stuart, that the match had been a disaster almost from the start—she did intend to let him know that she'd tried marriage once, and once had been enough, thank you very much.

Only she never got a chance to utter a sound, since James went right on.

"Think about it, Emma," he said in a low, urgent voice. "You'll get your money, and once you have it, you can do whatever you like with it. Give it to all the orphans and mission societies you care to. Just keep enough of it to live on, is all I ask. I can invest a percentage of it for you, if you like. You can live off the interest. At least that way it won't all go for a new roof on somebody's ancestral home—"

As if on cue, the door latch rattled, and Lord MacCreigh's voice called through the thickly paneled door, "Emma? Are you—"

In a flash, James had flung the bolt into place, resulting in a befuddled, "What the—" from the far side of the door. "Who locked this?" Lord MacCreigh cried. "Denham? Was it you? Open the door."

Emma, meanwhile, could only stare up at James, completely bewildered. She *thought* she'd heard him right, but she couldn't quite believe her own ears. "My lord," she said, worriedly. "Are you . . . did you just . . . ?"

"Don't you see, Emma?" James's amber-eyed gaze was appealing. "The money will leave you quite well taken care of for years and years to come, even if you do give half of it away, as I know you will. But if you marry one of them"—his gaze slid toward the door, upon which the baron, having apparently been joined by Cletus, now banged with energy—"they'll use the money for their own purposes. You wouldn't have to worry about that with me, of course, because I haven't any need of your money."

Now Emma was sure she had heard him correctly. But she could not, for the life of her, credit it. The earl of Denham—her husband's cousin—was now asking her to *marry* him?

Something of her astonishment must have shown on her face, since the earl added, after a beat, "We can, of course, have the marriage dissolved once you've received the money, if you like. That oughtn't to be a problem."

Now Emma had heard everything.

"*Divorce?*" she burst out. She wasn't at all certain which shocked her more: the fact that the earl of Denham had just asked her to marry him, or the fact that he had also offered, in almost the same breath, to divorce her afterward.

"Not divorce, Emma," he explained. "An annulment, stating that the marriage never took place at all. We wouldn't apply for it, of course, until after you've received the money."

But this explanation only served to astonish Emma even more. It wasn't only that the earl seemed so perfectly willing to allow his good name—of which he had every reason to be extremely proud—and fine reputation to be besmirched by the taint of a failed marriage. It was the casual, offhand way in which he seemed to consider the entire arrangement—as if it were just another one of his business deals!

Not, Emma told herself, that there was any reason for him to think of it as anything more. She certainly didn't fancy that the earl of Denham was in love with

her. James would never, in a million years, be romantically interested in a girl like her—a penniless orphan
whose tears he'd mopped up when she was little; an un-
titled nobody who'd had to depend all her life on the
kindness of her wealthy relations for her keep. The earl
of Denham only aligned himself with the finest, and
richest, beauties in London—all of whom, Emma had
noticed, back in 'thirty-two, had possessed shining
straight hair, not tightly curled locks like her own.

And he would certainly never purposefully involve
himself romantically with the impoverished widow of
his own cousin. Never!

But if he weren't in love with her, then—

"Why?" Emma asked, simply. She was, it had to be
admitted, too stunned at this point to formulate more
than one-word sentences.

"Why what?" James asked.

"Why—" Emma was extremely conscious, just at that
moment, of his closeness, of his imposing maleness. He
was a very large man—so much larger than Stuart had
been—and beside him, she felt insignificant as dander.

Still, she screwed up her courage and demanded,
"Why would you do something like this?"

For me, she'd meant to add, but had run out of
breath at the last minute. Something about his closeness, much as it had the night before, was making her
feel oddly light-headed. She told herself it was only because it had been so long since she'd last stood this
close to a man—a man who bathed with any regularity,
that is. It could not, she knew, be anything more than
that. Because, handsome as he was, she was not attracted to the earl of Denham. She could not afford to

be. There was too much she couldn't tell him, too much she could never let him know, for her to allow herself to feel anything but the remotest of feelings for him.

"Why, Emma," he said now, looking down at her with some surprise. "Why wouldn't I? You're family, after all. It's my duty to look after you."

"Duty?" She nearly choked on the word. Abruptly, her eyes had filled with tears. She couldn't say why, precisely. Perhaps it was the words, those same words he'd uttered the night before . . . that she was family. Family! That was certainly a word she had not often heard uttered in her presence. Family? She had no family now.

"Oh," she said. "I think you are going well beyond your *duty*, my lord, marrying me. It's hardly your *duty* to sully your perfectly good reputation with an annulment on my account. Doing so is going to significantly reduce your own marital prospects, later on."

James's lips twitched. "I'm not particularly worried about that," he said, with a smile that she thought looked wry. "I wouldn't trouble yourself on my account, if I were you."

She shook her head, truly perplexed. She still could not imagine what his motivation could be. To marry her without expecting a percentage of her inheritance, then go through the expense and trouble of an annulment, all for nothing—it made no sense, particularly considering what an excellent business sense James was purported to have. Why on earth would he do such a thing?

Then, as if he'd read her mind, James said gently, "Emma. I once did you a very great wrong. Won't you let me try to right it now?"

As he'd spoken, he'd lifted one of her hands in his own. That was all he did. Merely lifted her hand and held it there, between them. No doubt he felt how different her hand was now than it had been a year earlier, when he'd occasionally taken it to lead her in a quadrille. Now that hand was covered with calluses, hardened from doing her own laundry in ice-cold water sprinkled with lye. She had not danced a quadrille in months and months.

And yet if he noted a difference, he said nothing about it, just stood there, holding her hand and gazing down at her with those unreadable, unsettlingly golden eyes, oblivious to the shouts and thumps upon the door not two feet away from them.

And then, quite suddenly, the dizziness Emma had been feeling stopped. She was no longer puzzled or troubled. She understood exactly what the earl was doing. It was still astonishing—so astonishing that she was not quite sure she believed it. But there it was, all the same:

The earl of Denham was apologizing.

No, really. Not like the apology he'd tossed off the day before in front of the schoolhouse. This was different. This time he was well and truly apologizing for what he'd done to her—and to Stuart—a year earlier.

It was incredible, but it was true.

And it was proof that—contrary to what James himself had always asserted, back when she'd used to insist that through patience and education, thieves and drunkards might one day be reformed—men really could change.

The discovery was so amazing that for a moment,

Emma no longer heard Cletus's and the baron's thumps upon the door. She did not feel the damp chill that permeated Castle MacCreigh's walls. She was aware only of James, of his fingers on hers, of the clean smell of his shirtfront and the heat—oh yes, she could feel it again, just as she had the night before—emanating from him.

For just a few seconds, she was afraid. Really, truly afraid, though she could not think why she should be. It was true that the earl was an intimidating figure of a man, being so impressively large, and filled with good health and vigor. Why should that alarm her?

She didn't know. And she told herself she was being ridiculous. James was trying, at long last, to make amends for what he'd done. And hadn't Stuart always instructed her—along with the rest of his clergy—to forgive those who trespassed against them? That to err is human, to forgive divine? To turn the other cheek?

It would, she thought, be what Stuart would want her to do. And she owed his memory that much, at least.

How much of her decision was due to a feeling that she owed Stuart, and how much to the memory of that iron-hard thigh she'd felt the night before, pressed so insistently between her legs, Emma could not say. She told herself it was the former. Of *course* it was the former. She could not even believe she'd even *thought* of the latter. . . .

Pushing the memory of that thigh firmly from her mind, she said, tightening her fingers around his, "All right, James. I will marry you."

Chapter Seventeen

*J*ames, standing in front of Lord Chief Justice Reardon, could not quite believe what was happening . . . had not quite believed anything that had happened in the past half hour or so. For it appeared—it really did appear—that he had asked Emma to marry him.

And that, incredibly, she had said yes.

And yet the proof of this fact was there before him. Or rather, beside him. Because Emma was standing there, looking very serious in her gray dress with its worn lace cuffs, all of her concentration on the man in front of them—Judge Reardon, whose lips were forming the words that made up the civil marriage ceremony.

She did not appear to be aware, as James was, of Lord MacCreigh and his sister, standing to one side of the large, brightly lit hearth, and looking excessively displeased. Nor did she seem to notice Mrs. MacTavish, standing on the other side of that hearth and lifting a kerchief frequently to her streaming eyes as she wept at the highly impersonal words the judge was intoning. Beside her, her son Sean, who'd been named as witness to the ceremony, looked bored, as did Mr. Murphy.

But standing beside these two, Cletus MacEwan looked as if he, too, would have liked to weep. Never had James seen a man with an expression so glum.

And why not? For James didn't doubt that Cletus had genuinely worshiped Emma, and would have made her, if not a good husband, at least a highly devoted one.

Beside Cletus stood Roberts, James's valet. Roberts wore his usual expression of unruffled complacency. Surgeon in a duel, or witness in his wedding, Roberts served James faithfully and without comment, seeming to take his master's sudden decision to marry quite in stride.

How James envied his valet's calm, which he was certain he could never even begin to emulate. How could he? For he was marrying Emma. Emma Van Court, the toast of the season of 'thirty-two, the girl his cousin Stuart, against all sane reason, had won and wed.

And now she was his.

Well, for the time being, anyway. He was still kicking himself for mentioning the word *annulment*. But he had been so certain, looking down into her face, that she would never have conceded to his plan otherwise. For it had to have seemed so extraordinary, his proposing to her as he had. He had been astonished by it himself.

But no sooner had Judge Reardon made his highly

unorthodox suggestion than James had realized that here, at last, was his opportunity. How those words of Judge Reardon's—"By marrying one of 'em, of course"—had thrilled along his veins! As soon as he'd heard them, he'd known exactly what he was going to do. Perhaps he'd known all along. Perhaps that was why he'd been so determined to stay the night in Emma's cottage.

For this was, at last, his chance. His chance to prove to Emma that he was no longer the selfish, hard-hearted man he'd once been. She had changed all that, that day she'd run off with his cousin. She had taught him that all the money in the world couldn't buy him what he really wanted, couldn't stop what he most dreaded from happening. This was his opportunity to make amends for all that he'd done to her—though the truth was, he still believed her marrying Stuart had not been the wisest move.

But he regretted that he'd ever verbalized this belief to her, since it was exactly the sort of thing, he'd realized soon after, that would arouse the sympathy of a girl like Emma: Poor Stuart . . . Why, even his own family doesn't want to see him happy!

But oh, how glad he was that she had so stubbornly refused to follow his advice a year ago. For back then, she never would have agreed to marry him—had he had the sense to ask, which, of course, he had not. How blind he'd been, to both his own feelings and those of everyone around him! He saw that now. Why, back then he'd been everything an idealistic young girl like Emma Van Court despised—a wealthy, self-serving businessman, with no aspirations whatsoever except to accrue more money and see to his own personal gratifications.

But now. Now he was a changed man. A full twelve months of smarting from his own ill judgment had transformed him into the creature standing here before the judge, a man who was ready to do whatever he had to not only to make up for his past behavior, but to show the woman beside him that he truly was reformed.

And yes, he was well aware of his promise to annul the marriage. He had meant it, too. If Emma wanted an annulment, he would see that she got it.

But obtaining an annulment was a long and arduous process. Any number of complications might arise along the way.

For instance, a man's wife might happen to fall in love with him.

It was a gamble, of course. A risky one, too. And yet James felt, every time he glanced in Emma's direction and saw those deep blue, luminous eyes, fringed so thickly with those dark blond lashes, worth it. Well worth it.

And then suddenly Judge Reardon was saying, "Come, my lord. I realize this is all very rushed, and that a man might wish to have more time to consider his options, but I left a delicious luncheon for this and would personally like to return to it some time this week. Now, will you or won't you?"

James realized the all-important question that had just been put to him.

"I will," he said quickly, and glanced down to his right to see Emma looking up at him a little curiously.

After her own barely audible response to the justice's inquiry, Judge Reardon promptly proclaimed them, by the power invested in him, man and wife. Then, as James stood there, marveling at how quickly a person's fortunes could change—how just yesterday he would never have allowed himself even to entertain a fantasy of marrying Emma, only to find himself, today, her lawfully wedded husband—the justice barked, "Well, Denham? Are you just going to stand there? Or are you going to kiss the bride?"

James, startled, turned toward Emma, who'd reacted to the justice's question with a quick step backward.

"That," she said, "won't be necessary."

Mrs. MacTavish, however, having been cheated out of seeing her own son marry the curate's widow, would not allow herself to be cheated out of witnessing the bride and groom's first kiss as a married couple—probably not realizing it would actually be their first, and possibly only, kiss ever.

Accordingly, she laid two hands upon Emma's shoulders and gave her a mighty shove in James's direction.

"Oh, no, you don't," the innkeeper said determinedly. "You've got to seal the bargain."

The force of Mrs. MacTavish's push would have sent Emma, thrown completely off balance by it, sprawling, had not James stepped quickly forward, catching her in his arms before she struck the flagstones.

Lying in his arms, her face just inches from his, Emma looked wide-eyed up at James. And in those eyes, deeply blue as the ocean outside, James read an emotion that simultaneously perplexed and aroused him.

Bashfulness. Emma, for some reason, was feeling shy.

Of him.

"Well, go on, then, my lord," urged Mrs. Mac-Tavish. "Kiss the bride!"

James did not hesitate a second longer. What else could he do? He couldn't *not* kiss her . . . not with Geoffrey Bain looking on with such malice in his gaze. The baron might think he still had a chance.

He bent his head, conscious of that look in Emma's eyes—not to mention the stiffness with which she held her body, clearly unhappy with the position in which she found herself—intending merely to brush his lips against hers.

But something completely unexpected happened when James's mouth touched Emma's . . . something he was certain shocked her a good deal more than it shocked him. For he, at least, had always suspected that kissing Emma would be an experience not soon forgotten.

But Emma, he was quite certain, had never entertained a single thought about kissing him. Why should she? He was, after all, the love of her life's odious elder cousin, who'd set her family against her and once pummeled the face of her fiancé. No, it was unlikely Emma had ever considered what kissing James might be like.

And yet James was certain that he wasn't the only one who felt a quick, inexplicable jolt the moment their mouths touched. Even though he'd been expecting it—a man could not think as long and as often as he had about a certain woman's lips and not feel something of the kind when one day his long-held fantasy came true—it was still a shock, for it was so much stronger than even he'd anticipated.

But for Emma, who'd never in her life imagined a situation where she might find herself kissing the earl of Denham, the tiny spark that occurred when James's mouth met hers was as startling as a bolt from the blue. So startling, in fact, that when the earl raised his head, ending the kiss on a nicely chaste note, as befitted the occasion, Emma, her mouth still tingling from that first contact, promptly put both arms around his neck and brought his face down toward hers again . . .

. . . perfectly oblivious to the gaping faces all around them.

Well, who could blame her? Never in her life had Emma experienced anything remotely like what she felt when James's lips touched hers. Maybe the six months of widowhood she'd just endured had deadened her senses, but she was fairly certain that if Stuart had ever kissed her the way his cousin just had, she'd have remembered it.

And when James's lips met hers once more, she was sure of it. No, no man's lips on hers had felt like *this* before. Not that Emma was so widely experienced, so far as kisses went. She had, after all, only her husband's embraces to compare to. But kissing—among other things—had never been very important to Stuart, who'd frequently pointed out that it wasn't appropriate for a curate's wife to be as interested in physical demonstrations of affection as Emma seemed to be. And so she'd tried very hard to turn her thoughts to higher things.

But now, in the arms of Stuart's own cousin, Emma was discovering that keeping one's mind on higher

things was not at all easy when someone was kissing
you as expertly as James Marbury was kissing her. And
James Marbury *was* an expert kisser. There was no
doubt about that. His lips moved over hers with possessive greed—surprisingly possessive, considering they
had only been married for all of about thirty seconds.

Stuart's kisses had been neither greedy nor possessive. Whenever Stuart had kissed Emma, she'd been
quite sure he'd been thinking of something else—his
next sermon, or the fallacies in William Paleys's argument of the beneficent nature of God, or how he was
going to get the O'Malleys, whose marriage was only
common-law, to wed within the church.

Not so with Stuart's cousin. James kissed Emma as if
all he was thinking about was . . . well, Emma.

It was absurdly gratifying. Especially considering the
fact that for the past six months, very few people had
given much thought about Emma personally, but a
great, great deal of thought to the ten thousand pounds
she was to inherit upon her wedding day. James's interest, in contrast, was very personal indeed. *Entirely* personal. So personal that she could almost swear he
actually felt something for her. . . .

. . . something more than a desire merely to right a
wrong he'd done her. For didn't his arms, as she'd
slipped her own around his neck, tighten, straining her
closer to him? And couldn't she feel, through his
waistcoat and the bodice of her gown, his heart drumming very hard against her own? And wasn't there
something proprietary in his kiss, as if . . . well, almost
as if he felt he *owned* her now? It was perfectly
thrilling to be kissed in such a manner, as if James

were some conquering invader, and Emma his captive bounty. . . .

Not that Emma was ever given to such fanciful imaginings. Only . . . only how different things might have been, if Stuart had ever once kissed her in such a manner!

Emma was torn from these reflections by a sudden and very noisy throat-clearing that brought her, all too abruptly, to an awareness of where she was. Good Lord! Still in Lord MacCreigh's castle, and with all these people staring at her! How easy it had been to lose herself in James's embrace! How lovely to be supported by such strong arms, to feel such warmth radiating all around her, to inhale the clean scent of freshly laundered shirt!

Tearing her lips from James's, Emma blinked guiltily and rapidly in Judge Reardon's direction. He, at least, did not appear to be glowering with rage, as Lord MacCreigh, beside him, was. No, Judge Reardon appeared heartily amused.

"There," he said in a satisfied manner, snapping closed his book of civil ceremony services. "All's well that ends well. A perfect match, I think. She's wanting stability, which he has in spades, while he's wanting a bit of softening, which I have every confidence she'll provide. Now I'll return to my haggis, if it's all the same to you."

James, to Emma's great dismay, righted and released her. But when, to her utter mortification, she wobbled a little unsteadily on her feet, the kiss they'd shared seeming to have sapped every ounce of marrow from her bones, he slipped a steadying arm about her waist.

"Yes," James said, in his deep—and, she noted, completely unruffled—voice. "We've taken advantage of Lord MacCreigh's hospitality long enough—"

"Nonsense!" Fiona Bain's sweetly feminine voice rang out with only a hint of shrillness to indicate that she was suffering from anything like the unhappiness in which her brother, who'd retired to a deep chair by the fire to sulk, seemed enveloped. "You must stay for lunch. A wedding luncheon."

Mrs. MacTavish and her son looked hopeful. Even Cletus seemed to brighten a little from the gloom Emma's wedding had cast him in. A wedding luncheon? Such a treat was rare enough to be looked on with eagerness—particularly if it included a sampling from Lord MacCreigh's wine cellars.

But Emma didn't want to stay for a wedding luncheon, even if it included wine. Because of course this wasn't a *real* wedding . . . though only she and Lord Denham were privy to that particular little secret.

To her relief, James evidently agreed, since he said, "Thank you kindly, Miss Bain, but it will have to be some other time. Roberts, my cloak."

And sooner than Emma would have thought possible, she found herself inside Mr. Murphy's hearse, tucked between her husband—her husband!—and his valet, and headed away from Castle MacCreigh.

Only what a difference from when she'd approached the castle, just an hour earlier, and with fear in her heart, as she'd been expecting to find, upon her arrival, the scene of a murder. It was with an entirely different kind of anxiety that she descended King's Crag. This time, it was not a murder she feared, but something much less tangible.

She began to suspect the true nature of her anxiety, however, when they reached the village, and James called up to Mr. Murphy, "To Lady Denham's cottage, if you please."

Lady Denham? Was she here, too, then? Emma could not imagine what James's mother could possibly be doing in Faires. An elegant woman with a keen sense of style, the Dowager Lady Denham graced only the finest addresses, and was just about the last person Emma would ever expect to see in this part of the country.

It was only when Mr. Murphy directed his horses to make the turn toward her own cottage that Emma realized with a start that James hadn't been referring to his mother at all, but to her. *She* was Lady Denham . . . the new Lady Denham, anyway.

And somehow that, as neither the wedding ceremony she had just been through or the senses-rattling kiss that followed it, jolted her into the realization of what she'd just done.

Married the earl of Denham. She had *married* the earl of Denham. Never mind that it was a business arrangement only. Never mind that he had only done it to assuage the guilt he felt over the way he'd treated her and Stuart. She was married to the earl of Denham, a man she'd once been convinced had no heart—and certainly no conscience—to speak of.

Good Lord. What had she done?

Her heart in her throat, Emma leaned forward and cried, "Mr. Murphy! Mr. Murphy! Stop here, please."

James looked down at her as if she were mad. Well, and why not? She obviously was mad, if she'd ever thought, even for a second, that marrying him might not be such a bad idea.

"Emma," he said, as she gathered up her reticule and prepared to climb over Roberts—James seemed too imposing a figure to attempt to pass—to get to the door. "Are you all right?"

"Quite well, my lord," came Emma's terse reply. "Only I think I've left the children long enough. I really must get back to them." With murmured apologies, Emma managed to squeeze past her husband's—husband! Oh, Lord!—startled valet, and threw herself at the carriage door. It burst open, releasing her at last into the sunshine.

And away from James Marbury's amber eyes.

Hopping down from the hearse unaided, Emma turned back to look up at the two men still inside it.

"Thank you very much for marrying me, my lord," Emma said, because she felt that she ought to.

Then, perhaps because James's expression appeared so thunderstruck, she turned and fled, tearing off down the village street in the direction of the lighthouse.

James, watching as she ran, the bright sunlight bringing out the golden highlights in her hair, wondered just which of his past transgressions he was being punished for this time. Because it did not seem to him at all fair that, on the afternoon of their wedding, the ninth earl of Denham's new bride should rush off to teach school. She might, at the very least, have joined him in a glass of champagne.

James was not, he soon discovered, the only person—aside from Roberts and Mr. Murphy, of course—who'd witnessed Emma's bizarre behavior. Standing not far from the horse and carriage stood the young master Fergus, his head tilted at a peculiar angle as he watched Emma streak toward the school from which he was obviously delinquent.

Noticing the carriage, the boy changed the direction of his gaze, and now stared, his head cocked awkwardly, at James.

"Did I just hear Miz Chesterton say thanks for *marryin'* her?" the boy asked, in tones of great disbelief.

James was too tired—and truth be told, too humiliated—to dissemble. He said, "You did."

The boy whistled, low and long.

"Well," Fergus said conversationally, "that's one way of keepin' Lord MacCreigh from gettin' at 'er. If you can make it stick, I mean."

James found himself frowning down at the boy and quickly rearranged his features into something less moody-looking. "Stick?"

"Right," Fergus said. "The whole marriage thing, I mean."

"Of course I'll make it stick," James said, with some indignation.

"Right," Fergus said, with a grin that James found a trifle knowing for a youngster. "Well, good luck to you with that."

James glared at the boy, who had put his hand in his trouser pockets and was about to stroll off in the direction of the lighthouse.

"See here," James called after him. "What do you mean by that?"

Fergus glanced back at him in surprise. Or at least

James supposed the boy was looking at him. It was difficult to tell with the child's strange, unfocused gaze.

"Why, just what me mam always says," the boy said, with a shrug. "If you really want to win 'er—and I think you do—you'll have to woo 'er."

And with that the boy strode off, at a surprisingly brisk pace for one whose sight was so uncertain, leaving James, inside the village hearse, to wonder how it was that he had to come all the way to the wilds of the Hebrides to get the only piece, he was quite certain, of decent advice he had ever received in his life.

Chapter Eighteen

It seemed to take only moments for news of Emma's marriage to spread throughout the town of Faires. Mrs. MacTavish saw to that. No sooner had she returned from witnessing the ceremony at Castle MacCreigh than she quickly relayed news of it—and of the startlingly intimate kiss the two participants had shared afterward—to all she met. Soon there was not a person in Faires who did not know that the widow Chesterton was married at last, and that the ten thousand pounds that had been due to her upon her wedding would now go not to any local man, as the villagers thought just and proper, but to a complete stranger.

Or was he? Certainly the earl of Denham was a stranger to Faires. But was he a stranger to Emma? Word had it that he was a relative of the late curate, Mrs. Chesterton's husband. But though they bore a passing resemblance to one another, the two men could not be more different. Stuart Chesterton had been known for his poverty and piousness. Lord Denham had already shocked and stunned the village first by hiring Murphy's brougham at the stunning rate of two sovereigns a day, and then by challenging—yes, challenging—the baron of MacCreigh to a duel.

As if either of those things were not enough, there was the very tantalizing piece of information Mrs. Mac-Tavish would only deliver sotto voce, and then with many furtive glances from side to side to make sure no one else could overhear . . . though in fact by the end of the day, there was not a person in Faires who did not know this secret she felt so duty-bound to impart: that the earl of Denham had not, in fact, spent the night before in the room he'd hired from her. No, Murphy had dropped him at the widow Chesterton's cottage that evening, and had gone round to pick him up the following morning, as instructed.

In other words, Lord Denham and the widow Chesterton had spent the night together. *Before* they were married.

For which, according to many of Faires's female residents, there was only one explanation: Lord Denham and Emma had been lovers long before she had ever married his cousin and come to Faires.

It made perfect sense, of course. For hadn't Emma been something of a disappointment as a curate's wife? Oh, she had dutifully performed the normal responsibilities of her role—visited with the aged and the infirm; provided pies for the church fairs; helped the minister's wife with decorating for various church events.

But how often had she attended her husband's sermons? Only once a day. High Church as her husband might have been, Emma Chesterton was about as Low Church as a body could get and still call herself a churchgoing woman.

But it was the school Emma had insisted on maintaining for the village children after the death of the schoolmaster that had caused the most raised eyebrows. A woman, teaching? It had all been very well after her husband's death—a widow, particularly a childless one, could be excused for throwing herself into such work as a palliative for her loss. But Emma had started making plans for the schoolhouse well before her husband's death . . . some said, to the curate's disapproval. After all, Emma had both boys *and* girls in her schoolhouse, seated together, and not even on opposite sides of the room, but grouped by age and ability, an arrangement to which Mr. Chesterton would never have agreed.

It was after this that most of the villagers—including, it was said, the Reverend Peck's own wife, who, with a new little one of her own, hadn't time to cope with the young wife of her husband's late curate—quite washed their hands of Emma . . . though no one actually forbade their child from attending Mrs. Chesterton's school, and many even bragged quite openly about the progress their progeny were making under her tutelage.

But that, of course, had been before the arrival of the handsome and excessively wealthy earl of Denham, who not only, it appeared, knew Emma from her London days, but had had the temerity to sweep her—and her ten thousand pounds—out from beneath the noses of all of her good solid Scottish suitors.

What other explanation was there, really, except that

Emma and Lord Denham had once been lovers, but had been cruelly parted by fate, causing a heartbroken Emma to wed the earl's poor, pious cousin, and driving the earl—or so it was said by Mary, the hired girl at the Puffin Inn, who had a passion for novels—into the arms of a Parisian artist's model? It was only now—according to a dreamy-eyed Mary—that the earl had heard at last that Emma was free, and had come to Faires to fetch her home. No explanation was offered as to what had happened to the Parisian model.

By suppertime, most of the population of Faires had come to accept this explanation of the day's highly irregular activities. Most of the population with the exception of two people, that is. The first was the baron, who did not believe for a second that Emma could possibly love anyone but him. And the second was his sister, who did not believe that James could love anyone but her.

Not, of course, that the Honorable Miss Fiona Bain's acquaintance with the earl of Denham was of longer than a day's standing. Still, Fiona was the self-proclaimed reigning beauty of Faires. Her only competition for the title had been her brother's fiancée, who was happily gone now (and good riddance to that fast piece of baggage) and Emma, now a dried-up old widow, as anyone with eyes could see. Fiona had thought herself quite assured of the title of Most Beautiful Woman in Faires. It did not make sense that so illustrious—and good-looking—a personage as the earl of Denham should fall in love with anyone but her.

So it was with rage that Fiona heard Mary's tale of lovers parted, then reunited. It was, Fiona knew, patently untrue. She had been at the wedding. She had herself witnessed Emma's reluctance to wed the man—idiot girl that Fiona had always thought her. Hadn't Fiona been waiting her entire life, it seemed, for a man just like James Marbury to come strolling through her door? Hadn't her heart leapt when, only that morning, he finally had? How she'd planned, in those first few moments Lord Denham had stood in her home, their future happiness together, far, far away from this miserable country she'd been born in, and grown to hate.

She fastened her cloak with great umbrage, and tied her bonnet strings, almost with savagery, after hearing from Mary what everyone was saying. Emma Chesterton—now Lady Denham—had always seemed to Fiona a strange, contrary thing. For hadn't Mrs. Chesterton chosen Clara McLellen, and not Fiona, to be her particular friend upon her first coming to Faires? Or rather, Clara had chosen Emma, and Emma had not gone out of her way to avoid the girl, as Fiona had always tried to. Certainly Clara was her brother's fiancée. But she did not possess even an ounce of noble blood, whereas Fiona could trace her ancestors back to the fourteen hundreds.

But had that made Emma Chesterton even the remotest bit interested in her? Not a whit. How often had Fiona stumbled across the pair of them, Clara and Emma, speaking in conspiratorial whispers to one another in various parts of the castle? How many times had she encountered them on her own solitary rambles, walking side by side, Emma's head bent as Clara jawed at her? Lord only knew what Clara had been telling the curate's wife. Probably about how ill-treated she felt at Castle MacCreigh, and how much she hated Fiona.

Well, was it Fiona's fault that she knew her own place, even if her brother did not? Clara's father was, after all, in *trade*.

Fiona was willing to bet that Emma knew perfectly well what had happened to Clara, that night she'd disappeared. It was likely Emma even knew where she'd disappeared to. And two to one Emma had even encouraged the hussy to run off with Stevens, Geoffrey's valet. As if Fiona herself hadn't had her eye on him! Oh, he was a commoner, it was true. But what flashing dark eyes he'd had! Fiona could not quite blame Clara for falling for him, though her betrayal had hurt Geoffrey sorely.

Not that Fiona would ever be stupid enough to throw herself away on a mere valet. No, it was a man like Lord Denham she was saving herself for.

But now, thanks to Emma, her one chance at a good marriage was in ruins . . . just as Emma had, in becoming Clara's confidante, instead of Fiona's, destroyed her one chance at having a true friendship. Emma had done nothing since coming to Faires except make life more difficult for Fiona.

Oh, there were those stupid women—Mrs. Mac-Tavish, and even Mrs. Peck—who tried to say nice things about her: how Mrs. Chesterton had been so tirelessly helpful during the typhus epidemic, nursing so many even after she'd lost her own husband. How Mrs. Chesterton was so good with the children. How Mrs. Chesterton could always be counted upon to lend a sympathetic ear. And on and on.

Well, Fiona had certainly never had the benefit of

Mrs. Chesterton's sympathetic ear. Not that she'd ever asked for it, exactly, but really, one would think that, Fiona being the only noblewoman in the district, Emma might have made some effort at least to get to know her better. Clara had accused Fiona of being standoffish, but Fiona knew this wasn't true. She was merely naturally diffident. Men liked diffidence in a lady.

Well, this stealing of Lord Denham out from under her very nose was the last straw. Emma had gone too far this time, and Fiona intended to let her know it. There was nothing, of course, that she could do about James Marbury. He was lost to her forever. But she could still bring Emma down a peg or two. Just see if she couldn't.

The fact that evening had fallen by the time she set out for the lighthouse did not concern Fiona overly much. Her brother would simply have to wait for his supper, unless he cared to eat it by himself. He would be angry about it, of course, but when, since Clara had left, hadn't he been angry? And it wasn't as if he weren't already in the foulest mood Fiona had ever seen him . . . why else would she have fled the castle for the inn, if not to escape her brother's anger at having lost the one thing that had come in the past few months to mean anything at all to him, that thing being, of course, the widow Chesterton's ten thousand pounds?

Fiona did not blame her brother for being angry. By rights, that money—and the widow Chesterton—belonged to him. Just as the handsome and debonair James Marbury rightfully belonged to her.

As Fiona intended to tell Emma, and in just so many words.

But if the Honorable Miss Bain had hoped to find, when she finally crossed the threshold to Emma's schoolhouse, the new bride in high, and therefore more delightfully crushable, spirits, she was sadly mistaken. Emma was sitting beside the usual pile of slates, her face turned toward the high windows, though it seemed unlikely she was actually seeing the rosy flames of sunset that glowed there. She wore on her pretty face—though Fiona chose to refer to it as pinched—an expression of abject misery. Miss Bain felt a quick dart of delight course through her breast.

"Well, Mrs. Chesterton," Fiona said loudly, allowing the door to bang behind her. "Or should I say Lady Denham. You are certainly the talk of town. I don't suppose it would interest you to know what people are saying about you?"

Emma turned her head to look at the younger girl. Her blue eyes, usually so filled with mirth, were apprehensive.

"No," she said. "But I have a feeling you're going to tell me anyway."

Fiona laughed without humor. "You're right about that. If I were you, I would say good-bye to this little school of yours. I don't think you'll be allowed to continue teaching here much longer. Not after the scandal you've caused today."

Emma, much to Fiona's disappointment, did not even flinch. She merely looked around the room, at the benches and the slates, and said, sounding a little surprised about it, "No. I suppose you're right."

Fiona, who had never particularly liked Emma—any woman who would willingly marry a man intent upon living in a place like Faires, and a *curate*, no less, had to have something wrong with her—could not help feeling that this was all wrong. Emma was supposed to be gloating and superior. She had, after all, won: she would be escaping this wretched place well before Fiona ever would.

And yet she looked so . . . so small. Small and anxious.

Fiona, aghast that she might be feeling sorry for— sorry for!—her sworn enemy, turned even more waspish.

"Oh, what's the matter, then?" she demanded. "Don't try to tell me you actually *care* what Mrs. Mac-Tavish and the rest of the old biddies in this town are saying."

Emma responded merely by hanging her head . . . until, very faintly, the Honorable Miss Bain heard her say, in a tone of great despair, "What have I done?"

This was most unsatisfactory. How on earth was Fiona to make Emma feel bad when she was already sunk into such gloom? And what could she possibly have to be so depressed about? She was married to the handsomest—not to mention richest—man Fiona had ever met!

What Fiona did not know—and what Emma was not about to tell her—was that, yes, Emma was married to an extraordinarily handsome, and very well off, man. But it was only a business agreement, arranged so that she could finally get the ten thousand pounds she was owed, and so James Marbury could assuage his guilt over his treatment of his cousin.

Emma couldn't very well mention this to Fiona, who

could be trusted to go prating at once to Judge Reardon about the planned annulment . . . something Emma had a feeling the judge was not going to like one bit, and that, should he find out about it, just might cause him to hold onto the money that much longer.

And Emma needed that money. Now that it was within her grasp, it had occurred to her that there were so many lovely things she could do with it. Send John McAddams to college. Have a real school built—and a real teacher hired—for the children of Faires. And then there was Fergus, whose eyes had never, to Emma's knowledge, been looked at by a real physician. Who knew but that there might actually be a cure for whatever it was that ailed them?

Still, Emma was well aware that she was the talk of the town—that it was doubtful she'd be allowed to teach the children much longer. As if that were not enough, there was the shameful memory of her behavior that morning, when Lord Denham had kissed her, to contend with. Had any woman ever reacted to a kiss with more wanton abandon? She suspected not. She had acted like a complete and utter hussy, a veritable Mary Magdalene. What must James think of her? And her a widow of just six months' standing . . . and of his own cousin . . . and a curate, no less!

But the Honorable Miss Fiona Bain was oblivious to any of these misgivings of Emma's. All Fiona knew was that Emma Chesterton's ten thousand pounds, instead of going to her brother, who might have lent her a small part of it for a new bonnet or two, was going to a man who hadn't the slightest need of it, and who would doubtlessly keep Emma in new bonnets—not to mention fans—for decades to come, while Fiona herself hadn't had so much as a new hair ribbon in years.

Accordingly, Fiona opened her lips to say something particularly biting about Emma's gloom—"You might have waited until the body was cold," or something equally as heartless.

She was cut off, however, by the door behind her flying open and letting in a burst of brisk salt air.

The cruel jibe that had been on Fiona's lips died a quick little death the moment she turned around. For there, taking up almost the whole of the doorway, his shoulders were so broad, stood the earl himself, looking no less handsome than when she'd last seen him, eight hours earlier.

"Miss Bain," he said, mildly enough, with a nod to Fiona. Then, his hazel-eyed gaze flicking past her—as if, she thought with some irritation, she were not quite the prettiest girl in the room, which she knew she was—the earl said, "Emma, if you're quite ready, I've come to take you home now."

With what masculine energy did those words ring out! How they thrilled along Fiona's spine! How she wished some tall and handsome earl would burst into *her* room and inform her that he was there to take *her* home! *She* certainly wouldn't have reacted as Emma did, which was with a crimson blush.

"I am not quite through," the new bride said, in a politely distant tone that suggested none of the misery that had been apparent in her face and voice just seconds before, "checking the children's essays."

Lord Denham, instead of kicking over the row of benches before him, as Fiona knew perfectly well any of the local men might have done at being so addressed, merely closed the door and then, folding his arms across his chest, leaned his back upon it.

"Then I shall wait," he said, with just the faintest hint of amusement, "until you *are* quite through."

Emma, instead of having the sense to throw the wretched slates away and leap into the earl's embrace, as Fiona would have done, picked up the next slate and scrutinized it.

This, as far as the Honorable Miss Fiona Bain was concerned, was too much. She had always thought Emma a fool for having married Stuart Chesterton in the first place. Stuart, though undeniably good-looking, had talked a good deal too much about theology for Fiona's taste. Besides which he had been, after all, only a curate. What woman in her right mind would marry a curate? Even the Reverend Peck had waited until he had a ministry of his own before marrying the prickly, if ever proper, Mrs. Peck.

Now, however, Emma had had the good fortune to marry a man who was not only gorgeous and a nobleman, but also seemingly uninterested in religion. Why, the girl would never have to embroider another bolster for the church bazaar ever again, if she didn't care to!

And how did she behave? As if her husband were worse than a monster! It was almost as if . . . well, almost as if what Mary had been going around saying were true. As if the two of them really had known one another from another, previous lifetime. Only, far from being lovers, they'd been—

Enemies.

But that, Fiona knew, was ridiculous. Because who

could possibly feel anything but worship for the earl of Denham, a man who wore the most splendid, butter-colored breeches, and kept his collars turned very high indeed, and spoke not with a Scottish burr—how Fiona despised her own, and how many hours had she spent before her mirror, trying to correct her own speech habits—but with the deep inflection of a true Englishman.

Fiona could not stand by and watch such a travesty of justice. It was breaking her heart. Such a waste! Emma—who had the absurd temerity to prefer that harpy Clara McLellen's company during her country strolls, Fiona remembered bitterly, over her own—ought not to be allowed to get away with it. And if there was any justice in the world at all, she wouldn't.

"Well," Fiona said, refastening her cloak. "Good evening then, Lord and Lady Denham." It must be admitted that she spoke the last words with some malice.

Lord Denham held the door open for her. Fiona stepped past him and out into the mild evening air, but not without another pang of regret. For as she moved by him, she caught the faint but unmistakable scent of soap.

Why, she thought to herself, he even bathes!

And her jealousy of Emma Van Court Chesterton Marbury knew no end.

$\mathcal{I}$t was fortunate that the Honorable Miss Bain was not present then when, a half hour later, James held open the door to Emma's cottage, allowing her to pass through it before him. Because what greeted Emma on the far side of the door would have turned Miss Bain's blue eyes green with envy.

For Emma's cottage had been transformed. No, the broken Limoges had not been replaced. Not even James Marbury, so used to having his orders obeyed, could command porcelain to repair itself.

But the table, covered with a piece of linen so spotlessly white that Emma knew instantly it had never before been used, was set with a sparklingly clean service emblazoned with the earl's own monogram. Plates and bowls, cups and saucers, serving dishes and teapots, all of cream-colored china, bore the scarlet-and-gold crest of the earl of Denham. Crystal wine goblets gleamed in the firelight, and the ornate silver utensils at the twin place settings shined. The contents of a crystal decanter glowed ruby red, while curls of fresh butter lay waiting to be spread across golden, crusty rolls, still steaming from the bake oven.

But that wasn't all. No, there was much, much more. The copper cook pots hanging from hooks from those same roof beams gleamed in a manner Emma had not known previously that they could gleam, so tarnished had they been upon her purchasing them, secondhand, from Mrs. Peck. The cheerful fire on the hearth wasn't smoking in the least, causing Emma to realize that someone—surely not Lord Denham—had done something about the stubborn chimney flue. And over that fire, the simmering contents of a pot filled the small cottage with an appetizing odor quite unlike its usual smell of damp dog.

Carefully stirring what lay within the pot, Lord Denham's valet looked up as Emma came in and, laying his wooden spoon aside, said, "Good evening, Lady Denham. May I take your wrap?"

Emma stood where she was, still hardly daring to believe what her eyes were plainly telling her. It oughtn't, she knew, seem so strange to her. After all, Lord Denham was a man who enjoyed good food and wine. And it was, after all, their wedding supper. They could hardly eat apart on this night, of all nights. Not if they hoped to fool Judge Reardon and the rest of the island into thinking theirs was a marriage that would last longer than the time it took for Emma to collect her ten thousand pounds.

But the gleaming pots? The unclogged flue? The fine china that Lord Denham obviously traveled with, but which he'd gone to the trouble to transporting over all that bumpy road to her cottage?

She had not expected this. It was too much.

"W-what—" she stammered, hardly knowing how she ought to react. After all, there was Roberts, whom she'd known almost as long as she'd known James, stirring something over her hearth, and there was James himself, busying himself with closing the door behind them. James who was, for better or for worse—for better *and* for worse, Judge Reardon had said—her husband.

But James only said, "Chin up, Emma," and neatly undid her bonnet strings, then lifted the hat from her head and passed it, along with her cloak, to Roberts.

"You must be very tired," Lord Denham said, guiding her—unresisting—to the chair by one of the place settings. "Sit down. Drink a little of this."

He passed her one of the crystal goblets, into which he'd poured a little of the wine from the decanter. Emma brought the glass to her lips and drank without quite tasting what was, knowing the earl, probably a rare and obscenely expensive vintage. All she could think was, The pots! The flue! How long it must have taken them! For surely James must have helped. Roberts could not have done it all himself.

"Now, Emma," James was saying, as his valet heaped what appeared to be a large serving of Mrs. MacTavish's potato au gratin onto the plate before her. "We must have another serious discussion, you and I."

Emma stared down at the heap of potatoes steaming on her plate. They smelled amazing.

"You aren't going to like hearing what I have to

say," James was saying. "But I'm afraid I've got to say it just the same. I know how much you enjoy your, er, children. But I can't help thinking that perhaps a little break from your teaching duties might be in order. Hear me out before you say anything, please."

But all Emma had meant to say was thank you, as James's valet slid a small, roasted bird onto her plate. The words died on her lips, however, as she stared down at the squab. It was perfectly cooked. Never had Emma managed to prepare such a succulent-looking meal.

"If we are to get an annulment," James was saying, "it will be necessary for the two of us to do so in London. My solicitor is there, and he'll know best how to handle a case of this particular type. Your signature will of course be required, and it would be far quicker for you to go over the documents with him in person than for him to have to mail them to you from the city. God forbid they should get lost. I haven't a great deal of faith in the mail service from here to the mainland. It is my understanding that the weather can sometimes prevent the ferries from reaching shore for weeks at a time."

Emma nodded, but she was hardly listening. It seemed that the rational part of her brain had ceased to function. Instead of concentrating on what James was saying, she was remembering that Mrs. Peck had, upon their arrival in Faires, offered Emma and Stuart use of her charwoman—for the "heavy" work, she'd said. Only Emma had been forced to decline. She had not had the money to pay for any sort of household help. Besides, as Stuart had said, it was good for them to haul their own water and break up their own firewood. Honest work brought them, he'd said, closer to God.

Emma didn't know about that. But it had certainly brought her blisters.

This was, she thought to herself, probably the first time since she'd moved into the cottage that it had been completely and thoroughly cleaned by someone other than herself.

"What I propose," James went on, "is that we leave for London at once. Tomorrow, as a matter of fact. I would plan on at least a three-month stay. It will take at least that long, I believe, for us to collect the funds owed to you, and to start the paperwork necessary to annul the marriage. But you needn't worry about the children. I think that we can easily find an instructor who in the interim can . . . Emma?"

Emma tore her gaze from the food in front of her and brought it to James's face. "My lord?"

James was looking at her quizzically. "Are you all right?"

Emma shook herself. She could not help staring, however, at James . . . her husband, she reminded herself. He was her husband now.

But not really.

And yet it was somehow difficult to remember this when she looked at his face, and saw that mouth that earlier in the day had been pressed against hers with such possessiveness. Who would have thought that James Marbury was such a magnificent kisser? Oh, certainly he had never lacked for female companionship, but Emma had always credited this to his handsome looks, and even handsomer bank account. How was she to have known that beneath that coolly good-looking exterior beat the heart of such a passionate lover?

Or perhaps she only felt this because she was, as Stuart had often pointed out, so physically demonstrative by nature herself.

Slowly the words those lips—which had been capable of evoking such a shocking response from her when pressed against hers—had just been forming began to take shape in Emma's mind. Leave for London. He wanted her to leave for London.

With him.

Tomorrow.

"Absolutely not," Emma burst out, before she could stop herself.

Roberts, over by the fire, paused with a spoon poised in midair as he went to stir whatever was bubbling in the pot above the flames. Across the table, James cocked a single eyebrow.

"Really, Emma," he said, quite calmly. "If you think about it rationally, you'll see it's really the most sensible course of action—"

"And who'll see to the children's education while I'm gone?" Emma demanded. She did not know if the wine had served to clear her head, or if the initial shock of coming home to a clean cottage was beginning to wear off. But quite suddenly, she was herself again.

What she could not quite determine was what, precisely, James was up to.

"I know how you feel about, er, your children, as you call them," James said patiently. "That's why I suggest we hire a teacher—a proper schoolmaster—to look after them while you're gone—"

"That could take months," Emma said. "It isn't as if we were inundated with applications after the last one died, you know. Faires is hardly a popular spot with qualified academics. And I couldn't possibly leave before we found someone suitable."

She felt something that, though she wasn't certain, seemed to resemble fear. But that wasn't possible. Afraid? What did she have to be afraid of? Not of him, certainly. And not of London.

No. It wasn't fear. It wasn't fear at all. It was only that she had to think of the children. They needed her. They had no one else, really.

"You don't understand," she said, with some desperation. "The children *need* that school. For many of them, it's the only way they truly feel valued—"

"I am aware of that," James said. "That is why Roberts here has volunteered to take over for you until we find a replacement."

Roberts dropped the spoon. If, however, his master's words were a surprise to him, he gave no other indication. Instead, he murmured, "It would be my pleasure, my lady," and went to find a new spoon.

Emma, stunned, sank back in her chair. Well, there was no use denying it now. She was scared, all right. And not for the children, either. Did James have the slightest conception what he was asking of her? Go back to London? He couldn't know—not possibly—what he was saying.

Or did he? Was this all part of the change in him, this new James, the one who harbored this sudden desire to set things to right by her? Almost certainly.

But if part of his plan to do right by her included reuniting her with her family, well, he was just going to have to forget it. Emma couldn't possibly allow it. When she and Stuart had left London a year earlier, it had been with the understanding that, abandoned by both their families, they could never, ever return. Or at least, the only way Emma had sworn she'd ever return was when she'd proved her family wrong, that their dire predictions of the fate of her marriage had been for nothing. When she returned to London, she'd promised herself, it would only be as the happy wife of a fully ordained minister . . . and she'd planned on having at least half a dozen children in tow, to prove precisely how happy she and Stuart had been in their lives together.

Only now instead she'd be returning as a curate's widow—worse, a childless widow. Worse even, a childless widow who'd married her husband's own cousin . . . his very rich, very socially prominent cousin, the kind of man her family had wanted her to marry in the first place. The kind of man she'd never thought she'd marry, as Emma had always insisted she'd marry only for love, and only to a man who shared her determination to make the world a better place for the less fortunate.

Which of course meant she certainly couldn't explain to her friends and family why she'd gone ahead and married James. Even if she said she'd only done it so that she could collect money that was owed her— money that she had every intention of donating to charitable causes—they would want to know where the money came from, and why Stuart's killer had felt it necessary to leave her the money, which would only lead to uncomfortable questions as to why Stuart had been killed in the first place.

And Emma most certainly didn't care to discuss *that*. Not with anyone.

"Oh!" she cried, as this thought struck her. "Oh, James, I can't! Not back to London. Really, it would be too dreadful."

The earl of Denham looked very much as if he'd expected to hear something of the kind. He certainly seemed quick enough with a response.

"Emma, I can't possibly stay here. I have pressing business concerns back in London."

She blinked at him. Business concerns. Of course he needed to return to London. He had only come to Faires in the first place because he'd intended to have his cousin disinterred. Now that Emma had managed to squash that objective, why would he stay?

Why, indeed.

"Then by all means," Emma replied, feeling suddenly—and inexplicably—let down. "Of course you must go."

Absurd that she felt so disappointed. It was a very good thing that he was going! Then she'd need no longer worry about his inadvertently stumbling across the truth about that dreadful night Stuart died. . . .

What's more, if he went away, she need no longer look at that mouth, and recall the way it had felt against hers back at Lord MacCreigh's castle, and wonder, as she found herself doing time and time again, whether if he kissed her a second time, she might have the same reaction. . . .

No, it was all for the better this way. He should go

back to London, and she would go back to . . . well, being alone.

But better to be alone than for him to discover the truth, which, if he stayed, he surely would.

"You needn't concern yourself with me, you know," she said with all the bravery she could muster, when James hesitated in his response. "I shall be quite all right."

"Don't be ridiculous, Emma," James said, seeming to recover from his surprise at her eagerness to be rid of him. "No wife of mine—however temporary our union might be—is going to live alone. You are coming with me back to London, and I don't want to hear another word about it."

Emma's fear grew even more palpable. Back with him, to London? But that meant hours alone with him in a carriage . . . worse, nights together in cozy inns along the way. Who knew how long it would be before her curiosity over what had occurred when they kissed drove her to try the experiment again? "But—"

"Besides," James went on, as if she hadn't spoken, "if you were to remain here, Judge Reardon would be bound to notice that we're . . . well, not exactly living as man and wife. I am not at all certain he'd approve. He might even—"

"Hold onto the money," Emma finished for him, softly. James was right. It was exactly the sort of thing Justice Reardon *would* do. "Oh, but James, where would I stay in London? My family—I'm afraid my family, you see, would . . . Well, the way I left things—"

"I quite understand that your relations with your aunt and uncle are strained at the moment," James said, tactfully not mentioning, Emma noticed, his part in making them that way. "And after giving the matter some thought, I feel that, under the circumstances, we would best reside at my place on Park Lane—"

"With Lady Denham?" Emma couldn't help bursting out. "Oh, James, no! I couldn't bear it!"

Lord Denham looked surprised. It was distressing to note that even a look of surprise became him. "Was my mother such an ogre to you?" he wondered. "I rather thought the two of you quite got along."

"Oh, but that's just it," Emma said. "Lady Denham was always so kind to me." Kinder even, Emma supposed, than she ever deserved. She had, after all, done little to try to convince the dowager's nephew not to take such a risk, in moving to the wilds of the Hebrides. "I would hate for her to be deceived about the . . . well, the nature of our . . . er . . ."

"Union," James finished for her, calmly. "Yes, I see your point. Her elation at hearing I'd married at last might be a bit overwhelming. And she was always very fond of you. . . ."

Emma found herself blinking back tears. She couldn't, for the life of her, say why she suddenly felt like weeping, but there it was. She had always felt a tremendous liking for James's mother, and Stuart's aunt. Lady Denham, whom Emma had known for most of her life, had a large heart, and a very generous nature. . . .

But was it generous enough, Emma could not help wondering, to forgive her daughter-in-law for the crime that she had committed, some six months earlier?

"Perhaps," Emma said, reaching up furtively to dash away the tears that had gathered at the corners of her eyes. She hoped James did not notice this sudden welling of emotion, and take it as a sign of feminine weakness and lack of self-sufficiency. "Perhaps if we didn't tell her about . . . you know. The marriage. I don't like deceiving her, but . . . well, she is such a fine lady. I wouldn't like her to think ill of me." *More than she already has a right to,* Emma added silently to herself.

James said, "Naturally." Then, when Emma offered no more objections to his scheme, he nodded briskly. "Then it's settled. We'll leave for London in the morning."

And he reached for the decanter to pour more wine into her glass, quite as casually as if they'd just agreed to have bacon instead of ham with breakfast.

Flummoxed, Emma glanced in Roberts's direction. The valet was busying himself at the sideboard, putting away the remains of the potato au gratin. Really, but Roberts managed to give the impression that he didn't consider anything that had occurred in the past twelve hours at all extraordinary . . . almost as if his master married penniless widows every day of the week.

How Emma envied the valet's sangfroid! If only she could maintain an air of such cool disinterest. But that, she was afraid, was impossible. Why, only yesterday her greatest concern had been how to keep her rooster from roaming. Now, in typical fashion, her streak of bad luck had intensified to a point that her life was filled with such a myriad of problems, she did not know where to begin in addressing them. The fact that she was apparently leaving for London in the morning was the least of her troubles.

It was getting through this—her wedding night—that was of utmost urgency at the moment.

For it occurred to Emma that it was getting quite late in the evening. Yet James showed no signs of preparing to return to Mrs. MacTavish's. Even more startling, Emma could not remember whether or not he had asked Mr. Murphy to wait. Surely if the driver had been outside all this time, he'd be half asleep by now. And it was unforgivably rude of them not to have asked him in for a cup of tea.

And if he *wasn't* waiting outside, then what precisely did that mean?

"Shouldn't we," Emma asked, with forced brightness, "ask Mr. Murphy in, so that he can have a cup of tea before he drives you both back to the inn?"

She congratulated herself on the artistry of her query. It was polite, yet pointed.

The response it elicited, however, set her heart racing.

"I sent Mr. Murphy down the road to sup with Mrs. MacEwan," Lord Denham said, removing from his waistcoat pocket a pipe, and beginning to fill it from a small pouch. "At least until Roberts is through here, and joins him there. Then the two of them will drive back into town."

Emma threw an alarmed glance from servant to master, then back again. "But—" Her eyes widened to their limits. "But you can't mean to stay *here* for the night, can you, James?"

But James, leaning back in his chair and calmly lighting his pipe, gave every indication of doing precisely that.

"You can't expect me to stay at the inn, tonight of all

nights, Emma," he said, with some amusement. "After all, Justice Reardon has a room there. He might find it a bit odd, don't you think, the bride and groom spending their wedding night apart. You don't mind my smoking, do you?"

Distracted by the smoking question, Emma shook her head quickly. But inwardly, her mind was awhirl. James spend another night here at the cottage? But surely he didn't think . . . he couldn't believe that . . .

And then, glancing at his long, masculine form, stretched out somewhat uncomfortably in Stuart's chair, which was a bit too small for his cousin's bulkier frame, Emma told herself she was being ridiculous. Of course he meant to stay on the settle again. He could have no other intention in mind. Theirs was a titular union only, after all. Hadn't he been the one who'd suggested the annulment—suggested it almost in the same breath as he'd suggested marriage?

He meant to stay on the settle. Of course he meant to stay on the settle.

And yet just as she'd finished reassuring herself of this, the memory of that kiss—that blasted kiss!—*would* intrude to disrupt her thoughts. Supposing he kissed her good night? She would of course offer him her cheek. But supposing for some reason he missed her cheek, and ended up kissing her on the mouth again? Well, it could happen. And then supposing the same thing that had happened at Castle MacCreigh happened here, in the cottage? That his kiss rendered her once again completely senseless of all else? That it produced in her, as it had seemed to earlier in the day, that same wild, reckless longing to . . . to . . .

Well, Emma was not quite sure what James's kiss had made her long to do. Or rather, she knew, but the thought was entirely too shameful to admit. For it only proved what Stuart had always said about her: that she was too wanton by half. She really ought to turn her mind to higher things than physical pleasure.

But it was a very frightening thing, that the kiss of a man—especially a man like James Marbury—should arouse in her such an intense physical reaction.

And then she thought it might be better for her to retire at once, before Roberts left. Yes, certainly if Roberts were still about, there would be no question of anything but the chastest of good-night kisses. Surely she would not react in front of him as she'd reacted to James's kiss back at the castle . . . not twice in one day!

And so she rose—so quickly that she nearly upset her wineglass, but fortunately Roberts was there to steady it—and said, "Well, as tomorrow will no doubt be a very long day, I should like go to bed now. Good night, my lord."

She extended her right hand toward the earl, who, startled, climbed quickly to his feet.

"But surely it's early yet," he said, looking bemused.

"Yes," Emma said. "But here in the country we rise with the chickens." Or at least tried to, on the few occasions when the chickens had not run away. "Good night, my lord. And thank you. For the lovely meal. And for . . . well, and for marrying me."

The words, when she heard them, sounded exceedingly odd. And yet she meant them. It *had* been good of Lord Denham to marry her. He was putting himself out a good deal, and she wanted him to know that she appreciated it . . . while at the same time, she wanted to keep a certain distance—*needed* to keep a certain distance. Otherwise, she was fairly certain that this startling new attraction she was feeling for the earl might become rather hard to manage. Oh, why couldn't she turn her mind to higher things, as Stuart had always managed to so easily?

James, with a final puzzled glance at her hand, reached out and took it in his own. But instead of firmly shaking it, he raised her fingers to his lips—an oddly romantic gesture, Emma could not help thinking, as her pulse staggered and then started up again at the feel of those warm lips on her skin, for a man so notorious for being ruled by his head, and never his heart.

"Good night, Emma," he said. In the light from the enormous fire, James's face looked handsomer than Emma ever remembered seeing it. It was as if something had happened to soften those features, to lend a new youth to that mouth that had once been so hard and uncompromising, and tenderness to that gaze that had once held so much calculation.

Now, however, there was no hint of any emotion at all on the earl's face save the sincerest interest—that was the only word Emma could think of to describe it— in her welfare.

"Rest well," James said, his breath tickling her knuckles. His eyes, in the firelight, burned amber, like a cat's. No, more like . . . like a tiger's. Emma had seen a tiger once, at a private zoo James had taken her to, which he'd declared tediously dull. But Emma had not found it so . . . any more than she now found herself unaffected by James's touch.

Which was why she hastily tugged her fingers from his grasp and, with a hoarse, "Excuse me," flung herself from the room, which had grown suddenly far too hot for her comfort.

But if she'd expected to find peace and solitude in her bedroom, she was sadly mistaken. Oh, there was peace aplenty. But solitude? Not at all.

For in the center of her bed lay the stray dog Una, her thick tail thumping delightedly at the sight of Emma. That's because the dog was eager to show off her eight small, wriggling pups, each one of whom, only minutes old, still glistened from its journey down the birth canal . . . much of the contents of which had already been eliminated, and soaked deeply into Emma's bedclothes and mattress.

Emma, far from feeling the joyousness of such an occasion, merely clapped a hand to her mouth and, eyeing the mess, wondered with a sickening feeling where on earth she was going to sleep now.

Chapter Twenty

$\mathcal{I}$t was all going far better than James could ever have anticipated.

He could not, of course, have predicted that the dog would choose so fortuitous a night—and such a welcome place—to give birth. That much, at least, he could not take credit for.

But for the rest . . . well, that had been pure Marbury genius.

For earlier that day, after Emma had run off to her school, James had sat for some time back at his room in the inn, thinking hard about what young Fergus had said: *If you want to win 'er, you'll have to woo 'er.* It was somewhat extraordinary that a thirty-year-old earl should be taking advice from a boy not even half his age. But there it was. There was no doubting, James realized, that there was something to what the boy said.

And certainly he had not done very well a year ago, had he, operating under his own counsel? No, that had been a bloody disaster. All of his efforts to show Emma how foolish her dreams of saving the world were had only served to strengthen her determination to do so. In fact, James did not think it would be far wrong to say that he had, in his way, pushed her into the decision to marry his cousin. After all, what had his vehement opposition to the match done but propel the two of them even sooner into one another's arms?

Well, not this time. This time he would do it right.

It would, he considered, as he studied her profile in the flickering candlelight in his room at the Puffin Inn, be well worth it. For Emma van Court Chesterton was a woman quite unlike any he had ever known.

Take, for example, her reaction upon finding that her bed was, for tonight, anyway—and probably for a good long time, until the soiled mattress had had time to dry out, that is—perfectly unusable.

"It's quite all right," she'd hastened to assure him. "I'll sleep on the settle. You and Mr. Roberts may return to the inn for the night. Really, I insist."

And insist she had.

Only James wouldn't hear of any such plan. His reminder that Judge Reardon would wonder at the two of them spending their wedding night apart caused a pucker of worry to appear on his bride's face . . . a pucker that he could see now she still wore. Well, and why not? For before them stretched an expanse of white, feather-filled, and if not as luxurious as James was perhaps used to, then at least downright comfortable bed. It was the bed Mrs. MacTavish, when she'd shown him to the room the day he'd checked in, had explained was the best in the inn. And now it appeared that between him and Emma, only one of them was going to be allowed to use it.

"I'll take the chair," Emma said, one hand already resting possessively on the back of the small settee in one corner of the room. "I don't mind at all."

"Emma," James said, for what seemed to him to be the hundredth time. "We are both grown adults. I believe we can share a bed without either one of us being overcome by our baser instincts."

Emma, who upon being delivered to the inn—by Mr. Murphy, whom Roberts had walked to Mrs. MacEwan's to find, then sent to fetch them—had immediately disappeared into his lordship's dressing room, and emerged in a nightdress and the most threadbare of dressing gowns, which she wore with the seeming conviction that it was the fashion equivalent to armor, gave a sniff.

"I am quite aware of that," she said primly. "Only really, don't you think it would be better if—"

"No, I do not," James said, feigning tired impatience. Well, the impatience was not feigned. He was quite curious as to what was about to transpire. What he was not, was tired. Not in the least.

"I am finding your virginal modesty," he added, "quite trying, considering that you are in fact a widow, and not unaccustomed, one would think, to sharing your bed. Correct me if I am wrong about that."

Emma glanced at him sharply. "What do you mean?"

"Well, only that I am assuming you and Stuart used to share a bed."

"Yes," Emma said, her eyes very round in the candlelight. "But he was my husband."

"As," James could not help pointing out, "am I."

"Yes, but—" Emma blinked. "Well, you know what I mean. You aren't *really.*"

"But we don't want Judge Reardon to know that, now, do we?"

When she continued merely to stare down at the high featherbed, James added, "I thought we had a business arrangement."

"We do," Emma said, looking up, clearly stung. "Only I hadn't imagined it would include sleeping in the same bed."

"Well, it appears that it does now," James said. "The alternative, of course, would be that we go down that hall, knock on Justice Reardon's door, and tell him it was all a mistake. Then I'll return to London alone in the morning, and you can go back to teaching your little school—that is, if the town harpies will even allow you to continue to teach, knowing, as they seem to, that I stayed the night at your cottage last evening, when we were not, as we are now, man and wife. And you can of course return to fending off the advances of Lord MacCreigh and your other devoted suitors. It is entirely up to you."

She shivered, though the room was not terribly cold . . . even if without a doubt they would both be a good deal warmer in the bed than out of it. No, the shiver seemed to be at his suggestion, not the temperature of the room.

"No," she said, faintly. "No, I'd rather not."

"That's what I thought," he said. And then, because it seemed to him that it was high time one of them did so, he strode toward the bed, turned down the covers, and climbed into bed, his own dressing gown firmly tied and, he was all too grimly aware, likely to remain so.

Emma, still standing at the end of the bed, watched him, wide-eyed. She looked not unlike something otherworldly, small as she was, with her hair unfastened from the many pins it took to keep the heavy curls in place, so that it fell about her shoulders in waves of gold. The simple sight of her caused something to tighten inside James's chest. . . .

But then, it always had. Seeing her now, in a faded dressing gown at the end of his bed, he had no different a reaction than he'd experienced the first time he'd seen her come down the stairs in a real ball gown—not the muslin and pantaloons her aunt had kept her in until the age of sixteen. How could he ever forget the shock that had come over him the first time he'd seen Emma—funny, orphaned Emma—in actual décolletage, with her hair up, and that little self-satisfied smile upon her face, pleased by the reaction the sight of her had caused?

Only it wasn't his reaction that had pleased her. Heavens, no. It was Stuart—Stuart, who'd nearly dropped his punch glass—she'd watched so carefully, checking for signs of admiration.

And admired her Stuart had, though James had overheard his cousin warning Emma, a little while later, of the dangers of caring too much for material things like low-cut gowns and lace fans. How Emma could bear being preached to by Stuart every time she saw him, James had not been able to imagine, but he supposed that, considering that her admiration for his cousin had begun when she was very young, she hardly noticed it.

Or that, if she did, she enjoyed it, since any attention from Stuart had to be—to a girl who'd loved him as long as Emma had—better than no attention at all.

Looking at her now, in the candlelight, James realized that it made no difference whether Emma was in a ball gown or a dressing gown. Either way, in the plainest cotton or finest silks, she was the most beautiful woman James had ever known.

Glancing at her face, however, and seeing that it was still puckered with worry, he sighed.

"It's just for one night, Emma," he said. "At my mother's, we'll be in separate rooms, of course. Now come to bed. We've a long few days ahead of us."

And he rolled over and, with dampened fingertips, extinguished the single candle that had been lighting the small room.

Not until it was completely dark did she move. Only then did she come to the bed, under cover of darkness. She did not, James was aware, remove so much as a stitch of clothing, merely lifted the bedclothes and slid beneath them, her slight weight causing hardly a dent in the featherbed. He had only a brief whiff of lavender scent as her head sank into the pillow beside his.

And then there was nothing. Nothing except the soft, almost inaudible sound of her breath. And the heat, of course, that her small body generated, and that he could already feel pouring across the six inches of space between them.

Emma, lying stiff as a board in the darkness beside James, could only wonder, again, at how all of this had come to pass. How on earth had she ended up in bed with James Marbury? She could not begin to fathom it.

But it had happened—was happening—and there really did not appear to be anything she could do about it, short of throwing some sort of shrewish temper tantrum, which she was determined not to do. No, she was going to be every bit as adult and businesslike about the situation as James was being. She did not want him to think her some sort of prude. She was determined to behave in a grown up manner.

Except that—Oh! How nice he looked in his silk dressing gown! She was more glad than she could say that he had put out the light, and she no longer had to look at all that dazzling masculine beauty. Really, was it too much to ask that Stuart's cousin be average looking, or even merely as attractive as Stuart? Why did James have to be the handsomest man she had ever set eyes upon? Why did her gaze have to be drawn so irresistibly to the V where his dressing gown fell open across his chest, revealing a patch of such thick dark hair? Why was she left to wonder whether he wore a nightshirt beneath that dressing gown?

Of course, the greater question was why, when it came to James Marbury, was she suddenly so fascinated? Simply because of that kiss? Emma had never been conscious of James as a man—well, never quite *this* conscious—until that mind-searing embrace at their wedding. Before, he had simply been . . . well, James: dependable, occasionally reprehensible, James, Stuart's older cousin.

Except. . . .

Except that now, suddenly, James was so very much more. He had come to Faires in search of his cousin's grave. Instead, he had found his cousin's impoverished widow.

But had James turned around and gone back to London? Not hardly. Not only had he rescued her from what was turning into a very vexatious situation where Lord MacCreigh was concerned, but he had also attempted, in his own way, to provide for her in a manner that had never occurred to Stuart, whose mind never did have much of a practical bent. Not, Emma told herself, that she particularly needed James's—or any man's—help, except perhaps where Lord MacCreigh was concerned. Still, James seemed determined to see that she was taken care of, even at great inconvenience to himself.

And for that, she was very grateful indeed.

Only why was it that she couldn't think of all the kind things James was doing for her, rather than the way his lips had felt on hers? Why couldn't she concentrate on how thoughtful it had been of him to have that lovely supper prepared for her, rather than how nice he looked in a dressing gown? Had Stuart been right all along? *Was* she disgracefully wanton?

She supposed so. Why else was she so perfectly unable to keep her mind off the amount of heat radiating from James's side of the bed? Why else was she purposefully having to keep her fingers beneath the covers, to prevent them from setting off on an exploration of what lay beneath that dressing gown of James's?

Lord! What was *wrong* with her?

But wasn't this better, she told herself, than going to bed alone? All those nights she'd lain, cold and lonely, in the bed she and Stuart had shared, listening to the howling wind and roaring sea, and feeling so very insignificant, so very isolated and forgotten? Oh, yes, better this, a thousand times, than that.

Suddenly overwhelmed by a feeling of immense gratitude toward the man beside her, Emma heard herself breaking the stillness of the darkness around them by asking, softly, "James?"

For a moment, she thought he must have been asleep, since he didn't reply. How nice, she thought, to be able to drop off like that and not lie, as she usually did, awake for an hour or more before falling asleep, thinking about wantonness or, more often than not, her streak of bad luck and her delinquent rooster.

But James's deep voice startled her. He was not asleep. Not at all.

"Yes, Emma?" he said.

Emma, blinking in the darkness, instantly regretted having opened her mouth. Yes, she'd wanted to let him know how grateful she was for all that he'd done for her. But the midnight hour was never a good one for sharing confidences. Who knew what might happen under the cloak of darkness? What had she been thinking?

But it was too late now. She had to go through with it. He was expecting her to say something.

"Good night," she said, and then, quick as she could, she leaned over to press a kiss to his cheek.

A fact he quickly rectified with a simple turn of his head, capturing her lips with his own.

Chapter Twenty-One

The moment James's mouth touched hers, Emma stiffened and would have pulled away, had it not been for two things. The first was the fact that he had wrapped an arm about her—just one, but there was such firmness in his grasp, it seemed clear he was not going to be willing to let her go just then. And the second was that . . .

She didn't want to.

It was shocking, but true. Of course she understood the consequences of her actions. She was in bed with a virile and healthy man who, unlike Stuart, did not appear to have any moral objections to physical displays of affection. She had a very good idea what allowing James to kiss her might lead to.

And she didn't care.

She didn't. She couldn't. Not when being kissed by him felt so simply . . . well, heavenly. She could think of no other way to explain why she did not push him away.

But it felt so very nice, his mouth on hers, just as it had at the castle that afternoon. Who knew James Marbury could kiss this way? Not Emma, certainly, or things might have turned out very differently indeed, that season of 'thirty-two.

For wasn't it true that in spite of what Stuart had always said, physical expressions of affection were a large part of what love affairs were all about? Not that she imagined that James was in love with her . . . but certainly he was fond of her. Fond enough to marry her so that he could see her come into the fortune she was owed. Fond enough of her to kiss her so deeply that she could feel it all the way down to her bare toes. . . .

Perhaps Stuart had a point about physical demonstrations of affection. Because Emma was quite definitely feeling something that could be construed as wicked. It certainly *felt* sinful, the way James was holding her so tightly against him that she could feel the knot in his dressing gown pressing against her belly.

And like much of what was most sinful, it was also perfectly irresistible. So that when, a split second later, James slipped his other arm around her as well, and she was suddenly tumbled back against the mattress, with half his body resting heavily atop her, she did not even protest. That was how mindless his kisses made her.

And now he wasn't just kissing her lips, either, but her throat as well, his mouth roaming across her soft skin in the strangest manner, as if he could not kiss her enough, and yet also—this was the strangest part— almost as if he had already kissed her a thousand times. Emma could not imagine how this thought occurred to her, or where it came from, but there it was. Had he kissed her once this way in a dream? And had it been his dream? Or hers?

And odder still, her body reacted to his kisses as if familiar with them, even though James Marbury—or anyone else, for that matter—had never kissed her collarbone, never kissed her behind her ear. Their first kiss, after all, had only been that afternoon!

But tell that to her body, arching in a most shameful manner against his, as if greeting a long-lost—and most intimate—friend. Even Emma's hands seemed to have developed minds of their own, and were doing the most indescribably shocking things without her consciously willing them to . . . such as undoing the sash of his dressing gown, and slipping beneath the silky material to meet his cool, bare flesh.

Shocking behavior! And yet it didn't seem so. It seemed right, and good, and proper . . . which was how his lips felt on her neck—well, maybe not proper, but certainly *right*. And right was how his hands felt as they roved the length of her body, caressing and kneading and stroking through the thin material of her dressing gown . . . until quite suddenly, both their dressing gowns were gone, or at least parted, and her nightdress seemed to have disappeared, and she had the sense-shattering experience of his bare skin against hers.

And *that* was certainly right, since it was followed by an explosion of lips and tongue, as if they could not kiss each other enough. And when one of his hands moved to cup one of her suddenly bare breasts, well, that felt right, too. More than right. It felt divine. . . .

But not nearly as divine as when he dipped his head and put his lips where his hand had been. Never had Emma felt anything quite as glorious as the heat from James's mouth as his lips closed over a bare, sensitive nipple. Her fingers sank into his thick dark hair, and for a few heartbeats, she was convinced she'd gone to heaven. . . .

Until, a second later, one of James's big, strong hands brushed against a part of her that was even more sensitive. Emma's eyes flew open, though there was nothing at all to see in the near-total darkness. Now this, she thought to herself, in the part of her mind that was still capable of thought, is sinful.

Sinfully delightful.

The fingers she'd sunk into his hair slid to circle the back of his neck, while her other hand flattened against a broad shoulder, as if part of her wanted to draw him nearer, while the other strained to push him away. She could feel every sinew, every contour of him. She could not see him, but she could feel . . . and oh, what she felt! James's body was hard and taut, from his wide, muscular shoulders, to his flat stomach, down to his long, solid legs. His chest was covered with crisp hair that sprang back every time she tangled her fingers through it. He was big, so much bigger than Stuart had been . . . everywhere.

But that was not the only difference. Far from it. For James was a bolder lover than Stuart had ever been—bolder, or more experienced with women, or more interested, perhaps, in giving pleasure than merely receiving it. Almost before she knew what he was about, James had slipped one of those deft fingers of his inside her, and suddenly, sensations Emma had only been dimly aware existed swept over her like a tidal flood.

Gasping at the intensity of the warmth that suddenly spread over her body as James insinuated first one, and then another finger into the tight opening between her thighs, Emma was certain her racing heart was about to burst . . . particularly when, seconds later, he replaced his fingers with that part of him that she most desired—and yet partly feared. The prodding tip of his penis was smooth as velvet, but hard as marble. Clinging to his strong shoulders and feeling them shudder with the effort James was making to go gently with her, Emma—wanton creature that by now she knew she most certainly was—pressed herself against that hardness, and slowly, as his kiss grew more intrusive, she opened herself to him.

James entered her, and her first reaction was to gasp and strain away from him, certain something was wrong . . . and yet at the same time knowing it was right. This was *not* how it had been with Stuart. Not at all. Stuart had never filled her like this, until she was certain she was close to bursting. Stuart had never moved with such confidence, such consummate skill, again as if James had rehearsed this moment a thousand times in his mind. She could not be mistaken in this. . . .

But it was impossible. Because James could never have imagined that they might one day. . . . He had never given any sign that he—

He moved, just a fraction of any inch. But it was enough to send alarm roweling through her once more. She struggled to escape—from the frightening size of him; from the sudden realization of what she'd done; from the unfamiliar weight and smell and feel of him. . . .

And then she didn't want to be freed. James moved slowly within her, and all the glorious sensations she'd felt when he'd touched her there returned. She clung to him in wonder as he began to thrust himself deeper and deeper into her, gently at first, restraining himself, and then, hearing her appreciative gasps, with mounting urgency.

Emma's hips rose to meet James's, her need for release soon approaching the imperativeness of his. He was murmuring things to her now, words that in the heat of her passion she couldn't understand, and though she no longer resisted him, he had seized her hands and held them pinned to the bed, as if he was fearful she might once more try to slip away from him.

But escape was the last thing on Emma's mind. Her entire being was focused upon James, on his ragged breathing, the coarseness of the stubble on his chin as it raked her soft cheek, and above all, on the force behind each thrust, as he plunged so deeply within her that she feared for the integrity of the bed frame. Knowing her luck, the thing would collapse, and alert the entire inn to their nocturnal activities.

Her climax, when it came, was like nothing Emma had ever experienced before in her life. It seemed to her as if one moment, every nerve ending within her was taut with frustration, and the next, she was drowning, but in a good way . . . in a sea of sparkling fire and light, wave after wave of liquid flame pouring over her, causing her to shudder joyously from her scalp to the bottoms of her toes. Though she didn't know it, the cry she let out was as much a sob as a scream, and hearing it, James lost all semblance of self-control. She had not been imagining it when she'd sensed he'd made love to her before, in his mind. He'd rehearsed this scene thousands of times before, but never, never had he expected it to be like this, so perfect, so natural, so easy. . . .

He gave one final thrust, driving himself as deeply into her as he could, no longer conscious of whether or not he frightened her, seeking only release.

It came, washing over him in torrents, powerful spasms of relief, and he roared his pleasure with such force that Emma worried he'd wake the whole inn.

For a moment after he collapsed on top of her, all Emma was conscious of was the pounding rhythm of his racing heart, the heavy weight of his body against hers, and the breeze blowing in from the ill-fitting windowpane, cooling her fevered skin. It took a few minutes for the enormity of what had just passed to sink in.

But when it did, Emma realized with a sinking heart that those shoes she'd nailed to the Wishing Tree hadn't done the slightest bit of good. Her bad luck continued, unabated.

How were they going to go about getting an annulment *now?*

Chapter Twenty-Two

"Emma!" The Dowager Lady Denham cried, throwing her arms wide. "Oh, my dear!"

And Emma found herself snatched up and hugged with enough force almost to crack her spine. The Dowager Lady Denham was nothing if not effusive in her greetings.

In that manner, she was nothing whatsoever like her son. Portly and plain—but with a finely honed fashion sense and a great appreciation for art and beauty—the Dowager Lady Denham was one of London's most popular hostesses, not only for the excellent table she kept, but also because of her resounding good humor.

Emma was treated to an example of that good humor when, the great lady finally releasing her from that bone-crunching hug, she found herself being scrutinized from head to toe.

"She's too thin," James's mother declared, inspecting Emma, in her plain tartan gown and matching bon-net—both a season out of date—critically. "Doesn't she look thin to you, James? Whatever did they feed you up there, Emma? Air? You're thin as a whippet. Well, no matter. Cook will soon fatten you up again. Wait until you taste her—but my goodness, who is this?" Lady Denham paused as she happened to notice the small boy who'd been half-hidden by Emma's skirts.

Fergus, regarding James's mother from behind Emma's hip, replied shyly, his cap in his hands, "Fergus MacPherson, mum."

The Dowager Lady Denham, seemingly not at all taken aback at the fact that her son had brought back with him from Scotland not only his cousin's widow, but a half-blind beggar child, as well, extended a plump and dimpled hand toward the child. "I am very glad to know you, Mr. MacPherson."

Fergus, looking pleased, nevertheless hid his face in Emma's skirt. It wasn't, Emma knew, that the boy was shy. Lord knew Fergus had never known a moment of self-consciousness in his life. Rather, it was the grandeur of the house on Park Lane—the towering ceilings, the liveried footmen, the sparkling clean marble floors and ornately framed paintings—that was a little overwhelming. Compared to the thatched hut in which the boy had lived in Faires, the house James shared with his mother was like a palace. Even Emma, who had once known the town house well, found herself feeling a bit awed by it. It had been a long while, she realized, since she had been inside a building that felt anywhere near warm enough, and where the windowpanes were actually clean enough to see through.

No, Emma did not blame Fergus a bit. She wished mightily that she could hide her face as well . . . though not necessarily for the same reasons. She'd been wishing for several days now—since the moment she'd wakened in that bed at Mrs. MacTavish's inn and realized precisely what she had done—that she could have just pulled the covers up over her head and remained that way forever.

Slept with her husband. That's what she'd done. And while, in the annals of history, her sin might not seem like a very grave one, to her it was positively depraved. Because of course James wasn't really her husband. Well, he was in the eyes of the law, she supposed, but theirs was to have been a titular union only. So what had happened that night at the inn? She couldn't explain it.

Nor could she extract an explanation from James. She had not even been able to get him alone for more than a few seconds at a time since that fateful night: when she'd wakened the next morning, having tumbled into an exhausted sleep following their ardent lovemaking, she'd been alone. And had stayed alone, well alone, until, coming down the stairs to Mrs. MacTavish's dining room, she found her husband—*husband!*—already at table, and in the company of none other than young Fergus MacPherson . . .

. . . who, James smilingly informed her, without the slightest reference to the torrid night they'd passed together, was accompanying them back to London, so that a doctor—a noted specialist of problems of the eye, with whom James happened to be acquainted—could examine him.

Emma had been surprised to hear this, of course—

but not as much as she might have expected. This was clearly not the same James Marbury who'd strode into his mother's drawing room and given his cousin a punch that had sent him sprawling. This was a completely different James Marbury, one who seemed, without wishing to make a fuss out of it, to genuinely want to help others. The change that seemed to have come over James in the year since she'd last since him was a subtle one, but it was very much in evidence.

What Emma could not quite figure out was just what, precisely, was responsible for it. Men like the earl of Denham did not change . . . not just like that. Something had happened to James, something that made him marry impoverished widows and help young boys with vision problems.

But what that something was, Emma could not even begin to guess.

And so it had been the three of them—Emma, James, and Fergus—the whole of the way back to London. Never had there been a moment, jouncing along that road, when Emma happened to chance upon James alone, so that she could put to him the hundreds of questions burning in her mind, foremost amongst which was, What are we going to do now?

For he couldn't possibly think they could simply carry on as if nothing had happened. Something *had* happened, something that, to Emma's way of thinking, at least, was momentous.

But maybe to a man-about-town like James, it *had* been nothing. He was certainly *acting* as if it had been nothing.

How nice. How very nice that he could go about,

perfectly oblivious that what to him might have been a routine sort of night, had been to Emma an event of life-changing significance.

How very like a man.

Something, Emma was beginning to suspect, might actually be wrong with James Marbury. True, she had not seen him in a year, but in that year, he'd seemed to have grown into a completely different person. . . .

The person who, at that very moment, was lifting Fergus up so that he could examine the set of crossed swords that hung above the mantel in the east drawing room, swords that had belonged to James's grandfather. What, Emma wondered, had *happened* to James while she'd been away? For he was most definitely *not* the same James who had sunk his fist into the bridegroom's face, then gone to her aunt and uncle to warn them of her planned elopement.

She would ask Lady Denham. That was precisely what she'd do. She'd ask Lady Denham, the second they got a moment together, whether something had happened to her son in the past year. A sharp blow to the head, perhaps? Some other sort of near-death experience? There had to be *something*. Something to explain his exceedingly odd behavior.

And when Emma found out what it was, she hoped—sincerely hoped—that it would help her decide what to make of what had happened between them the other night. Because she still could not help feeling, at times, that it had all been a strange—but undeniably wonderful—dream. Certainly James had not laid so much as a finger upon her since, except of course to offer his arm as she alighted from their carriage, or a hand to help her into her seat. Perhaps it *hadn't* happened. Perhaps they *hadn't* actually made love like soul mates too long parted, wordlessly, but deep into the night. . . .

Right. And perhaps pigs would fly on the morrow.

Emma would not, in fact, be surprised if they did. Nothing would surprise her anymore. She was back in London, a place she never thought she'd set foot in again. She was staying in the earl of Denham's Mayfair town house, just a stone's throw from the house in which she'd grown up—and from which she'd been banished, for marrying a man not thought to be suitable husband material for a Van Court. And she was married . . . yes, married for a second time . . . to a man she'd once believed she detested above all others in the universe.

At least that part—the fact that they were married— was a secret of which only she and James were aware, she thought, with some comfort.

It did not take long, however, for her to realize that even about this, she had been deluded.

"Emma," James's mother said, reaching out to squeeze Emma's hand as the two of them stood before the large gilt-framed mirror in the room in which Emma was to stay in during her visit, and where she'd gone to tidy herself after their arrival. "I am so pleased."

Emma, trying to redo her coiffure, which had been ruined the minute she'd removed her bonnet, smiled at the Dowager Lady Denham, thinking that the older woman meant that she was pleased to see Emma after so long an absence.

"I'm happy to see you again, too, my lady," Emma

said. She wasn't lying, either. She had always had a soft spot for Stuart's aunt. "It's been too long."

Lady Denham had sunk into a deep, luxuriously soft brocade armchair, one of a pair in front of the huge marble fireplace at one end of the richly furnished bedroom to which Emma had been shown. James having disappeared into his library to look at the mail that had collected in his absence, and Fergus having been escorted to the nursery, where he'd been amazed and delighted by the collection of toys that had been saved from James's childhood—"For my grandchildren," Lady Denham explained, with a significant look that Emma did not understand just then—the two women were alone for the first time since Emma's arrival. Now, Emma realized, would be the perfect time to ask whether James had seemed himself lately, or if, perhaps, he'd suffered a fall from his horse. Emma was turning to ask just that when, to her amazement, she found the dowager weeping into a lace handkerchief.

Alarmed, Emma hurried to kneel beside the older woman's chair. "Lady Denham," she cried. "What is it? Are you ill? Should I fetch your maid?"

"Oh, no!" Lady Denham looked up with streaming eyes, but a smiling face. "I'm not ill, my child. Just so . . . so happy to see you again. We none of us parted last year on the best of terms, I know. You must understand, my dear, that it was only because . . . well, you were so young! The idea of the two of you going to live in the wilds of the Hebrides . . . well, I simply couldn't bear it."

"I know," Emma said quietly. "Please, Lady Denham, don't upset yourself."

"Honoria." Lady Denham patted Emma's hand. "You must call me Honoria now, my dear. And you must never, never think that I blame you for what happened to Stuart. When he made up his mind about something, nothing and no one could change it. And he died . . . well, he died happy, didn't he, Emma? Stuart, I mean? The two of you were happy there in Faires, weren't you?"

Emma, chewing her lower lip a little, nevertheless replied quickly, "Yes, of course, we were."

"I thought as much." Lady Denham's pale blue eyes, which were so unlike her son's changeable hazel ones, were soft. "How could you not have been? But I must say, Emma, I am glad to have you back home."

Emma, touched, gave James's mother a smile. "Oh," she said. "I'm happy to be here, too. I didn't think I would feel this way, but it is, I have to admit, good to be back. Tell me, Lady Denham—" She noticed the other woman's disapproving look, and corrected herself. "I mean, Honoria. Have you any news of my family? Has Penelope married yet? What of my aunt and uncle? Are they well?"

"Very well," Lady Denham said, drying her eyes with an effort. "And even though I rather get the feeling they were hoping that quite a different match would come out of our association, they could not be happier. They are coming over this evening for dinner. I hope you do not mind. But when they heard the news, they would not be put off, not even for a night."

Emma, trying to make sense of this information, asked, "You mean . . . you told them I was coming?"

"I? Oh, no, dear. Not me—"

They were interrupted by a tap at the door. Emma,

rising, called, "Come in," and a pair of footmen appeared, followed by Burroughs, Lady Denham's butler. The footmen were carrying an enormous trunk between them. Emma recognized the swirling monogram on its side at once.

"But that," she said, with some bewilderment, "is Lord Denham's trunk."

"Indeed, my lady," Burroughs intoned.

Emma, confused by the "my lady," but assuming Burroughs, who had served under James's grandfather, was growing slightly addle-pated with age, said, "Shouldn't it go in Lord Denham's room, then?"

"Oh, dear." The dowager had risen to her feet, and now flashed a guilt-stricken look at her butler. "I think they truly did mean to keep it a surprise, Burroughs."

"It would appear so, madam," Burroughs replied, with a smile he seemed to be trying to suppress.

Emma, glancing from James's mother to her butler and then back again, asked, with growing suspicion, "Meant to keep *what* a surprise?"

But before anyone could reply, footsteps sounded in the hallway, and James appeared in the open doorway.

"Oh, there you are," he said, his gaze on his mother. He held up a piece of ivory foolscap. "I've just received the most extraordinary thing in the post. I'm hoping you'll be able to explain it."

Looking as if she might burst with joy, Lady Denham nevertheless controlled herself and inquired, "Would it be an invitation from Lord and Lady Cartwright to a ball in your honor?"

James glanced down at the slip in his hand. "It would. But not only in my honor."

"No," Lady Denham said. Then, unable to restrain herself another moment, she burst out, "No, it's being held in honor of you and . . . your wife!" She turned shining eyes upon Emma and her son. "Oh, my dears! We know! We know all about your little secret! Judge Reardon told us all. Congratulations, children! We couldn't be happier for you both!"

Chapter Twenty-Three

*E*mma felt the ground move beneath her. She was quite sure of it. Either that, or her knees, which had always been perfectly serviceable in the past, suddenly turned to jelly.

In any case, she sank down heavily into the chair Lady Denham had just vacated, her legs no longer capable of supporting her.

"Justice Reardon *wrote* to you?" James looked as thunderstruck as Emma felt. "*When?*"

"Why, we received his letter a few nights ago." Lady Denham's smile faded a little. "Oh, now, James, you mustn't be angry. He said you'd wanted it to be a surprise, and I can understand that, under the circumstances, a little discretion is necessary. We certainly shan't, for instance, put out any sort of announcement just yet. Well, maybe something small, in the society pages. 'Lately,' you know, 'the ninth earl of Denham to Mrs. Stuart Chesterton.' Something like that.

Hardly anyone will *know*, darling. Stuart wasn't . . ."
She glanced at Emma. "Well, not many in our set knew
him terribly well. He was so often at his books, you
see."

James did not appear to have heard his mother. He
was gazing down at the invitation in his hand, but he
did not seem actually to be seeing it. "That interfer-
ing old cuss," was all he said, and it was clear—to
Emma, anyway—from his tone that he was referring
to Justice Reardon.

But Lady Denham didn't seem to realize it, as she
cried, "Oh, now, you mustn't go blaming the
Cartwrights, dear heart, they're our oldest friends,
after all. And everyone is just so pleased. You should
have heard the Van Courts when they were here the
other night. They could hardly contain themselves,
they rushed over the minute they received their letter—"

Emma, her fingers tightening on the arms of her
chair, cried, "My aunt and uncle? He wrote to *them*, as
well?"

"Why, of course," Lady Denham said. She looked
from Emma to her son in confusion. "You aren't angry,
are you? I thought it was terribly sweet of him. Justice
Reardon, I mean. He seems a very conscientious, likable
man."

James's only response to this statement was a bitter
laugh. Emma wished she could see, as he seemed to,
even a hint of humor in the situation. But the whole
thing seemed to have turned from a dream—a strange
dream, true enough, but still, one in which Emma had,
if only for one night, felt, for the first time in her life,

completely and thoroughly loved—to a hideous nightmare.

Well, and hadn't that been what she'd wakened to, the morning after her wedding? A nightmare in which the man who had come to her in the night with so much passionate abandon seemed barely able to acknowledge her presence in the light of day?

"It was naughty," Lady Denham went on with a teasing smile, "very, very naughty of the two of you to think you could get away with such a thing. A secret marriage! Why, I can understand you're not wanting to advertise the fact that you'd married so soon after poor dear Stuart's death, but really, to try to hide it from *me!* Why, you had to know that *I* would understand."

"Mother," James said, but not soon enough. Lady Denham went on, gaily, "After all, anyone who saw the way the two of you fought—like cats and dogs!—that season of 'thirty-two would have known you were destined for the altar someday—"

"Mother!" James's handsome face, Emma noted, had gone an interesting shade of umber. Or perhaps it was only a trick of the spring light, trickling in from the tall windows behind her chair. For what on earth did *he* have to blush over?

"Pshaw," Lady Denham said, waving a dismissive hand at her son. "I used to see the way you two looked at one another across a ballroom. . . ."

Emma wished heartily that the floor beneath her chair would open up and swallow her whole. While it was true that James and she had sparred publicly and often in the past, Emma had not been aware that anyone besides Stuart—particularly her new mother-in-law—had ever taken note of these sometimes heated exchanges. And certainly they had not been, as Lady Denham seemed to interpret them, signs of anything more than two disparate individuals trying to sway one another to their own way of thinking. There had been, so far as Emma knew, no longing looks across any ballroom . . . at least, not coming from *her* direction.

And certainly James had shown no sign, that Emma had ever seen, of having felt anything for her but a sort of brotherly tolerance . . .

. . . until recently, that is.

But that, Emma was quite sure, had been her fault. After all, she'd been the one who'd started it all, with that good-night kiss. A simple kiss, that was all it was supposed to have been. But she was clearly too carnal a creature not to give in to her baser desires, and that night, what she'd desired more than anything was to see what lay beneath the satin of James Marbury's dressing gown.

Well, she'd found out—and it wasn't any wonder he could hardly look at her. What he must think of her!

"So we'll leave the trunk here, then, my lord?" Burroughs tone was interrogative, but he seemed supremely confident of a positive answer. Which, in fact, he received—to Emma's utter disbelief.

"Of course," James said, and then, without another glance in Emma's direction, he added, "I had better go and see about the boy's appointment with Dr. Stoneletter. . . ."

And he actually turned and left the room, without so much as another word.

Oh, dear. This wouldn't do at all. Shocked by her wantonness or not, James simply had to talk to her now. They couldn't possibly let things stand as they were!

Pushing herself from her chair, Emma said to Lady Denham, "Excuse me for a moment, my lady." Then she took off after James at a run—the servants, who stared after her astonishedly, be damned!

Hearing her heels clacking on the parquet behind him, James turned at the head of the stairs, saw her, took one look at her face, and assumed an expression of grim authority.

"Now, listen, Emma," he began, before she could get a word out.

But Emma was having none of it. She seized him by the arm and swung him, with all her might, into the nearest available room—which happened to be Lady Denham's morning room, but that was of no consequence. It was a private room, with a door she could close—which Emma promptly did, before whirling upon James.

"No, *you* listen, James," she hissed, keeping her voice low with an effort. "We can't ignore this. We have *got* to talk about it. I know you don't approve of me— God knows, I'm not too happy with myself, either—but you are not leaving this room until we've decided what we're going to do now."

James, assuming an expression of mild amusement, folded his arms across his chest. Emma tried not to notice how this caused the muscles in his shoulders to bunch up in a manner that was really most appealing, but which the widow of a curate hadn't the slightest bit of business noticing, for all the owner of those muscles happened to be her husband.

"And just," James asked, in a maddeningly sardonic tone, "what is it that you did that you think I disapprove of, Emma?"

Emma, to her mortification, felt her cheeks turning crimson. "Are you going to make me say it?" she whispered. "You know perfectly well. It was my fault, I admit it. I shouldn't have kissed you. But you were there, too. I can't be held entirely to blame."

James said, in that same dry tone, "Emma, I'm not blaming you for anything. Quite the contrary."

Not at all certain, in her state of embarrassed confusion, what he meant, Emma could only respond by shaking her head and asking, frantically, "What do you propose we do now?"

He raised one of his dark eyebrows. "I haven't the slightest idea," he said. "What do *you* propose we do, Emma?"

Emma's jaw sagged for a moment. She realized almost at once that her mouth was hanging open, and snapped it closed in a hurry.

"What do *I* propose?" she hissed. "This was *your* scheme from the beginning. What do *you* propose?"

"I propose," James said, unfolding his arms and slipping one hand inside his waistcoat pocket, from which he drew a watch and eyed it, "that we have tea. I myself am particularly hungry. And after tea, a bit of rest might be in order. I understand your entire family is coming over for a late supper to celebrate our happy nuptials."

Emma stamped a foot with enough energy to cause

the many glass ornaments, perched upon shelves about the room, to tinkle ominously.

"Oh, how can you make a joke out of this?" she cried. "Can't you see Judge Reardon has ruined everything? Your mother knows! The marriage was to be a secret from her, and now she knows!"

"Yes," James admitted, putting his watch away again and reaching up to rub his chin. "She does, doesn't she?"

But he was not showing the kind of outrage such a betrayal seemed, in Emma's mind, anyway, to warrant.

"James, how are we to get an annulment now?" Emma wanted to know. "Your mother is telling everyone! She is clearly over the moon about it. She asked me to call her Honoria! She even said something to me earlier about *grandchildren!*"

James dropped his hand away from his face, looking surprised. But not, as she might have thought, about his mother's hopes for his future offspring.

"Oh," he said, his hazel eyes hooded so that Emma could not read the expression in them. "You still want to go through with the annulment, then?"

Emma's jaw dropped once more. And this time she didn't snap her mouth closed right away. She was far too stunned to think of social niceties just then.

"James, are you *mad*? Of *course* I still want to go through with the annulment!" She eyed him warily. "I mean . . . don't you? That *was* the plan, wasn't it?"

"Well, you'll have to excuse me, but I rather thought the plan had changed." James spoke as mildly as if he were discussing a plan to take a new phaeton round the park for a spin. "It did seem to me as if the other night you were rather . . . liking the idea of being married to me."

Emma felt her cheeks go up in flame once more. That he could refer to what had passed between them in so offhanded a manner . . . well, it was no wonder he had reached the age of thirty and was still unmarried!

Except, of course, that he *was* married. That was the problem.

"What happened the other night," Emma managed to croak, her embarrassment so complete, it seemed to be choking her, "was a mistake. I thought I'd explained. I didn't mean . . . well, I didn't mean for it to . . ."

James, however, did not appear to be suffering from any embarrassment whatsoever. He looked down at her with the same cool detachment he seemed always to exhibit—except, Emma was in the peculiar position of being able to point out, when he was in the throes of sexual passion.

"I'm sorry you think so," he said politely. "I had rather thought . . . but I see I was wrong."

Emma, feeling her pulse quicken (though why this should be so, she could not imagine), asked, "You thought what?"

But James didn't say anything more—at least about his private feelings. Instead he said, "Judge Reardon's letter has made things awkward, but it's hardly call for panic, Emma. I see no reason why we shouldn't proceed with our plan, if that is your desire. My mother will be disappointed, of course, but she will get over it, as will, I'm certain, your family. So long as you are confident there shan't be any, er, unexpected fruits of our union. . . ."

Emma nearly choked. Though she'd hardly have thought such a thing possible, her embarrassment deepened until it seemed even her toes, in her well-worn boots, were curling with it.

"I see," he said, observing Emma's reaction with raised brows but no sign of any great emotion. "Well, perhaps we might want to forego any sort of decision until that particular question has been settled."

"I . . ." Emma hardly knew what to say. It seemed something should be said, and yet she didn't know what. "I don't want you to feel you have to . . ."

Now he did show emotion. He frowned at her with disapproval. "Emma," he said, severely, "do you really think that if you found yourself pregnant with my child, I should fail to—"

"I wouldn't want you to feel obligated," Emma interrupted quickly. "I—"

It was James's turn to interrupt. "You needn't trouble yourself on that account, Emma," he said. "I have always rather fancied fatherhood. But should you find, however, that it is not to be, the annulment is yours, so long as you haven't any compunction about perjuring your immortal soul."

Trust James to bring up so drily the fact that what had happened that night in Mrs. MacTavish's inn would make swearing that the match had never been consummated not just difficult, but an outright lie.

"I myself," he went on, "have never been particularly bothered about the final destination of my immortal soul anyway. Now is that all, Emma? Because I need to finish that letter on young master Fergus's behalf, and there is your bank to be consulted, as well, in preparation for Judge Reardon forwarding the money owed you. . . ."

Emma stood in the center of the flowered pile that carpeted Lady Denham's morning room, feeling, for reasons she couldn't say, disappointed. Why on earth she should feel that way, when she had in fact gotten everything she'd asked for, she could not imagine. Certainly she wasn't feeling any sort of feminine indignation over the fact that James hadn't fought her on the idea of the annulment.

And yet. And yet he seemed remarkably improved since the last time she'd seen him, that fateful night she'd told him of her and Stuart's plans to elope. . . .

Emma shook herself. What in heaven's name was she thinking? Was she so totally swayed in her feelings for the man just because he'd happened to arrange for one her pupils to see a doctor? Or had her attitude gone through so notable a change because of the man's prowess in another arena?

Well, it would not continue. Of that she was certain. He had told her to be an adult about this. Well, she would be an adult, as businesslike and coldhearted as he was.

And so she said, putting her shoulders back, "Thank you, no, Lord Denham. That is all."

Still, when James, with a polite nod, turned and left the room, Emma had to sit down for some time before she felt recovered enough to face his mother once more. She even had to tell herself, again and again, that all this would be over soon—assuming that, as her previous marriage had proven, she was not the child-conceiving type. No, soon she'd be able to go back to her peaceful life in Faires and never, if she chose not to, see James Marbury again.

Or so she told herself.

And for a while, she even managed to believe it.

Chapter Twenty-Four

It was, James decided, going well.

Justice Reardon had helped enormously, though James doubted the man knew it. The more people who knew about the match, of course, the more difficult a time they were going to have extricating themselves from it.

Which was exactly the last thing James could ever imagine wanting . . . to be extricated from marriage to Emma Van Court.

Even now, as he sat in his mother's drawing room, watching his bride as she became reacquainted with her family—for all the world as if the last time she'd seen them, it had not been to declare she was marrying against their wishes, no matter what they said—he could not quite believe his good fortune. He had gone to Scotland to find a body, and ended up bringing home a bride.

And not just any bride, either, but the very woman

who had for months and months haunted his dreams and plagued his heart. James could not imagine what he had done to deserve such a rich reward. He only knew that he'd won it at last, and he was determined to guard it diligently.

Even against Emma herself, who, he was convinced, did not know her own heart as well as perhaps she thought she did.

James, watching her as she made a remark to Penelope that caused the latter to throw back her head and laugh (Penelope, James could not help noticing, was taking great pains not to let on how mortified she was that her younger cousin had married not once, but twice now, while she herself had yet to marry a first time), thought, not for the first time, that it was perfectly amazing that the Van Courts, who were among the most cultured and wealthy families in London, but not exactly the most philanthropic, should have raised a girl such as Emma. She was, in every way, as unlike her cousin as day was unlike night.

And it wasn't just the plain gray dress she wore—James's first call, in the morning, would be to his mother's dressmaker, to commission a trousseau for his bride, who, though even in gray the loveliest woman in the room, was quite outshone by her cousin's gold silks and heavily jeweled wrists.

No, Emma had always been different from the rest of her family. Perhaps because of the early deaths of her parents, or perhaps merely because of something innate within her, she had always been excessively sensitive to the plight of others—from the linnets she'd found in the garden after a storm, and begged James to put back in their nest, then later to the poor starving peoples of Papua New Guinea for whom she'd begged alms of him. It was no wonder that, from an early age, it had been Stuart she'd worshiped. Besides a pale face and a habitual expression of melancholy—traits, James knew, irresistible to a young girl—he had also, like Emma, owned a burning desire to help the less fortunate.

But James, like Emma's aunt and uncle, had never taken her infatuation with his cousin very seriously. Indeed, James had always felt it would die a natural death when Emma discovered that Stuart was, by nature, far more interested in spiritual unions than physical ones.

Unfortunately, however, this discovery never seemed to occur. In fact, at precisely the time James was expecting to be called upon to mop up Emma's tears of heartbreak over Stuart forsaking her for the church, he found himself being informed by her of their intention to elope. Which was not how things were to have gone at all.

What he had been thinking, a year ago, when he determined that she would eventually come around to seeing him, and not his cousin, as her perfect match, James could not imagine. While he had been declaring his conviction that the poor should be left to fend for themselves, Stuart had been busy winning Emma's heart with his unfaltering faith in God and unending charitable impulses. It wasn't any wonder that in the end she'd chosen Stuart. How much more glamorous to a girl like Emma was a life of poverty and discomfort in the Hebrides than a pampered existence as the wife of an earl!

But earls, James was now determined to show her, were in a far better position to help the less fortune-favored than penniless curates.

He had already done an admirable job—or so he fervently hoped—of showing her that earls made better lovers than curates. Though he was not, unfortunately, privy to Emma's thoughts on that matter, he did not think she could have any complaints in that department—despite her continuing insistence on this annulment he now regretted ever mentioning in the first place.

But how else was he to have convinced her to marry him? For Emma had not yet forgiven him—or so he feared—for his behavior that afternoon in his drawing room. Nor had she any way of guessing his long-held secret love for her. She could not have known that, all the time she was sighing to him about his cousin, he was sighing to himself about her. . . .

But Stuart was gone now. Emma was free to marry—and to love—again. And Emma needed loving . . . needed it badly. For Emma was, as he'd discovered from the moment he'd kissed her back at Castle MacCreigh—and perhaps always known—a highly passionate sort of girl, the kind who seemed to enjoy kissing, and similar entertainments, very much. So much, in fact, that it was no great difficulty to get her to forget everything else, in her desire to go on being . . . entertained. It was a quality rarely found, in James's experience, in ladies of distinction, but always highly appreciated on the rare occasions it turned up. That Emma should be such a creature did not surprise James, but it did, once again, make him curse his past behavior toward her. That he had let such a woman go was an unforgivable sin, in his opinion. It would not happen a second time.

But the road to marital bliss with Emma Van Court Chesterton was not going to be an easy one, James knew. This was made all the clearer when, at the end of the long evening of celebration with the Van Courts— though *celebrating,* perhaps, might be too strong a word for the sentiments of Emma's aunt and uncle, who, though they had accepted the dowager's invitation readily enough, seemed somewhat stunned that it was apparently Emma who was to be the next Lady Denham, and not Penelope, whom they had been thrusting beneath James's nose since the girl had been barely out of the schoolroom—he and Emma were at last alone together in the pleasant room in which his mother had put them. Emma, having emerged from the dressing room in the familiar threadbare robe, had pointed imperiously at the set of brocade-covered chairs before the fire and asked, "Are you taking them? Or shall I?"

James could not help casting the bed, piled high with snowy white coverlets, a longing glance.

Unfortunately, Emma caught it.

"James, what can you be thinking?" she cried. "We cannot sleep in that bed together. You know what happened last time. If we're to get an annulment, we cannot . . . well, we cannot continue in that manner."

James, likewise clad in a dressing gown—he'd had to see to his own wardrobe, what with Roberts back in Faires managing Emma's school and her dog's new litter—sat down on the edge of the bed to remove his slippers.

"I don't see why I should have to get a crick in my neck from sleeping all night in a chair," he said, "when there is a comfortable bed a few feet away." It was a gamble, he knew, to go on in this way. But a man had to fight for what he wanted. "And besides, what difference does it make now? We've committed the sin once already. A few more times couldn't get us in any hotter water. Or hellfire, I should say."

Emma did not laugh. It was as if she had worn herself out, forcing herself to put on the gay facade of a happy bride for her family, chattering happily about mutual acquaintances, and maintaining, all the way through the soup, after the melon, even up through the cheese course, an air of giddy joy.

He supposed such a display was necessary, considering that the last time Emma had seen Arthur and Regina Van Court, it had been in their own family's library, with her uncle warning of the perils of an injudicious marriage and her aunt fretting over what the earl of Denham must think of her, confiding in him such a ridiculous plan. If either Emma's uncle or aunt were conscious of the irony of the fact that, a year later, their wayward niece was now married to that same earl, they did not mention it. They were all that was obliging . . . though James wasn't fooled, and knew Emma could not be either. Had she returned to London merely as Stuart's widow, and not the earl of Denham's bride, her reception by her family would not have been nearly as welcoming.

As it was, the effusiveness of that welcome seemed to have been a little wearing on the bride. That, coupled with their arduous journey from Scotland, had tired her. He could tell by the slight traces of violet beneath her sapphire eyes. It had been a long, eventful day.

Still, she wasn't about, it appeared, to back down from this fight.

"It's wrong," she said. "And you know it. But if

you're going to be that way about it, fine. I'll take the chairs."

And she stomped toward the bed and yanked the silk coverlet from it.

James watched as she attempted to make a semblance of a bed between the two chairs.

"You're being ridiculous, Emma," he said. "As two adults, we should be perfectly capable of sleeping in the same bed without anything . . . untoward happening, you know."

"Ha! Where have I heard *that* before?" Emma asked.

"You," James could not help pointing out, "were the one who started it, you know."

He had the satisfaction of seeing her face turn pink in the firelight.

"Well, you needn't concern yourself about it happening again," she said, primly folding herself into the small, distinctly uncomfortable-looking bed she'd made. "As I will keep a safe distance from you tonight."

"Your concern," James remarked, "for my immortal soul is much appreciated. But I really do think it's too late, Emma. The damage is done. I don't see what it matters, if I'm to burn in hellfire anyway, whether we sin once or a thousand times."

When, from the twin chairs, there was no response, Emma having pulled the silk coverlet over her head, apparently out of a desire to end the conversation, James only gave a shrug and, sliding beneath the cool sheets, admitted, "Well, I suppose you have a point."

No response from the twin chairs. James, amused, folded his hands behind his head and gazed at the royal blue canopy above his head.

"After all," he said, "chances are that the more we . . . how did you put it? Oh, yes, *continue in that manner* . . . the more likely we are to be caught. Progeny, after all, would be incontrovertible proof of our sin."

From beneath the coverlet came a small sound. James, studying the lumps in the coverlet, uncertain which one indicated the place where her head was, said, "What was that, my love?"

She flung the coverlet down from her face. Her blond curls making a halo—of which she seemed perfectly unaware—around her head in the firelight, she said with some asperity, "That has nothing to do with it."

"Are you sure about that?" he asked, with another arch of his brow.

"Very sure," she replied.

"Well," James said, enjoying himself more, he knew, than he ought to. But there was something about her indignation—and she was so often indignant with him—that he found immensely entertaining. It was a far cry from the fawning interest of the Honorable Miss Fiona Bains and Penelope Van Courts of the world. "There's something noble about your sentiment, I suppose. But as there's every possibility that the damage is already done, I really feel I must point out that your sleeping in a chair can't be good for him."

Emma knit her brow. "Good for whom?"

"My son and heir," James said. "You might very well be with child already, you know, Emma."

Emma's cheeks turned an interesting shade, but her expression—one that seemed to clearly indicate that she thought very little of him indeed—did not change.

"Your concern is noted," she said. "But if I were capable of bearing children, don't you think I'd have done so already? I am, after all, a widow."

James answered with some surprise, "But you were only with Stuart for a short time." Something in the tone of her voice had already warned him that on this territory, he would do well to tread carefully. Penelope Van Court had said something about it as well, he'd noted, in the dining room. Upon seeing Fergus, she'd laughed, "Well, he can't be yours, can he, Emma? He's much too old." Emma, who had laughed a good deal—though in not the most convincing manner—throughout the evening, had not laughed at all then.

Sensing that this might be an issue about which Emma could not joke, he added, "The two of you had hardly half a year together. I am, of course, not well versed in matters such as these, being, as you are well aware, a bachelor. But it is my understanding that it's been known to take twice that long—even longer—for some women. It isn't uncommon, Emma."

"All the more reason," came Emma's prim response, "for me to stay in this chair, far away from you, then."

And James realized belatedly that, in his efforts to lend balm to a wound he was only learning just now even existed, he had perhaps only caused further pain. As he lay in the semi-darkness, listening to the soft hiss of the fire Emma was curled up before, he couldn't help allowing his mind to wander down a dangerous path—one near which he'd hardly dared let himself venture, these past twelve months. And that was to wonder just what, precisely, had gone on in the bedroom between Stuart and Emma.

For Emma was, as he knew now only too well, not a

passive lover. She seemed to him to possess a healthy appetite for sin.

But Stuart? James could not see it. He could not even picture the two of them together—and not because he didn't want to, though of course he didn't. He simply could not envision Stuart and Emma . . . like that. Knowing what he did now about Emma's very great interest in that arena—and knowing Stuart as he did— James could not imagine that their union had been a successful or happy one.

Still, he could not blame Emma for having been drawn to his cousin. She could have had no way of knowing what lay in store for her in *that* direction. She had been, after all, only just out of the schoolroom at the time, as blissfully ignorant of the marital arts as most girls of her age and station. It had been up to her aunt and uncle to protect her from an injudicious match. And they, despite James's efforts, had failed miserably to do so.

And were, he felt, every bit to blame for their niece's current situation.

A situation, however, that he felt was not as grave as Emma herself might believe. Because while she probably considered herself in a pathetic state—having to endure a titular marriage to a man who'd once betrayed her, in order to collect the inheritance due her from her husband's murderer—James knew differently. She was, though she was apparently completely unaware of it, loved, and very dearly so. One of these days he was going to have to make this fact known, since apparently his actions were not saying it clearly enough.

But not yet. Certainly not now that he'd caught a

glimpse of the gaping wound she'd kept so carefully hidden until now. She still had a good deal of healing to do before she could raise her head and see the world again as a safe and welcoming place. All she had known from it this past year was hurt. She would not, he was certain, be receptive to any declarations of love, from him or from anybody else, until she had begun to feel confident of herself again—really confident, and not just this mask of confidence that she had put on for her family and all those who might have reason to utter those four most detested words in the universe: *I told you so.*

He could afford to wait . . . this time. He had waited a year ago, and look where it had gotten him. The love of his life had married another.

And yet the news was not all grim. For, twelve months later, wasn't it he that she was married to this time?

No. He could afford to wait. His patience, he was convinced, would be rewarded. At some point—perhaps only a few weeks from now—she wouldn't be smarting so badly, and she'd look up and realize that he had changed.

And with that knowledge, he hoped, would blossom something a little stronger than the friendship he knew they already shared. Friendship and mutual attraction. For he knew, much as she might care to deny it, that she desired him. Though her lips might say the opposite, her body told the truth. Could it be very long before she started to listen?

In the meantime, at least she was sleeping not twenty feet away from him, instead of all the way across the country.

A fact that weighed, more and more heavily, on James's conscience as the night wore on. It was perfectly ridiculous, her sleeping in those chairs. He would be damned before he'd sleep in them, but the alternative was to retire to some other room, allowing her to have this one to herself, and that would never do. His mother would never let him hear the end of it.

Which was why, round about midnight, he finally gave up, flung back the sheets, and went quietly to the twin chairs before the fire.

She was asleep, but how she'd managed to get that way, he couldn't imagine. Pure exhaustion, probably. Her head was tilted at a peculiar angle that would, if he allowed it to continue in that position much longer, prove painful come morning.

With a sigh, James bent down and, gathering her up, silk coverlet and all, lifted her from the twin chairs.

She woke instantly.

"Put me down," she commanded, in a voice roughened by sleep.

"I will," James said. "In the bed, where you belong."

Her response was unhesitating. "James," she began, but he shushed her.

"Quiet now," he said. "Or you'll wake my mother up and send her and Lord knows how many other people barging in here. Then they'll find out the truth about us and no doubt feel duty-bound to inform Judge Reardon, and you'll never see your ten thousand pounds, or the lovely school you intend to build with it."

This sobered her.

"How did you know about the school?" she asked.

"You talk in your sleep."

She looked shocked. "I do not!"

"You do," he said. "But I'm still willing to share my bed with you, just the same."

She blinked at him warily. "Fine," she said, at length. "But no kissing—"

This, of course, was too perfect a taunt to resist, and a second later James was kissing her as thoroughly as he knew how—which, given his long and varied experience in that venue, was quite thoroughly indeed. Emma responded as he'd known perfectly well she would, first by stiffening rebelliously in his arms, then relaxing by degrees, until moments later, she'd wrapped both her own arms around his neck and seemed to melt against him, her mouth falling open against the onslaught of his lips. It was easy after that to lay her back upon the bed and, pulling away the coverlet, replace its warmth with his person.

Emma, as he sank down atop her, seemed to recover herself a bit, and murmured something against his lips. But then his hand dipped beneath her gown, his fingers seeking out and then finding one of her smooth round breasts, and whatever she'd been saying was lost in an appreciative sigh. And when with a knee, he parted her legs, placing an iron-hewn thigh against the slick crevice where her legs met, Emma, though she tried to resist it, could not help sighing again, feeling the pleasant wave of desire that passed over her at the sudden contact.

She gave up after that, all the fight gone from her trembling limbs. It was as if he possessed a magic touch that rendered her compliant to his whims. She didn't care if they stayed married or not, so long as he kept touching her there, sending such delicious sensations through her body.

James felt her surrender and took full advantage of it. Perhaps it wasn't fair, this power he now knew he had over her, but he wasn't about to feel any guilt over it . . . not while he had her exactly where he'd been wanting her all day. Inching up the hem of her night-dress, he caressed with his hand now what he'd previously stroked with his thigh, eliciting soft murmurs of pleasure from Emma, who, in some distant part of her mind, thought it could only be wrong, making love like this to another man under what had once been her husband's roof. But then she remembered that James was her husband now. Besides, it didn't seem to matter where they were when James wanted her. He always seemed able to make her want him, too.

Before she was fully aware of what he was about, James had abandoned his dressing gown, and suddenly, that part of him that she had at first found so alarming for its size the first time she'd encountered it, but which she had since grown to appreciate most fondly, branded her thigh. With a boldness she hadn't previously known she possessed, she took hold of it and guided it into her, gasping as he filled her, even as he had gasped when her fingers had curled around him.

Then they were together, in the way that only two people who were truly compatible could be—even if one of them was too stubborn to admit it. Still, Emma had not had the wildly diverse experience in these matters that James had, and so could not know how rare it was, this perfect fit.

But she seemed more than ready to admit the pleasure the two of them were capable of giving one another, after his repeated thrusts soon sent her over the edge, into that place she'd only been with him. There might have been a good deal she'd have been ready to admit, after that.

When James, too, found release, he collapsed atop her and they lay in a damp pile, breathing hard and barely able to see one another in the darkening room, as the fire had all but gone out. Still, when he finally slid from her, James's green-eyed gaze sought out her azure one, and he asked, affably, "Now will you stay in bed like a good girl?"

To which she responded merely by burying her face in his neck.

But that was good enough for James.

Chapter Twenty-Five

"The blue suits you," Regina Van Court declared. "But then, blue's always suited Emma. Hasn't it, Penny?"

Penelope Van Court, eyeing the pile of gowns that was growing ever larger on a nearby settee, merely pressed her lips together. Standing on a footstool in the center of the room, Emma supposed this was all very hard on her cousin. Penelope had always had a great eye for fashion, and though her parents had never denied her a thing it was in their power to give, they could not give her what she most longed for.

Which was, of course, a husband. All Penelope cared about was no longer having to wear the white and pale pinks young unmarried women were relegated to in a ballroom. Seeing Emma, two years Penelope's junior, being fitted into an evening gown of the boldest blue imaginable had not done much for the eldest Miss Van Court's mood.

"I suppose," Penelope said, and she rose from her chair and strolled toward a nearby window, her back to the puddles of vermilion and emerald and gold dotting the room behind her.

Emma, a worried expression on her face, watched her cousin pass by. How could she tell Penelope, who cared so much for clothes and other fripperies, that it was just a facade? That her marriage was a sham, a trick, a mockery . . .

Or was it? The way things seemed to be shaping up, her marriage to James appeared to be turning into quite a normal one—or at least, what Emma took to be a normal marriage, her first one actually having been quite different.

But Emma didn't suppose that anything she said to Penelope would make a difference. The girl seemed determined to be unhappy—and Emma could not exactly blame her. Never had Emma seen as many gowns, bonnets, corsets and petticoats and slippers as the Dowager Lady Denham's dressmaker had brought with her the morning after Emma's arrival in London. It was as if the earl had bought out an entire dress shop.

And perhaps he had. When Emma had stepped with perfect innocence into the room, expecting to find only her aunt and cousin come to call upon her and James's mother, her eyes had nearly bulged from her head.

"Oh, no," James had said, laying a hand upon her back and propelling her gently back toward the door through which she'd just backed up. "For better or for worse, Emma, you're my wife, and though you look perfectly charming in them, I can't have you going about in your gowns from 'thirty-two. People will think me a skinflint."

But Emma, knowing full well how much a wardrobe like the one spread out before her cost, was quick to reply, "Supposing you donated the cost of the clothes to the poor. No one would dare call you a skinflint then."

"Supposing you act, just for one morning, like the wife of an earl. I might reward you by directing a cheque to be issued to the Society for the Improvement in the Quality of Life for the Sandwich Islanders, or whatever organization it is that you are lately supporting." At Emma's surprised look, he added, "I am not, as you very well know, opposed to helping the poor, my dear. I would prefer merely to help them help themselves. Give a man a fish . . . well, I'm sure you know the rest."

Then, kissing her on the forehead, he left her to the tender ministrations of Madame Delanges and his mother, while he escorted young Master Fergus to his first appointment with the esteemed Dr. Stoneletter.

Thinking of the exchange now—and the other, much more heated (and a good deal more physical) one they'd shared the night before—Emma wondered at James's behavior. It wasn't her imagination. He was actually acting . . . well, in a loverlike manner. There was no other word for it.

But that was absurd. James Marbury was not in love with her. He had never expressed anything but disapproval of her the entire time they'd known one another. This extraordinary thing that seemed to happen whenever they kissed . . . well, that she could not explain. But

292 • *Patricia Cabot*

it certainly wasn't love. Passion, perhaps. But passion was a far cry from love.

Still, this hardly explained his kindness toward her. And Fergus. She supposed she could deny it no longer: James Marbury, whom she'd once thought the most hard-hearted man she had ever met, had softened in the year since last she'd seen him.

How and why she could not say. It surely wasn't on her account. She had been nothing if not contrary to him, since that first morning she'd looked out her window and spied him in her vegetable patch. Well, except for the time they'd spent in bed together. It was very difficult to be contrary, Emma was discovering, when James was in a dressing gown . . . or out of it, as often as not.

"Oh!" The Dowager Lady Denham clapped her hands, bringing Emma out of her revery. "That is the one! You must wear it tonight, to the Cartwrights!"

Emma's aunt seconded that opinion. "It brings out her eyes beautifully." To Madame Delanges, she said, "Can you have it ready by eight?"

"But of course," the plump Frenchwoman exclaimed. "Agnes, Mary. *Allez, allez.*"

The two seamstresses scurried to help Emma from the basted gown. As they were doing so, Penelope, by the window, suddenly exclaimed, "Here's another one, Lady Denham."

"My word," the amiable dowager cried. "I had no idea James was so popular. We haven't even made a formal announcement, and already the wedding gifts are pouring in. I can't think where we shall put it all."

Emma, who had received only a single wedding gift

for her first marriage—and that had been the Limoges James had so thoroughly demolished—could not help but feel a pang upon hearing this. Would she, she wondered, have to return all of these gifts after the annulment? She supposed so.

Still, whenever she remembered James's look of surprise the day before when she'd brought the subject up— "You still want to go through with the annulment, then?" he'd asked her—she wondered. Wondered why she'd said she did. Because she didn't. She was quite sure of that now.

Except of course she had to. There was the truth about Stuart, for one thing. Were James ever to find it out, he would never consent to remaining married to her. It was simply too awful.

And besides, earls needed heirs. Something at which Emma had proved to be no use whatsoever. Making heirs, that is. Oh, James had tried, she knew, to make her feel better on that account, but it was no good. She knew the annulment would have to go through. It would not be fair to James, otherwise.

"Wait," Penelope said, still at the window. "This isn't a delivery. It's . . . well, I don't know *what* it is."

"Come away from the window, love," Emma's aunt called. "You're in the draft. You won't want to come down with another one of your sore throats, you'll miss the ball."

"Emma," Penelope, not budging from the window, called. "This appears to be one of yours. You always did collect the oddest people. This one seems to be a large redheaded person who goes about in a kilt and long black cape."

Emma, slipping into the old gray gown with the tattered lace trim, paused with an arm half in, half out of a sleeve. *"What?"*

"Do you know someone like that? Because he's just got down from a carriage with an equally redheaded young woman and another, rather scruffy-looking boy. They are just about to ring the bell."

Far away, a bell did ring, and Dowager Lady Denham cried, "Goodness! Emma, are these friends of yours? Shall we admit them?"

"You certainly can't keep them out," Penelope cried, with a little of her old spirit, from before Emma had committed the perilous sin of marrying before her. "I never saw a man in a kilt who actually looked as if he knew how to wear one. I am prodigiously interested in meeting this one." Though of course Lord MacCreigh's kilt was not the reason behind Penelope's interest in meeting him. The fact that he was tall and appeared to weigh over ten stone was all that mattered to her. Penelope knew that at the ripe old age of one and twenty, she could no longer afford to be discriminating where potential husbands were concerned. "Let him come in, Lady Denham. This should be extraordinarily entertaining."

Emma did not think so. Emma did not think so at all. For what in heaven's name could Lord MacCreigh be doing here in London? He could only have come to stir up trouble. And trouble, Emma did not need.

The dowager must have observed the look of distress on Emma's face, since she laid a hand to her cheek and said, "Oh, dear. I really do think—"

But when Burroughs threw open the door at that

very moment and announced the baron of MacCreigh and his sister, the Honorable Miss Fiona Bain, Penelope was quick to inform him that they would all be delighted to see the Bains, and asked that Burroughs bid them wait in the drawing room, where the ladies would be happy to join them as soon as Emma's gown had been put to rights.

And then there was nothing for it. Because Emma could not refuse to see the Bains now that they already knew she was at home.

Strange as it was to see her old acquaintances—dare she call them friends?—from Faires, Emma was not prepared for the meeting, particularly when she spied, standing in the corner with his cap in his hands and a very nervous expression on his face, young John McAddams, her best scholar, whom she'd had such high hopes of someday seeing admitted to college.

The explanation for how he, of all people, had come to be standing in the earl of Denham's drawing room was quickly given, after stilted, slightly bewildered, greetings were exchanged.

"Lord Denham's orders, ma'am," John said shyly. "Or I should say, my lady. He sent word that he'd gotten me an interview for Oxford, and paid my passage here for it."

Emma barely had time to register this incredible piece of information before Fiona was adding, in her silkiest voice, "And we, of course, couldn't let the boy travel alone, so we thought we'd come along. It's been so long since we were last in London." The girl's blue eyes flicked across the tastefully papered walls and heavy velvet drapes. Emma hadn't the slightest doubt that this was the grandest room the Honorable Miss Fiona Bain had ever stood in, though the younger girl would never have let on any such thing—any more than she would let on the true reason for their visit. It was James, Emma knew, and James alone that had drawn Fiona to London, just as it was Emma that had drawn Lord MacCreigh there.

Oh, what a tiresome pair they were! Emma wondered what the baron had pawned to pay for their passage. Doubtless some family heirloom. And all in the hopes of finding her marriage to the earl in shambles, so that the pair of them might profit in picking up the pieces.

Not that either of them were about to admit to any such hopes. "We came to do a bit of shopping," Fiona said, ever so casually.

Emma believed this about as much as she believed in the man in the moon. But she was beyond feeling rancorous toward the other girl. All she could think about was John McAddams, and how he had come to be on Park Lane. James had done it. James had arranged it all. And she could not remember saying a word, not one word, to him about the boy. How had he known?

More importantly, why had he done it? Emma felt the most peculiar rush of warm feeling toward her husband, a man whom she'd once suspected of having an abacus where his heart should be. Never had she seen a person so changed as James Marbury.

And there was a part of her that could not help wondering if it were possible—even the slightest bit possible—that he had done it for her.

Her thoughts were interrupted, however, when Fiona

said, "And of course we also came to see how married life was suiting the new Lady Denham."

Emma, jolted from her thoughts, could not help replying, a bit confusedly, "Seeing as how I've been married less than a week, I am hardly an adequate judge on the matter."

"I can tell you," Lady Denham said, with her usual warmhearted loquaciousness. "The newlyweds are head over heels for one another. I never saw two people so in love. Now, Lord MacCreigh, may I offer you a glass of sherry?"

Geoffrey Bain, who had probably never sipped sherry in his life, looked as stunned as Emma felt, but for entirely different reasons. Never seen two people so in love! Surely Lady Denham was only seeing what she wanted to see . . . or trying to make Emma's guests feel at ease. It was an understandable sentiment, since both Lord MacCreigh and his sister—not to mention poor John McAddams—seemed quite out of their element.

James? In love with her? Of course not. *Of course not.*

And yet how else to explain Fergus? And now John? Not to mention this marriage, which certainly could not have been in James's best interests.

"You still want to go through with the annulment, then?"

It was all Emma could do to make simple conversation with her guests, her mind was in such a whirl. Penelope, however, was only too willing to help. Her interest in Geoffrey Bain only increased upon her closer inspection of him, Penelope finding him, Emma supposed, imminently more interesting than the assortment of nasal-voiced, thin-shouldered suitors she usually encountered. Spotting the ornamental dirk Lord Mac-Creigh wore, Penelope asked a number of questions about it, almost managing to bring the baron out of the despondency he had sunk into upon hearing from Lady Denham that Emma's marriage to her son was not the total and complete disaster he'd evidently been hoping for—and planning, perhaps, to rescue her from.

Emma, for her part, had to hand it to the Bains. They were not siblings easily to give up on a plan once undertaken. Emma, though married to another, just might yet be convinced to give the baron a try. Well, and why not? Ten thousand pounds, as Emma well knew, was ten thousand pounds.

Her husband, Emma was not particularly surprised to learn, did not find the Bains' sudden appearance in London at all amusing. His expression, in fact, upon returning home to find these esteemed guests in his drawing room was a very dark one indeed. Though he welcomed John McAddams graciously enough, he could not be as warm to the Honorable Miss Bain, who nevertheless made every attempt to thrust herself into his notice, until Emma was quite embarrassed for the girl.

And James had barely a civil word at all to say to Miss Bain's brother. At his earliest opportunity of getting Emma alone, in fact, James demanded, "What are they doing here? Tell me you didn't invite them."

Emma, shocked at the suggestion she would ever encourage Lord MacCreigh's interest in her, hastened to assure him she had neither invited the Bains, nor expected him to take them under his charitable wing, as it appeared he had young John McAddams. This appeared to mollify James not at all. And her stilted attempts to thank him on behalf of John McAddams— for his generosity there had been most unexpected, so much so that Emma hardly knew how to put into words what was in her heart, which was a sincere and abiding gratitude, equaled only to her complete confoundment that he should do something so kind—were brushed aside. His ire had been raised, and it only soared higher when Penelope, clearly taken by the manly and morose baron, who, unlike the other young men of her acquaintance, neither quoted Byron nor looked likely to do so, asked innocently, "And what are you and Miss Bain doing tonight, my lord? Do say you are not engaged. For we are all going to a ball in honor of the newlyweds, and I do think it would be great fun if you came with us."

Both Regina Van Court and the dowager were duly horrified by this, but there was little they could do once the words were spoken, save send a note to the Cartwrights apologizing for the addition to their party. James, however, was so overcome with rage that he had to leave the room for a half hour altogether. Emma, herself not liking the smirk that appeared upon the baron's face, would have followed her husband, if only to keep him from smashing something, but she was distracted by Fergus MacPherson, who took that moment to burst into the room modeling his new spectacles, of which he was immensely proud. Though Dr. Stoneletter had not held out much hope of Fergus's ever regaining the sight he'd lost, the boy declared, there was a very good chance of his holding onto the vision he was in possession of, so long as he completed certain "exercises" and wore his new glasses religiously.

Good news indeed, and a happy little celebration ensued, in which heavily frosted tea cakes—Fergus, it appeared, had already made fast friends with Lord Denham's cook—were passed round. James returned in the midst of this, looking more like himself, though Emma could not help casting nervous looks in his direction now and then, wondering if he had his pistols with him. He had, after all, challenged Lord MacCreigh to a duel once before. What was to keep him from doing it again?

Fortunately the rest of the visit from the Faires contingent passed without bloodshed, and finally Lord MacCreigh and his sister decided they needed to return to their hotel in order to change for the ball (John McAddams eschewed an invitation to the Cartwrights', finding his lordship's library a good deal more appealing than London's current crop of debutantes).

And if Lord MacCreigh had hopes of lingering for a fraction of a second longer than he ought over Emma's hand while bidding her adieu, or passing her any sort of love letter—this last would have been highly unlikely, as Lord MacCreigh had a strong dislike for the written word—these hopes were dashed by the fact that James stood with a hand upon her waist, the very picture of the possessive husband. In fact, if Emma had not been so stunned by the events of the past hour, she might have joked at his turning out to be the jealous type.

But there was nothing, that she could see, to joke about. There were too many other things to consider, too much to feel. What she needed, she thought, was a walk—a nice brisk walk along the seashore, such as she would have taken back in Faires, to think things through.

But she wasn't back in Faires. There was no seashore in London. And wives of earls did not go walking by themselves, in any case.

And so she kept to the house, finding instead a quiet window in the middle of a deserted back staircase at which to stand and try to figure out what, precisely, she was feeling.

It had been a very long time since she had stood and gazed out at Park Lane, the street on which she had grown up. It had not changed much, however. The same elegantly clad, attractive people alighted from the same well-turned-out carriages. The horses pulling those carriages were better fed—and probably better treated—than most of her students back in Faires. At one time, such a thought would have filled her with despair. Now it only caused her to wonder why the people of Faires did not attempt to do more to improve their lot. Ignorance was perhaps the greatest cause of their troubles. The fact that so many of them had objected to her school, because of its mingling of the sexes, for instance. And what about their insistence that the Bible was the only book worth reading, and so long as they went to church of a Sunday and had Gospel read to them, what was the point in learning to read themselves? To say nothing of their stubborn reliance on whiskey as a cure-all. Good Lord, Emma had attended births at which the mother-to-be had been deeper in her cups than the baby's father!

Had she, Emma couldn't help wondering, made the slightest difference in the lives of the people she and Stuart had been so determined to save? Certainly John McAddams was in a better place now—but that had been through James's beneficence. And Fergus? The same.

No, about the only thing that Emma could tell she and Stuart had accomplished by going to Faires was Stuart's death. It was sad, but it had to be admitted. As a missionary, Emma had been a complete and utter failure.

And even if she took her ten thousand pounds and sunk it into a school and possibly even a hospital in Faires, would any of it do a bit of good? Would the villagers change their ways at all? She did not think so. Not the older ones, anyway. The young ones though . . . well, for the young ones, there might still be hope.

As if he'd read her thoughts, one of those young ones appeared at her side with a "Miz Chesterton? What're you doing?"

Emma looked down and was amused to see Fergus, his eyes very large behind his new spectacles, looking up at her inquisitively.

"Oh," she said. "Only thinking."

"About Lord Denham?" the boy asked.

Emma could not help laughing, albeit nervously, at that. For James, of late, never seemed very far from her thoughts anymore. It was odd that Fergus should have mentioned that.

"No, not about Lord Denham. Why?" She hoped she sounded more lighthearted than she felt. "Should I be thinking about Lord Denham?"

"Well, I'm sure he's hoping you might," the boy informed her, conversationally. "After all this wooing."

"Wooing?" Emma looked down at him with a perplexed smile. "What are you talking about?"

"I told him if he wants you, he'll have to woo you." Fergus, regarding the step on which he stood with some fascination—undoubtedly it had been some time since he'd last seen much of anything, so even a back staircase held for him a certain charm—hopped from it to the one below it on a single foot. "If he wants to make it stick, I mean."

"You and Lord Denham," Emma said slowly, "discussed me with one another?"

"Oh, aye," Fergus said, with a shrug. "I told 'im, 'If you want to make it stick,' I said, 'you better woo 'er.' "

Emma, a curious feeling, quite unlike any she had ever known, creeping through her, asked in a hoarse voice, "And does he? Want to make it stick, I mean?"

Fergus rolled those previously nearly sightless eyes.

"Miz Chesterton, you might be the one needin' the spectacles. I'd loan you mine, only Dr. Stoneletter said never to take them off, 'cepting at bedtime."

Emma, transfixed by this information, could only stare down at the boy, perfectly speechless.

"I think he's done a rum job of it," the boy observed at length. "I mean, bringing John here, and getting me my spectacles, and all of that." Another hop down the stairs. "I know you loved Mr. Chesterton." Hop. "But he always hollered at us for playing ball too near the church." Hop. "I don't think he ever even really loved you, not properly. Not like 'is lordship." A final hop, and then Fergus, looking very small, and yet strangely

304 • *Patricia Cabot*

authoritative, turned toward her to add, "Never seen a man so in lerve. That's what me mam said. And she should know. She's 'ad three husbands. Well, got to see Cook about a cake. G'bye."

And then he was gone.

And really, what could Emma do after this extraordinary exchange, but sit and cry her eyes out for half an hour?

Chapter Twenty-Six

It wasn't true. It couldn't be true. James Marbury, in love with her?

No. It was impossible. Fergus had misunderstood. And yet.

And yet, what about what he'd done for Fergus? And for John? And making his own valet stay to run the school, and look after Una, and oh! She blushed to think of it now. Even James putting up with that wretched cow!

He had gone to all that trouble, and she had never once stopped to think why . . . not really. She had merely accepted it, almost as her due. After all, he had wronged her. He owed her.

But for what? What wrong had he really done her, after all? He had gone to her family when she had been about to make what turned out, in the end, to be a rash and ill-considered decision. Stuart had *died* in Faires.

James, she knew now, had been right to go to her

uncle. He had been right to try to stop her. If she had stayed in London—if she had waited—perhaps Stuart would be alive today.

And certainly she would not be in the position she was now, of being the sole heir to her husband's murderer.

But that James might have done it all because he loved her? No. James had never given any sign, in all the time she'd known him, that he harbored feelings stronger than amused tolerance for her. She had certainly never heard any protestation of affection cross his lips. Quite the opposite, in fact. He was forever arguing with, often even criticizing, her.

Except in bed. The thought crept inexorably into her consciousness, and once there, rang like a bell. Except in bed. Except in bed.

Was that why, when James kissed her, he was capable of stopping her breath and mind both at once, so that she could neither breathe fully nor think rationally? Was that why, when he came anywhere near, her heart staggered and seemed nearly to stop? Had he been trying, all this time, to express a love for her physically that he could not, for whatever reason, bring himself to say verbally?

Or was he merely so skilled and experienced a lover that he was able to make her feel all these things, while he himself felt nothing? She was not, she knew, the most sophisticated of young women—James's past paramours had surely been far more accomplished in the bedroom arts than she was—but surely even a relative innocent like herself ought to be able to tell the difference between making love and . . . well, faking love.

And there had never been anything the slightest bit

fake—that she could tell, anyway—about what had occurred between her and James in bed.

But was she really so stupid—so mulishly bull-headed, just as Aunt Regina had always accused her of being—that it had taken a small child finally to make her realize why?

The sad answer to that question was yes. Oh, yes. She was that stupid.

But what was she to do now? How was she to feel? For she seemed incapable of feeling anything but the strongest astonishment, not just at Fergus's revelation, but at her own reaction to it. That was all. Just astonishment. James Marbury, ninth earl of Denham, loved her . . . had loved her, perhaps, for some time. What other explanation was there for what she now realized to be such highly loverlike behavior?

Why hadn't he said anything, though?

Perhaps because he thought she despised him.

And yet surely he'd been able to tell how wildly attracted to him she was. How else to explain why, whenever he touched her, she seemed to melt? He aroused her the way no other man of her acquaintance ever had, despite the fact that she abhorred his politics. He knew. He had to know how she felt.

So why hadn't he said anything?

Oh! It was infuriating! Infuriating and ridiculous. She wouldn't think of it anymore. Fergus could not have known what he was saying.

Except, of course, in her experience, Fergus had always known precisely what he was saying—one of the few people she had known of whom this could be said, the only other that she could think of being . . .

Well. James.

"You still want to go through with the annulment, then?" The words rang through her head. Was that why he'd asked? Not because of what they'd done, but because of what he felt?

She was sitting at her dressing table wondering this, while the dowager's maid wrestled with her hair, when the bedroom door opened, and in walked James.

He had changed into an evening jacket, black as jet. His hair was still wet from a bath. He looked devastatingly handsome.

And that's when she knew, with a little inward groan, that she could deny it no longer.

She loved him.

He had teased and goaded her, frustrated and vexed her, at times even enraged her. But never had he not been there for her. Never had there been a time—except when she'd gone to him to tell him she was marrying another—when he had not done all he could to see her happy.

"I'll just be a moment, my lord," Pamela, the dowager's maid said, giving the last of the many pins Emma was wearing in her hair a determined push. Then, with a smile of satisfaction at the reflection in the great gilt mirror before them, Pamela said, "You do look a picture, my lady." Then concern creased her kindly features. "But you've gone quite pale! Have you taken chill?"

Well might Pamela inquire, for Madame Delanges had taken a good deal of trouble, it seemed, to see that as much of Emma's shoulders and bosom as could tastefully be exposed were so, the blue gown dipping to a décolletage that was not just daring, but downright architecturally unsound.

But it was not exposure to the elements that had caused Emma's color to fail. It was the sight of her husband, a man with whom, she was suddenly realizing, she was hopelessly in love.

"Let me see if I can find you a pretty shawl, so you don't take cold," Pamela said, with a reassuring pat on Emma's bare shoulder. Then, dipping low, the maid added, for Emma's benefit alone, "And her ladyship's got a pot of rouge that will take care of the rest."

Unfortunately for the maid, the master had hearing keen enough to catch even the lowest of whispers. "I think not," he said, in a smoothly casual tone, as if he were declining the offer of a cigar. "No wife of mine is going to go parading about in face paint."

Pamela, casting a conspiratorial wink in Emma's direction, merely curtsied and uttered an "As you wish, my lord," before scurrying from the room with an ill-suppressed giggle.

How Emma wished she could summon a giggle of her own. But she felt wholly serious, more serious than she had ever felt in her life.

"Let's hope that these will add some color to your cheeks," James said, in the same casual tone he'd used before, as he approached the dressing table. He laid a long, black velvet box in Emma's lap.

But Emma's mind was too full to notice something as mundane as a jewel box on her knees. Her gaze roved worriedly along James's face, searching it for some hint that what Fergus had said was true.

But all her exploring look produced was an eyebrow cocked in her direction. "*Have* you taken cold, Emma?" James asked. "Because you look a little peaked."

What was she to do? What was she to say? She certainly couldn't come out and ask him, "James, is it true that you love me?"

And how devastated she would be if his response was a laugh, or worse, an outright denial.

She shook herself and looked down at the box. "No," she said, to her hands. "I'm all right."

Then she opened the lid.

Dozens of sapphires, as blue as her dress—and, though she didn't know it, her eyes—sparkled up at her. The necklace, with matching earrings, was the most beautiful thing she had ever seen.

"And before you go berating me, Emma," James said, plucking up the stones and, moving behind her, lowering them around the smooth white column of her throat, "about how the money might have been better spent sending some poor missionary to a miserable tribal village in Swahililand, allow me to assure you that these stones have been in my family a good deal longer than either of us has been alive. I had nothing whatsoever to do with their purchase. But I must say"—this he added as he inspected Emma's reflection in the great gilt-framed mirror—"I personally support the expenditure."

How he could speak so blithely while feeling anything like what Emma herself was feeling, she could not determine. Perhaps, if what Fergus had said was true, he'd been aware—fully aware—of his feelings longer than she, and so had had more practice at concealing the truth.

In any case, whatever color she'd lost came flooding back into her face at the compliment. Emma, her gaze lowered, reached up to lay her fingers upon the smooth, cool stones. "Thank you, James," was all she could manage to say.

"You look lovely," her husband assured her. And then he was reaching for her new, ermine-lined cloak, saying, "I've no more desire than you to attend this ghastly event, but short of feigning illness, I see no way out of it. And though you looked pale before, I see no evidence of it now. We'll just put in an appearance, and then be home again, quick as we can."

Emma stood and allowed him to slip the furred garment over her shoulders, his fingertips grazing her bare skin. Was this, she wondered, how it was, then? Love? Because it didn't seem familiar. What she had felt for Stuart had never felt like this, this sweetly gnawing ache. Why, there had been times when she had gone quite out of her way to avoid the kisses Stuart had but rarely bestowed. Now she was quite certain she'd walk barefoot through fire just to feel James's lips on hers once more.

"Lovely!" cried the dowager, bringing Emma from her revery as James led her down the stairs to where his mother waited. "My dear, you make an exceedingly beautiful bride. James, you could not have found a prettier wife in all of London."

"No," James replied, with his customary dryness. "I had to go all the way to the Hebrides to find her."

This brought gales of laughter from the Dowager Lady Denham, who was in a mood, apparently, to laugh at everyone and everything. She laughed at the footman who missed his step and nearly sent her tumbling into a puddle as he helped her into her place in the chaise and four. She laughed at the housemaid at the Cartwrights' who accidentally trod upon her hem as she was helping to remove her veil. She laughed at Emma, who still wore a blush so deep, she did not need to stand in the ladies' dressing room and pinch her cheeks to make them redder, as her cousin Penelope and the Honorable Miss Fiona Bain, arriving at close to the same time, were doing. The dowager even laughed at her own son when, seeing the ladies emerge into the crush of the Cartwrights' ballroom, he hadn't arms enough to offer them.

Fortunately the Honorable Miss Bain, in a simple white gown that, though a few seasons out of date, nevertheless set off her flaming hair and excellent figure, was almost immediately snatched up to dance, and by no less esteemed a personage than the duke of Rutherford's heir. Fiona, perhaps to her advantage, had no idea of the pedigree of her dance partner. Though she looked a little put out to be dragged away from James so quickly, it was still a thrill for her merely to be under such a dazzlingly high ceiling, from which no discernible rainwater dripped—quite a contrast to life in Castle MacCreigh.

And as for Penelope Van Court, she had only to appear on the ballroom floor before she was claimed by Geoffrey Bain, who, though keeping a close and jealous eye on Emma, was nevertheless not foolhardy enough to waste his time on a woman whose hand—and fortune—seemed so firmly, despite all his efforts to pry them loose, in the possession of another.

Emma watched the couples whirling around in front of her without seeming really to see them. Her mind was still in a fog from all that she had heard and realized the past few hours. She felt the hands that shook hers in congratulation, and smiled like an automaton in response to each wish for her future happiness. But she could concentrate on nothing except the man standing beside her, his hand likewise being squeezed. What, she could not help wondering, did James think of all this? If what Fergus had assured her was true, he could only be hearing each word of congratulation with bitterness, thinking, as he must, that with the pending annulment, their wedded bliss was soon to turn acrimonious.

Worse, if he did not love her, how laughable all these heartfelt blessings must seem!

Still, though Emma could not enjoy herself, and did not think James was at all as comfortable as he was pretending, there was no doubt that the dowager was in her element. Never had Emma seen James's mother with brighter eyes or a wider smile. Seizing every hand that was offered to her as the Cartwrights' guests moved down the receiving line, the dowager grew more and more effusive in her replies to the well-wishers. "Couldn't be happier," was the phrase Emma heard Lady Denham use to describe her son, again and again. Couldn't be happier, she wondered, because he was married at last to the woman he loved? Or couldn't be happier because that was how he wanted his mother to think him? For James was doing a very good job of playing the joyful bridegroom, keeping a hand anchored at all times at Emma's waist, and smiling more broadly than she had ever seen him smile.

The only time Emma saw that smile crack in the slightest was when in response to someone's question as to just how the happy couple had come to be the happy couple, the dowager cried, "It was the strangest thing! I couldn't have been more surprised myself. He went to Scotland to fetch Stuart, you know, but came back with a bride instead. A sad business, to be sure, but with a very happy ending, I think." Then, quite suddenly, the dowager turned to James and Emma and asked them, "My dears, when are we to expect Stuart? Is Roberts seeing to that?"

Emma felt as if something had caught in her throat. Unable to utter a sound, she merely looked at the dowager, feeling all the color drain from her face.

"Mother," she heard James mutter. "Not now."

But the Dowager Lady Denham, in her high spirits, did not seem to realize she had brought up a subject over which there might be any friction between her son and new daughter-in-law. "I had Billings go ahead with the engraving. It will be small, but meaningful, I think."

Suddenly it seemed to Emma as if the ballroom had tilted—like the deck of a ship. She blinked at it, wondering how on earth everyone kept from lurching to the side, as she felt she was about to do.

"Mother," James said, and now he was not muttering. "That's enough."

Lady Denham, who had not a cruel bone in her body, and had genuinely not realized that what she was saying might be a cause of pain to anyone, looked from her son to his new bride, then said, the smile wiped from her face, "Oh, dear. I am sorry. I don't suppose it is something that ought to be brought up in a ballroom. Only it seems wrong to me to have Stuart so very far away. I know how happy he would be to know that the two of you—his two favorite people in the world—have found happiness with one another. He would want to be kept close by, don't you think?"

But if the dowager had meant for her words to comfort Emma, she'd failed badly in her endeavor. For suddenly, not only was the room tilting, but Emma was having difficulty breathing. Tears shone in her eyes, though she did her best to hide them.

Still, James noticed. It would have been hard for him not to. The wave of guests had ebbed. Everyone was either on the dance floor or crowding around the refreshment tables. He had only to glance down to see her face, drained again of all color, she was certain, and her blue eyes swimming in what she was certain was an unattractively pink haze.

"Emma," he said, and the arm around her waist tightened. . . .

He didn't understand. How could he? She knew what he must be thinking. That she was crying because of Stuart . . . that she still loved Stuart, and that any mention of him, or his grave, brought on such a wave of misery that she could not help but weep.

If only he'd known the truth! A truth she never dared tell him. . . .

"I really must," Emma said, with all the brightness she could muster, hoping against hope that the tears with which her eyes were brimming didn't choose this moment to overflow, "return to the ladies' dressing room for a moment. My slipper has become unlaced."

And then she made her escape. She managed it only because at that moment a late-arriving guest, a business associate of James's, hurried up to him, eager to pump the bridegroom's hand. James was distracted long enough for Emma to dart out from beneath his arm, past the dowager, and down the hall, where mercifully she found only deep carpets and potted palms.

Sinking onto the first bench she saw, Emma buried her face in her hands, praying that the swaying of the floor would stop, and that when she took her hands away, she'd find herself back home . . . back home in Faires, where, it was true, she'd been the unluckiest of souls, but where at least she would not have to confess to the man she loved what she knew now that she was going to have to confess to James.

Chapter Twenty-Seven

It was as Emma was telling herself this that she heard a cry and, looking up, saw a dark-haired girl in a lovely velvet gown tear around the corner and disappear. It was with no little shock that Emma saw the baron of MacCreigh, of all people, thundering after her.

He stopped short when he saw Emma. For the first time since she'd known him, Emma saw that Geoffrey Bain was wearing not his look of perpetual disdain but an expression of profound confusion.

"That," he said to her, in a voice she had never heard him use before, "was Clara."

Emma, her surprise making her forget for the moment her own troubles, looked back. But the dark-haired girl had dived into the ladies' dressing room.

"My lord," Emma said, slowly. Mercifully, the floor had righted itself, and Emma no longer felt the sickening sensation that she was aboard the deck of a storm-tossed ship.

Instead, she felt a sickening sensation of another kind.

"Don't say it wasn't she," Lord MacCreigh said urgently. "For I know it was! I would know that hair anywhere."

"You recognized her hair," Emma said. "But did you see her face, my lord?"

"I didn't have to," Lord MacCreigh assured her. "It's Clara's shape, her walk, her hair—Go to her, Emma. Fetch her out. She liked you. She'll listen to you. Tell her she need not be afraid to speak to me. Tell her I only wish to know that she is alive and safe. . . ."

Emma, deeply troubled, stayed precisely where she was. "My lord," she said in a low voice, "that was not Clara."

"Of course it was," Lord MacCreigh cried. "Why else would she have run from me?"

It was on the tip of Emma's tongue to say that of course the girl had run. She had doubtless been terrified by the redheaded man who was after her, calling her by a name that was not in fact her own. For Emma knew, as no one else did, that Clara would never be seen again.

"You're wasting time, Emma," the baron said, striding toward her bench. "It was her, I tell you. I always knew she and that rascal Stevens had headed for London. Anyone might disappear without a trace in a city this size. Go and see why she will not speak to me. She'll tell you. She told you everything. . . ."

Emma did not move from her place on the padded bench. "Lord MacCreigh," she said, tiredly. "I really do not think—"

"It was she!" The baron began to pace the length of

the hallway, his gaze never leaving the door to the ladies' dressing room. "Emma, why do you doubt it? It was Clara, I swear it."

"No," Emma said. She could not keep the sadness from her voice. "I'm sorry, my lord. But it was not."

Lord MacCreigh made a frustrated sound and whirled around, seemingly intent upon heading back to the ballroom from which he'd just come.

"Fine," he said. "If you will not fetch her out, I will get Fiona to do it. Only stay where you are, will you please, and see that she does not try to sneak past ere I return—"

"Lord MacCreigh," Emma said. Then, after a deep breath, she added, "Geoffrey."

That stopped him in his tracks. He turned to look down at her, his expression not so much curious as full of shock at her using his Christian name for the first time. "Emma?"

She patted the empty spot on the bench beside her. "Sit here," she said. "There is something I must tell you. Indeed, there is something I ought to have told you long ago, only . . . well, a friend made me promise not to. But I think it better . . . well, I think it better that you know the truth."

The baron, who had not much color beneath his freckles at any time, seemed to go even paler than usual. Still, he did as Emma bid, lowering himself onto the bench beside her.

"You startle me, Emma," he said in a nervous voice. "You look . . .well, you don't look well."

Nor do you, Emma wanted to say. And when she finished telling him what she had to, he would look even worse. But there was nothing she could do about that.

"Lord MacCreigh," she said, gravely. "That could not have been Clara you saw just now. Because Clara is dead."

Lord MacCreigh looked, just for a moment, stunned. Then he looked stern.

"Emma!" he said. "That you, of all people, should listen to common village gossip! Don't tell me you believe that sordid tale about me slaying the pair of them, and tossing them down the cistern—"

"No," Emma hastened to assure him. "No, my lord, I do not. I never did. Because, you see, I know the truth. And the truth is that poor Clara really did die—"

But Lord MacCreigh only shook his head. "Emma. This isn't like you! I know you don't want me to cause a scene at your party, but really, to tell such a tale as that—"

"It isn't a tale," Emma said. She spoke in the same gentle voice she used with the children, when she needed to break bad news to them. "Clara died six months ago, my lord, during the typhus epidemic. I'm very sorry, but she asked me not to tell you. She didn't want you to—"

To her surprise, Lord MacCreigh sprang to his feet—so quickly that he very nearly upset the bench that two of them had been sitting upon. He stood before her, ashen-faced and incredulous.

"You lie," he said. His face had contorted into a mask of such disbelief that a couple rounding the corner saw them, and turned hastily back. Lord MacCreigh, however, did not notice.

"You could not have seen her six months ago," he said. "She ran off longer ago than that—"

"I know," Emma said, quietly. "But she came back."

"Impossible!" the baron cried. "If she'd come back, I'd have known of it!"

"She had reason not to want you to know," Emma said. Her eyes had once more filled with tears. "Oh, Geoffrey, I am sorry. But she did not want you—you, of all people—to know. . . ."

When she did not continue, Lord MacCreigh looked down at her with wounded eyes.

"Know what?" he asked.

Emma shook her head, her eyes bright with unshed tears. "I can't tell you. I'm sorry, but I swore to her I wouldn't tell . . . she wanted to keep it from you, most of all."

Lord MacCreigh stared. Then he took a quick step back, running a hand raggedly through his red hair and making it stand up almost on end.

"Are you telling me—" He seemed hardly to know what he was doing, which was pace before her like a madman. "Emma, are you telling me that all this time—all these many months—you knew that Clara was dead . . . that she was dead, and not of my own hand, as everyone has been saying . . . and *you kept it to yourself?*"

What could Emma do but nod? Because it was quite true, what he was saying.

"You could," the baron said, stopping suddenly in front of her, "have exonerated me with one word, and yet you chose to say nothing?"

"I didn't choose not to," Emma said, quickly. "I told you, she made me swear—"

"You knew all this time?" the baron roared, "and yet you said nothing?"

It was perhaps unfortunate for Lord MacCreigh that the earl of Denham should have happened to choose that particular moment to turn the corner in search of his wife and come across the pair of them. It could not, of course, have looked any worse for the baron, who was looming over the new Lady Denham in a manner that could only be construed as frightening, and who had, in fact, just shouted at her in an extremely ungentlemanlike manner.

Still, when he noticed the earl striding toward him, the baron did take a hasty step away from Emma, with a murmured, "Now, Denham, it's not what you think."

Even Emma sprang from her seat with a cry of, "Oh, James, no!"

But it was too late. It was much too late.

Chapter Twenty-Eight

"You needn't," Emma said, as she slipped in front of her dressing table, "have hit him that hard."

James disagreed. "He was threatening you. What was I to think, except that you were about to be assaulted?"

"By Lord MacCreigh?" Emma shook her head. "At the Cartwrights' dinner dance?"

"I don't think it an unreasonable assumption," James said. "He is, after all, rumored to have done far worse."

Emma began to remove her hairpins. "He was just upset," she said. "He had received some very bad news."

"How was I to know that?" James asked. "All I saw was that Geoffrey Bain, a man who once wanted to marry you, was behaving in what looked to me to be a highly threatening manner. And what"—James watched his wife carefully from where he'd gone to stand with one elbow upon the mantel, trying to ignore the throbbing in his right hand—"kind of bad news had he received anyway?"

She glanced at his reflection in the mirror before her, then looked quickly away. "He thought he'd seen Clara," she said. She'd picked up a hairbrush, and now she held it a little too tightly.

"Clara?" James's eyebrows came down in a rush. "His fiancée?"

"Yes," Emma said. She kept her gaze on the horsehair bristles of the brush.

James moved, a little impatiently. "How is that possible? She ran off with his valet, and he murdered her for it. Didn't he?"

"No," Emma said. "He didn't. That story was entirely made up, all rumor and conjecture. Well, the part about her being murdered, anyway."

"Really?" James raised his eyebrows. But the truth was, he wasn't very interested in discussing Geoffrey Bain's romantic travails. He wanted to talk about his own. Unfortunately, he did not think Emma at all inclined to agree with him that now would be a good time to discuss anything of the sort.

Not that he blamed her. He'd seen the way she'd looked when his mother had mentioned Stuart's grave. How he wished he'd thought to warn the dowager off that particular subject sooner. But so much had happened since their arrival in London, there had never been a moment, really, when it had come up . . . the real reason for his having gone to Faires in the first place, that is.

Wretched, wretched mistake! For clearly, the subject of Stuart's death was still a painful one for Emma. . . .

She sat now with her head bent, the silver-handled hairbrush in her hand. Somewhere in the house, a clock chimed the hour. It was early yet. They had left the Cartwrights' directly after James's altercation with the baron, without saying good-bye to anyone. Even the dowager, unaware of what had transpired in the hall-way, was still at the ball. When he'd left him, the baron had been taking his comfort in the arms of Emma's cousin Penelope, who had chanced upon the scene and been justly horrified—and sympathetic to, as far as James was concerned, the entirely wrong person.

But, really, how much could a man be asked to bear? For it wasn't only the ghost of her first husband James felt he had constantly to fight for Emma's affections, but now it was apparently redheaded barons as well.

"So was it Clara?" James asked. "That MacCreigh saw?"

"No," Emma said, softly, still not meeting his gaze. "It wasn't. Clara is dead."

James, surprised, said, "But I thought you just said—"

"Lord MacCreigh didn't kill her," Emma said. "The typhus did."

Confused, James said, "Really? But then why does everyone—"

"Because I never told anyone before," Emma said. She kept her eyes on the hairbrush in her lap. "About what happened to Clara. What really happened to her. She asked me not to. She made me swear . . . but now. Now I think I must because . . . Oh, James." She looked up then, and he saw that there were tears shining her eyes. "It's about Stuart. And Clara."

James stared. Really, but the last thing he'd ever expected to hear was that there was a connection between his cousin and Lord MacCreigh's fiancée. It so startled him that for a moment, he did not think he could have heard Emma right. He said, "I beg your pardon?"

"Yes," Emma said, putting down the brush. "We've got to talk about Stuart. It's wonderful that you've never asked me to before, but I think now . . . well, I think now we'd better."

"I rather gathered," James said, longing for nothing more than to take her in his arms and kiss away the pucker of worry he saw once again clouding her brow, "that you didn't want to talk about Stuart."

"I didn't," Emma said. "But now I do."

"Well." James dropped his arm from the mantel and wished he could ring for Burroughs. A whiskey, he felt, was what he needed at this juncture. He felt he lacked the courage to face stone cold sober what he feared was coming. MacCreigh's fiancée, and his cousin Stuart? It wasn't possible. It really wasn't. But it might . . . might . . . explain a few things. "Please don't let me stop you."

She sat on the dressing table stool, her head still bent, her gaze evidently on her lap. Closer inspection, however, revealed that her eyes, as deep azure as the jewels around her neck, were unseeing. What Emma was looking at, he didn't know.

"He was killed." Her voice, which had always had a husky quality to it that he'd found restful compared to the shrill voices of all the other women he'd known, shook. Whatever Emma was about to say, it was costing her. Costing her far more, he realized, than ten thousand pounds.

"I know that," he said, gently. "By that O'Malley fellow."

"You know how," she said. "But you don't know why. It was at the height of the typhus epidemic." Emma kept her gaze on her hands. "Mrs. O'Malley— well, they weren't really married, but that's what we all called her, to be polite—was dying. Tom O'Malley came to us because Reverend Peck was at some other house—I don't remember where now—and he felt . . . it was time. For the last rites. He was beside himself, Mr. O'Malley was, with grief. For even though he and Ginnie—that was her name—had never married, they had been together for a good many years, and he truly did love her, in his way.

"But Ginnie . . . well, she was always an odd woman. An infrequent churchgoer. Stuart used to plead with her to attend more often—or at least to let Reverend Peck marry her and Tom. But she would only laugh—well, she was odd. She had a great love for nature. She used to torture Stuart, asking him, If the Lord created the earth and all that was on it, why couldn't her prayers be heard in the sheep's meadow just as clearly as in a church?"

She broke off and turned suddenly to face him.

"When we arrived at her home that night—I went too, to see if I could do anything to help—Ginnie wasn't the least bit delusional. She was dying—so thin, so gray and gaunt I hardly knew her. But her mind was as sharp as ever. When Stuart got to the bit about renouncing sin . . . well, she said she wouldn't, because in her mind, she hadn't committed any sins that she could think of. When Stuart reminded her that, in fact, her life with Mr. O'Malley had been one long continuous sin, as they had never married, she only laughed. . . ."

The tears spilled out now, but Emma seemed unconscious of them as they splashed upon her palms, upturned in her lap.

"Of course Stuart said that if she would not ask forgiveness of her sins, he could not give her absolution. He started . . . he started packing up his things. He was very tired. Everyone we knew, it seemed, had someone dying in their family. It was . . . it was horrible. But still. Still, he should have given some thought to Mr. O'Malley's feelings. He should have . . . but he didn't. And when Mr. O'Malley saw that Stuart really meant to go, he . . . he . . ."

She broke off. James took a step forward, anxious to stem, if he could, the flow of those tears.

"Emma," he said, his hands going out to grasp those smooth white shoulders.

But she held up a hand of her own, warning him away from her.

"No," she said in a voice clogged with tears. "No. I've got to say it. Mr. O'Malley hit him. Just the once. But Stuart struck his head on the corner of the hearth, and he . . . he died at once. And the worst part of it is, James, when Mr. O'Malley hit Stuart, I was glad." She gave an astonished laugh through her tears. "I was actually glad. Because I liked Ginnie, and I'd wanted to hit Stuart myself, for being so sanctimonious."

She'd stopped crying. The tears were still there, glistening on her face, but her eyes were clear again, as was her voice as she said, "But I never wanted him to die. It was . . . well, it was horrible. Mr. O'Malley turned himself in at once. He was the one, in fact, who went for help. He had no reason, with Ginnie gone— she went just minutes after Stuart did—to live anymore. The villagers—Mrs. MacTavish and her son, the MacEwans—came and got me, and Stuart, and took us both back to the cottage. The next day . . . the next day, they told me there was . . . was some problem with finding a burial site for Stuart. Mr. Peck said there were no plots left in the parish cemetery, except group plots, because of the high number of deaths from the typhus. I . . . I didn't know what to do. I was half out of my mind, I suppose. I knew nothing would do for Stuart but a grave on consecrated ground, but—"

"Emma," James said, but again she held up a hand to stop him from saying anything more.

"It was the night after Stuart died that she came back," she said. Her gaze was far away, and James realized she was seeing something that happened in the past, not what lay before her in the present. "Clara, I mean. She'd disappeared a few months before. I knew where she'd gone, because she'd confided in me. We were friends. She was . . . she was my only friend, for so long, on the island. Things with Stuart . . . well, they weren't easy, as you can imagine. We had nothing— nothing but what the Pecks gave us. I . . . I wasn't as well prepared for married life as perhaps I ought to have been. No, don't say anything." James shut his mouth. "It was . . . It wasn't what I expected. Being married to Stuart, I mean."

She took a deep, trembling breath. "But at least I had Clara. She was a friend, when I needed a friend. It was she who gave us the Limoges, you know. Clara was well off, but her father had always been rather overprotective of her. When Lord MacCreigh began courting her, it was the most exciting thing that had ever happened to her. Of course she said yes when he asked her to marry him. Anything to get out from under her father's thumb."

Emma sighed. "But then, upon coming to Castle MacCreigh, she met Sean Stevens—the baron's valet. He was very handsome, and charming, and I suppose the idea of having a rich bride like Clara was as appealing to him as it was to Lord MacCreigh. I would like to think that Mr. Stevens liked Clara a little. . . . She certainly loved him. And eventually, when he asked her to run away with him, Clara said yes. She told me she was going to, but made me swear not to tell anyone—not even Stuart—that I knew where she'd gone. They were to elope—and about time, too, since she was already with child by him. Once they were safely married, Clara said, they'd return to her father's house as man and wife. . . ."

James knew what was coming before Emma said it. It was all too familiar a tale.

"I didn't hear from her again until the night after Stuart was killed. It was a rainy night . . . there was a bad storm. And I was sitting in the front room of the cottage with . . . with his coffin. Stuart's, I mean. The next day I was going to have it buried, with or without Mr. Peck's permission, in a grave by itself. I had already consulted Mr. MacEwan and Mr. Murphy, and they'd promised to help me. . . ."

Emma took a deep, trembling breath. "There was a knock at the door, and when I went to open it, thinking

it was one of them—Mr. MacEwan, or his mother perhaps, come to keep me company—I was shocked to see
Clara standing there, soaked to the bone and pale as
death, with a belly swollen out to here. . . . And she was
sick. Not just because the baby was coming, but because she had it. Typhus. I knew it the minute I saw
her."

"Emma," James said, horrified. "You didn't—"

"What else could I do?" she asked, swinging her
gaze, filled with hot tears, toward him. "She was my
friend. My only friend. Of course I took her in. Mr.
Stevens—the cad—had abandoned her. Clara had been
too ashamed to go home. How she lived, she wouldn't
say, but I can't imagine, judging by the state her clothes
were in, that it had been too pleasant. I put her in my
bed—the bed Stuart and I had shared. She had the baby
there . . . a girl, with Clara's dark hair. It was healthy,
too. But Clara . . ." Emma's eyes went dark with sadness. "She knew she would not recover. She had fought
the disease so long, trying to stay alive to deliver the
baby. She couldn't fight it any longer. She was too worn
out. All she wanted—all she asked of me—was to find a
good home for her baby, and never to tell anyone—anyone at all—what had happened to her. She thought it
would hurt her father—and Lord MacCreigh—too
much to know the truth. Although I doubt it ever occurred to her that people would think Lord MacCreigh
murdered her."

James had lowered himself onto the edge of the bed.
He'd had to, for he wasn't at all certain he could have
gone on standing after Emma's horrifying revelation.
He sat there now, staring at her, his mind awhirl.

"And the baby?" he asked.

"Oh," Emma said, brightening a little. "I wrapped her up and took her to Mr. and Mrs. Peck. I left her on their doorstep, then pounded on the door and ran. I watched from their barn. Reverend Peck opened the door and found her. Mrs. Peck took her in. She'd been desperate for a child of her own. And that's exactly how she's been passing Olivia off—they called her Olivia. As their own child." Emma smiled ruefully. "I'm the only one who knows the truth; of course the Pecks aren't aware of it—or of who Olivia's poor mother really was."

James cleared his throat. He didn't want to ask the next question, but he felt he had to. For at long last, the connection between his cousin and Clara McLellen was becoming clear.

"And her body, Emma?" he asked gently. "What did you do with the mother's body?"

Emma's glance at him was filled with anxiety.

"What *could* I do?" she asked. "It was winter. The ground was frozen solid. I couldn't bury her myself." Emma looked miserable. "She'd asked for so little. Just my word of honor not to tell, a home for her daughter, and . . . and a proper grave."

James could not help but smile. He tried to restrain it. But the corners of his mouth twitched, just the same. Emma looked at him, waves of agony seeming to pass over her.

"Oh, James, don't," she said. "It was too awful of me. But what else could I do? And I did figure, well, that Stuart was beyond caring. . . ."

"About sharing his coffin with an unwed mother?"

James was definitely smiling now. "I should say not. Did Murphy or MacEwan suspect?"

Emma, however, could see nothing amusing in the matter.

"No," she said. "At least, they didn't seem to feel the extra weight."

"Emma," he said. After such a tale, it was wrong that his heart should be soaring. But there it was. The true reason that Emma had been so reluctant to have Stuart's body disinterred was actually a relief to him, after what he'd been imagining . . . which was that Emma still loved her first husband so much, she could not bear to have his eternal rest disturbed.

He felt like singing.

But since that would hardly be appropriate, under the circumstances, he settled for saying, "Well, it's quite true it would have been something of a shock to the undertakers, to find two bodies in a coffin when they were expecting only one. But Emma, for heaven's sake. Why didn't you simply tell me?"

"I promised I wouldn't," she said. "Promised Clara, I mean. And well . . . it wasn't a very respectful way to treat Stuart. I thought . . . honestly, I thought you'd be very angry. Like you were that day I first told you . . ."

"Ah," James said, when her voice trailed off. "That day. Yes. I was not, perhaps, at my best that day."

"No," Emma said, looking surprised. "No, you were right—well, not to hit Stuart. That was wrong. But you were right to try to keep us from eloping. I . . . I was angry at you at the time. And for a long while afterward. I even hated you for it—but not, perhaps, for the reasons I always thought I did. Still, I realize now you were completely and totally right. Because you see, if we'd listened, Stuart might still be alive today."

James, staring at her incredulously, asked, "You think that's why I did it? For Stuart's sake?"

This, as nothing else he'd said to her so far that evening, seemed to sink in. She looked up, blinking rapidly, like someone newly wakened.

"W-wasn't it?" she stammered. "I mean—"

"I loved Stuart," he admitted, readily enough. "Like a brother. But like a brother, I was perfectly aware of Stuart's faults. He's lucky he even lived through that night you told me about your plans to elope with him. But not, Emma, because it was him I was worried about losing. Far from it."

Her eyes, blue as forget-me-nots and wide as pennies, stared up at him in bewilderment. "Then . . . I don't understand. What, then?"

He stood then, and went to kneel beside her chair. He reached out and took her hand in his—her left hand, the one that wore his signet ring, since he'd yet to secure a proper wedding ring for her.

"Is it so hard for you to believe?" he asked, with an attempt at a lightness he didn't feel. Indeed, his heart was thudding heavily inside his chest, like war drums, he thought, warning him away. And yet he couldn't turn back now. Not and still call himself a man.

"It was you I was afraid of losing, Emma," he said, tightening his fingers around hers, as if even now she might slip away, though she was sitting not a foot from him. "That's why I did it."

"Impossible!" And now he did lose her, for she'd

pulled her hand from his and leapt up from the stool to face him in defiant indignation. "Now you are . . . well, I don't know what. But you didn't love me, James. You *didn't*. I *know* it."

"Then you know nothing," James said, not defensively, or even angrily. Just tiredly, because that was how he felt. It was not, as he'd once thought it might be, a relief to admit his heart's deepest secrets. It was only very, very tiring. "I loved you since the moment you left the schoolroom. Only Stuart got to you first."

"This is . . . this is . . . Well, I don't know what," Emma declared. "But you could not have loved me, James. If you had, you'd have come for me, not Stuart, when you finally heard he was dead."

Climbing to his feet, James crossed the space between them in a single stride. "How could I have faced you after that? I assumed you were in London, with your family. I never dreamed, in a million years, you'd still be in Faires. I thought I'd have time, be able to work out how I was going to approach you."

"It was so hard then," she said, in a wounded voice, as her blue eyes searched his face, "to admit you felt something for me?"

"Admit I was in love with the wife of the man I thought of as my brother? Yes. It wasn't as if, Emma," he said, as gently as he was able, given that he felt like something that had been flayed alive, "you'd ever given me the slightest bit of encouragement. You were very clear about your feelings for me."

"And you, yours for me," she retorted, just as rawly.

"Was I?" He gave a rueful smile. "Emma, when a

man who's been denied nothing his entire life is suddenly faced with the fact that the one thing he wants above all else, he can't have, he'll say just about anything to convince himself he never wanted that thing in the first place. But believe me when I say, Emma, I can no longer remember a time when I did not want to make you mine."

She reached up to wipe, with the back of a wrist, the newly formed tears that were trembling on the ends of her long eyelashes.

"That's impossible," she said, though her tone was not tearful at all but scornful. "If that were true, why did you mention the annulment, that day at Castle MacCreigh?"

"Would you have married me, Emma," he asked, gently, "if I hadn't?"

She sniffed. And raised her gaze to the ceiling. And seemed to debate something within herself.

When finally she brought her gaze back up to his, it was unreadable. But the set of her mouth he recognized. Emma was determined.

And when Emma was determined about something, the world—as James well knew—had better watch out.

"What about now?" Emma wanted to know. "Do you want the annulment now?"

"I never," James said, taking a step forward, "wanted an annulment in the first place."

But again, Emma raised a hand to stop him from coming any closer. She still looked determined, but there was pain in her eyes as well.

"You would stay married to me," she asked, in a shaking voice, "after everything I just told you? James,

I desecrated your cousin's coffin. And I did nothing to stop the man who killed him. Stuart is dead because of me."

"Stuart is dead," James informed her, "because he lacked the sense God gave a chicken. Now stop crying, and come here."

"I'll make a terrible wife," Emma assured him, backing up warily as he came forward, one hand stretched toward her. "I can't seem to do anything normal wives manage with ease. Even produce heirs."

"That's what entailments are for," he said. "Now come here." And he captured one of her hands in his. Then, like a fisherman reeling in the day's catch, he pulled her, by degrees, toward him.

"James," she said warningly. But even as she said it, she wondered what she could be warning him about. He knew the worst of her, and still seemed to want her. And God knew she wanted him. The fact that Fergus had been right—that James, it turned out, had always loved her, and loved her still—was causing her heart to perform some interesting gyrations beneath her ribs. She seemed to be having trouble catching her breath, and she did not think she could blame that on the tightness of her corset.

When James, not taking his gaze off hers, lifted the hand he held and pressed it to his lips, her breathing troubles became acute.

"James," she gasped.

But he would give no quarter. Instead, he moved his lips from her fingertips to the white skin on the inside of her elbow. Emma gazed down at the bent head, at the tumble of dark hair, feeling the firebrand of his mouth against her skin as it crept higher and higher up her arm, until, just as she was certain her thumping heart would burst, his lips finally found hers.

They kissed deeply in the firelight, tongues and lips entwined, until Emma suddenly gave a shaky laugh and placed a hand on either side of his face.

"Are you real?" she asked, though she knew the answer perfectly well. She could feel his realness between her hands, the hard planes of his face, the bristles of new razor stubble against her palms.

"I was about to ask the same of you," James said, his deep voice unsteady. "I think, to reassure ourselves, we ought to make a thorough investigation."

Off came the blue ball gown, and his elegantly cut evening clothes. Emma admired the swell of muscles in James's bare back, the hard, broad shoulders, the thick biceps and lightly haired forearms. Truly, she thought, he has the body of an angel. . . .

And all at once, that body was pressed hotly against her, and his hands were tugging at her camisole.

And the mind, she added wryly to herself, of a devil.

"How do you get this thing off?" James demanded, wrenching at the ties that held her camisole closed. But before Emma could reply, he'd broken the slender ribbons, and with a self-satisfied sound he dipped his head to her breasts, taunting her nipples into stiff readiness with his tongue, while backing her, with single-minded purpose, toward the bed.

Emma fell back against the soft coverlet with a sigh. This, then, she thought to herself, is what it means to be married. James had been too polite to ask, but she thought he probably knew that what she had had with Stuart had been nothing at all like this. Certainly Stuart had never, as James was doing now, run his lips along her stomach, the bristles on his chin scraping the sensitive skin. Emma did not even suspect what he was about until she felt his tongue between her thighs. Then her back arched so suddenly that she nearly launched herself from the bed.

"What are you doing?" she gasped. He didn't respond. It was, after all, perfectly obvious what he was doing. But she thought she felt him smile against her. He was doing things to her with his tongue that, she was quite certain, were probably frowned upon by the church.

And just as she was sure she'd been pushed to the brink of sanity, James lifted his head.

And then he was inside her, seeming to fill her to the point of overflowing. Though she was unaware of it, she closed so tightly around him that it was difficult for James not to lose himself right away in her warmth. He managed to hang on, however, until suddenly Emma, with a strangled cry, arched against him, and he felt her pulsating around him, and he, too, was lost.

Emma's last thought before being swept away by that tide was to fling both hands over James's lips to stifle the roar of pleasure she knew would burst from him. She couldn't be certain whether or not she succeeded, because she was far too caught up in her own climax to notice.

But when a few minutes later a tap sounded at the door, and the dowager's voice called, "James? Emma? Are you in there? I thought I heard you. Wasn't it simply a lovely party?" Emma knew she hadn't been successful.

James, who was not recovered enough to reply in a normal voice, appealed to Emma. She called, without even giggling very much, "Yes, Lady Denham. A very lovely party indeed."

Chapter Twenty-Nine

"$\mathcal{I}$ welcome you all here today," declared Lord High Chief Justice Reardon, who had put on his finest wig for the occasion, "to the Stuart Chesterton School for Children. It is with great pleasure that I declare this school officially . . . open."

And then he struck the side of the brick structure with a bottle of champagne. The heavy green glass shattered instantly, and sent white foam running down the side of the building. James was not the only one in the crowd who considered it a waste of a perfectly good bottle of champagne. But he clapped along with everyone else—after his wife elbowed him, that is.

And then they were surrounded by residents of the village of Faires who wanted to thank them for their generous donation of a school that would be open to every child in the district, or to wish them well, or merely to look at them. For it was not often that the residents of Faires got to gawk at an earl and his lady.

Barons and their wives they saw with alarming frequency, as Lord and Lady MacCreigh spent a good deal of time in the village, now that repairs to the castle roof were under way. Lady MacCreigh—née Penelope Van Court—claimed her ears rang constantly with the sound of masonry.

And the Honorable Miss Fiona Bain—now Lady Harold, wife of the heir to the duke of Rutherford— they saw rather often, as Lady Harold liked nothing better than to parade down the streets of Faires in her new London finery.

But Lord and Lady Denham were not regular visitors to the area—though money seemed to flow from their Mayfair home and into the area at a fairly steady pace. The school was only the first of the establishments they had built in Stuart Chesterton's name. A clinic was to follow, which one day would be staffed by one of the first Oxford graduates Faires had ever produced, young John McAddams, and would also include a nursery wing that would, ironically, be completed at around the same time Lady Denham was to enter her confinement.

Not everyone, however, was pleased with the many improvements the couple had wrought to the ramshackle fishing village. Mr. Murphy was alarmed when, thanks to the new construction, a good many vehicles began showing up, rendering his hearse fairly useless, except for the purpose for which it had originally been built. And as, for the moment, no new epidemics had broken out, business was appallingly slow. The last time, in fact, his services had been called upon was when Lord and Lady Denham asked him to remove from the ground the coffin of young Mr. Chesterton, whose corpse he and Cletus MacEwan had, many months before, lowered in secret into the soil beneath the Wishing Tree, space in the church graveyard being scant.

Murphy had been handsomely rewarded for his efforts by Lord and Lady Denham—for removing the coffin, and then for transporting it to the waiting undertaker. But he still didn't understand why, when he'd paid a call upon the undertaker a while later to see if there'd been any new business, there'd been *two* brand-new coffins—better fitted for a prince than a curate—in the back room, where there ought to have only been Mr. Chesterton's.

But two coffins were placed on the ferry to the mainland, and two coffins arrived, Murphy had to suppose, at the churchyard at Denham Abbey. It seemed an extravagant waste of money to Murphy, having two coffins where there ought to have been only one, but then, it wasn't any of his affair. The rich, he'd always felt, were quite a breed apart, and he couldn't be bothered to try to understand them.

Mr. Murphy wasn't the only resident of Faires, however, who had cause to wonder at the earl of Denham's extravagance that day. Young Fergus MacPherson could not help but think the new school was a scandalous waste. Now that he had his spectacles, and could see all that he'd been missing, it was quite impossible to lure the boy into any schoolroom, however clean and shining. He had far too much exploring to do in the local hills, which he took to wandering with the pick from Una's litter, a ginger-colored mutt he took to calling Roberts the Second, after the valet who'd so gallantly taken over Emma's teaching duties—and who'd been so vastly relieved when Lord Denham had finally hired a permanent schoolmaster, and sent his valet home to London.

It was during one of these rambles with Roberts the Second that Fergus happened to spy Lord and Lady Denham standing beneath the Wishing Tree, hanging up pairs of their own shoes, quite as if they were not English nobility but a simple pair of newlyweds, anxious to begin their married life together, and looking for a little bit of luck to pave the way. The whole thing, in Fergus's opinion, was just a waste of perfectly good shoes, since, judging by the way he saw the earl kiss his lady when he thought no one was looking, fortune had already more than blessed this particular bride.